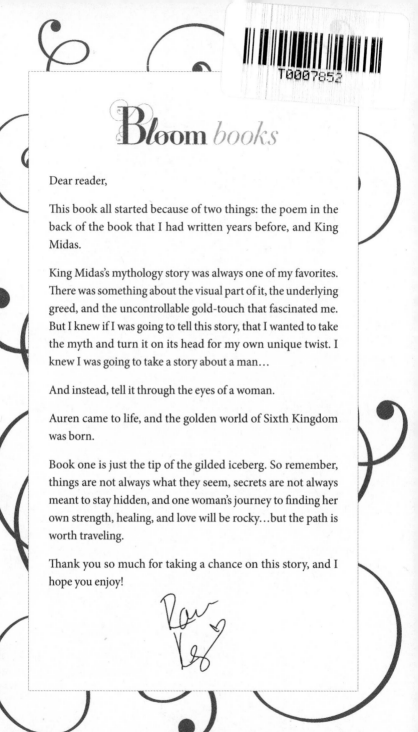

Bloom *books*

Dear reader,

This book all started because of two things: the poem in the back of the book that I had written years before, and King Midas.

King Midas's mythology story was always one of my favorites. There was something about the visual part of it, the underlying greed, and the uncontrollable gold-touch that fascinated me. But I knew if I was going to tell this story, that I wanted to take the myth and turn it on its head for my own unique twist. I knew I was going to take a story about a man…

And instead, tell it through the eyes of a woman.

Auren came to life, and the golden world of Sixth Kingdom was born.

Book one is just the tip of the gilded iceberg. So remember, things are not always what they seem, secrets are not always meant to stay hidden, and one woman's journey to finding her own strength, healing, and love will be rocky…but the path is worth traveling.

Thank you so much for taking a chance on this story, and I hope you enjoy!

GILD

RAVEN KENNEDY

Bloom *books*

Sourcebooks and the colophon are registered trademarks of
Sourcebooks. Bloom Books is a trademark of Sourcebooks.

Published by Bloom Books, an imprint of Sourcebooks
P.O. Box 4410, Naperville, Illinois 60567-4410
(630) 961-3900
sourcebooks.com

Originally self-published in 2020 by Raven Kennedy.

Cataloging-in-Publication Data is on file with the Library of Congress.

Printed and bound in the United States of America.
VP 10 9 8 7 6 5 4 3 2 1

To the ones who try, but can't see the stars.
Keep looking up.

Orea

SECOND
KINGDOM

WALLMONT

GALLENREEF

ELLIMERY

FIRST
KINGDOM

HIGHBELL

SIXTH
KINGDOM

SEVENTH
KINGDOM

ABOUT THE BOOK

THE MYTH OF
KING MIDAS REIMAGINED.

This compelling and dark adult fantasy series is as addictive as it is unexpected. With romance, fae, and intrigue, the gilded world of Orea will grip you from the very first page. Be immersed in this journey of greed, love, and finding inner strength.

Please Note: This series will contain explicit content and dark elements that may be triggering to some. It will include explicit romance, mature language, violence, non-consensual sex, emotional manipulation and abuse, sex trafficking and assault, and other dark and potentially triggering content. It is not intended for anyone under 18 years of age. This is book one in a series.

CHAPTER 1

I lift the gold goblet to my lips as I watch the show of naked flesh through the space between my bars.

The lighting is low, deliberate. Just a crackle of flame over promiscuous shapes that move in warm tandem. Seven bodies working all to one sole release, while I'm here, apart, like a spectator for a sport.

The king called me in here a couple of hours ago when he started getting hot and heavy with his revolving harem of concubines—also known as his royal saddles. He decided to have his pleasure in the atrium tonight, probably because of the acoustics in here. To his credit, the moans really do echo nicely.

"Yes, my king! Yes! Yes!"

The skin around my eyes tightens, and I quickly gulp more wine down and force myself to look away and take in the night sky instead. The atrium is huge, and all of the walls and the domed ceiling are made entirely of glass windows, so it's the best view in the palace. That is... when it stops snowing long enough to see anything.

Right now, there's a snowstorm like usual. White flakes fall from the sky, a promise to cover the panes by morning. But for now, I can see a faint hint of a single star high above, peeking out from between the oppressive clouds and looming white. Always, the puffy, frozen vapor stands sentinel over the sky like a miser, stealing the view from me and hoarding it to itself. But I have a glimpse, and I'm thankful for that.

I wonder if at one point, past monarchs from forgotten times built this atrium so they could chart the stars and decipher the stories that the gods left for us in the sky. But then nature thwarted them, those sentry clouds mocking their effort and blocking truths from us.

Or perhaps the long-dead royals just built this room to see the glass frosted over and blizzards whipping around while they could stand in here, untouched by the vast, white cold. Orean royals are arrogant enough to do something like that. Case in point...my eyes flicker over to the king who's currently balls-deep in his saddle while the others flaunt and play for his pleasure.

Maybe I'm wrong though. Maybe this space wasn't built for the purpose of us looking up, but for the gods to look down. Maybe those old royals brought *their* saddles up here too, as a visual offering for the heavens to enjoy the debauchery. Based on some of the stories I've read, the gods are a horny bunch, so I honestly wouldn't put it past them. I don't judge them, though. The royal saddles are very talented.

Despite the fact that I'm being forced to watch and listen to the lewd acts right now, and despite the fact that the top of the dome is usually blocked with snow, I still like coming in here. It's the closest I ever get to being outside, or feeling the wind on my face, or having my lungs expand with fresh air.

Bright side? At least I never have to worry about my skin getting chapped from the wind or shivering from the snow. The snowstorm *does* look cold, after all.

I try to keep a positive outlook on life, even if I am in my own person-sized birdcage. A pretty jail for a pretty relic.

"Oh, Divine!" one of the saddles—Rissa, I think— cries out in bliss, pulling me from my thoughts. She has a husky voice and blonde hair, beauty effortlessly held on her face.

I redirect my gaze to the scene in front of me, unable to help myself. There are six saddles doing their best to impress. Six is the king's lucky number—since he's the ruler of the Sixth Kingdom of Orea. He's a bit obsessive about it, really. At any given time, I see the number surrounding him. Like the six buttons on every shirt that his tailors make for him. Or the six spires in his gold crown. The six saddles he's fucking tonight.

Right now, five women and one man are catering to his carnal needs. The servants brought up a bed so that he could be comfortable while he's getting his thrill. It seems like a big hassle for them to take apart the enormous bed, walk up three flights of stairs, and then put it back together again, only to have to remove it again later. But what do I know? I'm just the king's *favorite saddle*.

I wrinkle my nose at that term. I prefer it when people call me the king's favored. It has a much nicer ring to it, though it still means the same thing.

I'm his.

I kick my feet up on the bars in front of my cage, settling back on the cushions beneath me. I watch the king's ass flex as he plunges in and out of one of the girls beneath him, while two more women kneel on the bed on both sides of him so that he has full access to their bare breasts, which he's currently kneading, two-handed.

The king is a breast man.

I look down at my own chest, which is currently wrapped in gold silk. It looks more like a toga than a dress, the strip of fabric clasped together at each shoulder and then cascading down, belted with gold loops at the waist. Gold is all I wear or touch or see.

Every single plant in this atrium that used to be fertile and green is now lifeless and metallic. The entire room, other than the clear glass of the windows, is gold. Just like the golden bedding the king is fucking on right now, gold flakes peppered into the wood grain of the bed frame. The gold marble of the floor, darker veins burnished into it like frozen, silty streams. Gold doorknobs, gleaming

4

vines creeping up gilded walls, metallic columns holding up all the wealth as they reach for the archways.

Gold is a big theme here in King Midas's Highbell Castle.

Gold floors. Gold window frames. Rugs, paintings, tapestries, cushions, clothing, dishes, knights' armor, hell, even the pet bird is frozen in lifeless shine. As far as the eye can see, everything is gold, gold, gold, including the entire infrastructure of the palace itself. Every stone and rung and pillar.

The exterior of the castle must be glaring when the sun hits it. Luckily for everyone who lives outside of the palace, I don't think the sun has actually ever come out to shine on it. If it's not snowing, it's sleeting, and if it's not doing either, there's usually a blizzard on the way.

The bell here always tolls with a warning when there's a blizzard coming, warning people to stay indoors. And that enormous bell in the tower that sits at the highest point of the castle? Yep, that's solid gold too. And damn, is it *loud*.

I hate it. Its peals are noisier than a hail storm on a glass ceiling, but with a name like Highbell Castle, I guess *not* having an annoying bell would be blasphemy.

I've heard that people can hear it ringing from miles and miles away. So with the loud bell and the dazzling gold, Highbell Castle is a bit garish from its spot perched on the side of this snow-covered, rocky mountain. King Midas doesn't believe in subtlety. He flaunts his renowned power, and the people either bow in wonder or hunger in envy of it.

I walk over to the edge of my cage to pour myself more wine, only to find that the pitcher is empty. I frown down at it as I try to ignore the squeals and male grunts going on behind me. A different saddle—Polly—is getting ridden by the king now, her sex noises grating on me like an aching tooth scraped over ice, while jealousy cringes inside my chest.

I *really* wish I had more wine.

Instead, I snatch up the grapes on my cheese and fruit platter and stuff them in my mouth. Maybe they'll ferment in my stomach, and I can get a little quasi-drunk from it? A girl can hope.

Stuffing in another mouthful for good luck, I walk back to the corner and settle down on the plush gold pillows on the floor. With one ankle crossed over the other, I watch the writhing bodies as they put on their lovely performance for the king.

Three of the saddles are new, so I don't know their names yet. The new male is standing up on the mattress, totally naked, and great Divine, he is pretty. His body is molded to perfection. I can see why the king chose him, because with those chiseled abs and effeminate face, he's *very* nice to look at. It's clear that when he isn't servicing Midas, he's working out to sculpt his each and every muscle.

Right now, he has his forearms braced on the top beam of the four poster bed frame, and a female saddle is perched on it like a squirrel on a branch, her legs spread wide as he eats her out. Their balance and showmanship can't be ignored.

The third newbie is on her knees in front of the male, sucking his length like poison from a snake bite. And... wow, she's *really* good at that. Now I know why she was chosen. I tilt my head, taking mental notes. You never know when something like this can come in handy.

"Your cunt is boring me," Midas suddenly says, making Polly quickly get out from under him. He spanks the boob girl in front of him. "You're up. I want your ass."

"Of course, my king," she purrs before spinning around and dropping onto her knees, her ass high in the air. He plunges into her with the slick juices of Polly still on his cock, and the woman gives off a moan.

"Faker," I mumble under my breath. No way that felt good.

Not that I would know firsthand. I've never been breached *down there*, thank Divine.

The sounds in the room intensify when a couple of the saddles orgasm—either faking it or real—and the king slams harshly into his female before finally spilling his seed with a grunt.

Hopefully, he'll be well and truly done this time, because I'm tired and I'm out of wine.

No sooner does the woman collapse beneath him than he smacks her on the ass again, this time in dismissal. "All of you can go back to the harem wing. I'm done with you for the night."

His words interrupt the rest of the saddles, cutting short their own releases. The male is still rocking his erection, but none of them complain or pout or ignore his command. To do so would be pure stupidity.

They all quickly disentangle themselves from each other and walk out naked in a single file line, some thighs still wet and sticky. It's been a long night.

I wonder if the saddles will finish things off themselves in the harem wing. I wouldn't know, because I'm not allowed in there, so I don't know their dynamic when the king isn't around. I'm not allowed to go *anywhere* unless I'm in my cages or in the presence of the king. As his favored, I'm kept locked away and safe. A pet to be protected and kept.

I watch Midas carefully while he pulls on his golden robe as the last saddle walks out. Just the sight of him standing there, barely dressed and satisfied from his sensual pleasures makes my stomach tighten.

He's beautiful.

He's not muscled, because he has a very plush life, but he's naturally slim and broad shouldered. Young for a ruling king, Midas is only in his thirties, the edge of youth still softening his face. He has tanned skin, despite the fact that all it ever does is snow and rain here, and his hair is blond with reddish honey tones, the scarlet hue more pronounced in the candlelight. His eyes are a deep brown, and there's a presence about him—a charm. It's his charm that always gets me.

My gaze travels further down, over a tapered waist and the outline of his softening length that I can still see beneath the silky fabric.

"Getting an eyeful, Auren?"

At the sound of my name, I jerk my attention away from his crotch and up to his smirking face. My cheeks go warm, though I play off my embarrassment. "Well, it *is* a nice view," I tell him with a lift of my shoulder and a wry curve of my lips.

He chuckles and then begins strutting over to the bars of my cage at the back of the atrium. I love when he smiles. It gives me the crawling caterpillars in my stomach—not butterflies. I'm jealous of those free-flying bitches.

His eyes run over me from my bare feet all the way to my chest. I'm careful not to move from where I'm seated, even though I want to fidget under his scrutiny, my head tilted up in expectation. I've learned to stay still because that's what he likes.

His gaze runs over my body in a slow stroke. "Mmm. You look good enough to eat tonight."

I get to my feet fluidly until the fabric of my dress cascades down to skim over the tops of my toes, and then walk over to the bars in front of him. One hand curls around one of the delicate bars that separates us. "You could let me out of this cage and have a taste." I'm careful to keep my tone playful and my expression sultry, though my gut burns with want.

Let me out. Touch me. Want me.

My king is a complicated man. I know he cares for me, but lately, I've just been wanting...more. I know that's my fault. I shouldn't want more. I should be happy with what I have, but I can't help it.

I wish Midas would look at me the way I look at him. I wish his chest would beat with yearning as mine does. But even if he could never give me that, I wish he'd simply spend more time with me.

I know that's an impractical thing to want. He's a king. Constantly being pulled in a thousand directions. He has duties that I can't even fathom. The fact that I get any attention at all should be something I celebrate.

Which is why I bury the want, a shovelful of snow covering the craving with numbing weight to hide in my depths. I distract myself. I flounder. I fill up my hours with whatever I can. But no matter how many people I see every day, I still wake up lonely and go to sleep the same way.

It's not Midas's fault, and it's pointless to pout about it. That would get me nowhere—and I live in a cage, so going nowhere is my expertise.

Midas's smirk widens into a grin at my cheeky words. He's playful tonight, a mood I don't often get to see, but love when I do. It reminds me of how we were when we first became friends. When I was just a lost girl and he swept in to show me a different life, the way he smiled at me and reminded me how to curve my own lips.

Midas takes another sweeping look over my figure, my skin warming in flattery at his pleased attention. I'm shaped like an hourglass, with a generous chest, hips, and butt, yet that's not what people notice when they first look at me. I'm not even sure *he* notices it either.

When people look at me, it's not to appreciate the curve of my shape or to decipher the thoughts in my eyes. No, they're only preoccupied with one thing, and that's the luster of my skin.

Because it's *gold*.

Not gold*en*. Not tan. Not painted or dipped or dyed. My skin is real, shimmering, satiny, gilded gold.

I look just like everything else in this palace. Even my hair and irises glimmer with a metallic sheen. I'm a walking gold statue, everywhere except for my gleaming white teeth, the whites of my eyes, and cheeky pink tongue.

I'm an oddity, a commodity, a rumor. I'm the king's favored. His prized saddle. The one he gold-touched and keeps in a cage at the top of his castle, my body bearing the mark of his ownership and favoritism.

The gilded pet.

I'm the darling of King Midas, ruler of Highbell and the Sixth Kingdom of Orea. People flock to see me just as much as they come to look upon his gleaming castle worth more than all the riches in the entire realm.

I'm the gold-plated prisoner.

But what a pretty prison it is.

CHAPTER 2

My *tiredness is forgotten with* Midas standing in front of me.

All of my focus is on him, my every nerve aware of his attention. As Midas continues to watch me, I take the opportunity to look over the handsome planes of his smooth face, the determined edge of his eyes.

The longer I look at him, the more I forgive him for bringing me up here tonight. For making me be a bystander of the pleasure I took no part in as he spread the thighs of his saddles.

Midas raises a hand and slips his finger past my bars. "You're so precious to me, Auren," he murmurs, voice low, tone tender.

I freeze, my breath contorting in my chest like a stiff, sharp bevel that scrapes my nerves into awareness. He carefully draws closer until a finger trails down my cheek. My skin tingles at the contact, but I continue to hold perfectly still, too nervous to even flutter my eyelids closed in case that tiny movement would make him stop touching me.

Please don't stop touching me.

I desperately want to lean forward and nuzzle against him, to reach through the bars and touch him back, but I know I shouldn't. So I stay still, though I can't keep the eager glint from shining in my gold eyes.

"Did you enjoy watching tonight?" he asks, his fingers carefully trailing down to skim the edge of my plush bottom lip. My mouth parts, breath demanding as it wraps around the pad of his thumb, heat drawing in heat.

"I would enjoy participating more," I reply, extremely mindful of how his fingers move with my mouth as I speak.

Midas brings his hand back up so that he can touch a piece of my hair. He rubs the strands together, watching the way they glimmer in the candlelight. "You know you're too precious to pile you in with the other saddles."

I give him a tight smile. "Yes, my king."

Midas drops my hair and taps me on the nose before pulling his hand out of the cage. It takes a lot of self-control to stay still, to not arc my body toward him like a branch bending to the call of the wind. He breezes past me, and I want to bend.

"You're not like one of the common saddles to be ridden daily, Auren. You're worth far more than them. Besides, I like you always there, watching me. It makes me hard," he says with a heated gaze.

It's funny how he can make me feel both immense desire and crushing disappointment at the same time.

Even though I shouldn't, I push back. I blame the coiling forlorn want in my stomach. "But the other saddles resent me, and the servants talk. Don't you think it would be better if you let me participate one night, even if all I do is touch *you*?" I ask. I know I sound a bit pathetic, but I yearn for him.

His brown eyes narrow on me, and just like that, I know I've overstepped. My stomach tightens for an entirely new reason now. I've lost him. I've torn the playfulness off like a ragged strip of parchment.

Handsome features harden, charm cooling like snow over coals. "You are my royal saddle. My favored. My precious," he lectures, making my eyes drop down to the edges of my toes. "I don't give a forged fuck what the servants and saddles say. You are mine to do with as I wish, and if I wish to keep you in your caged quarters where only I can get to you, then that is my right."

I shake my head at myself. *Stupid, stupid.* "You're right. I just thought—"

"You are not here to have thoughts," Midas snaps, cutting me off in a rare harsh discipline that makes my breath catch. He was in such a good mood, and I ruined it. "Do I not treat you well?" he demands, flinging his arms up as his voice cracks through the vast room. "Do I not bestow every comfort to you?"

"You do—"

"There are whores in the city right now, living in squalor, pissing in buckets and humping in the streets to make a coin with their cunt. And yet, you complain?"

My lips clamp shut. He's right. My situation could be so much worse. It *was* worse. And he saved me from it.

Bright side: The fact that I'm the king's favored gives me lots of advantages and protections that others don't have. Who knows what would've happened if the king hadn't rescued me? I could be owned by horrible people right now. I could be living where disease and cruelty runs rampant. I could be fearing for my life.

After all, that was my existence before. A victim of child trafficking, I lived for far too long at the hands of bad people. Saw too many vile things.

I ran away once, lived with the only kind people I'd ever met since my parents. I thought I'd escaped the brutality of life. Until raiders came and ruined that too. My life was going to be pushed right back into misery, but Midas swooped in and saved me.

He became my shelter from the harsh, biting violence always raining down on my beaten soul, and then he made me into his famed figurine.

I have no right to complain or demand. When I think of how I could still be living...well, the list pretty much just goes on and on with *lots* of other really unpleasant things, and I don't like to think about that. I get indigestion when I think of my past, so I prefer not to. After all, indigestion doesn't mix with the amount of wine I drink every night. That's why I'm a bright side kind of girl.

The second King Midas sees the contrition on my face, he looks pleased with himself that he was able to redirect my line of thinking. His eyes soften again, and his knuckles come up to brush against my arm. If I was a cat, I'd purr.

"That's my precious girl," he says, and the worry knotted up in my gut loosens a bit, because I *am* precious to him, and I always will be. He and I, we have a bond no one else understands. No one else can. I knew him before he wore the crown. I knew him before people bowed to him in reverence. Before this castle gleamed with gold. Ten years I've been with him, and that decade knotted the string between us.

"I'm sorry," I tell him.

"It's alright," he soothes, one more stroke over the bones in my wrist. "You look tired. Go on back to your chambers. I'll call for you in the morning."

I frown as he pulls away. "In the morning?" I fish. He doesn't normally call for me until after the sun has set.

He nods as he starts to turn and walk away. "Yes, King Fulke is leaving tomorrow to return to Ranhold Castle."

It takes a lot for me not to visibly sigh in relief. I can't stand King Fulke of Fifth Kingdom. He's a sleazy, crass old man with the power of duplication. When he uses his power, he can duplicate whatever he touches exactly once. It doesn't work on people, thank Divine, or I bet he would've tried to duplicate me ages ago.

If I never see Fulke again, it would be too soon, but he and my king have been allies for several years now. Since our kingdoms border each other, he comes here a few times each year, usually with wagons full of things for Midas to turn to gold. Once he gets back to his own castle, I'm sure Fulke duplicates it all. He's gotten *very* rich off of Midas's alliance.

I'm not sure what my king gets in return, but I highly doubt he's making Fulke rich out of the kindness of his heart. Midas isn't exactly known for being selfless, but hey, when you're a king, you have to take care of yourself and your kingdom. I don't fault him for it.

"Oh," I reply, knowing what this implies. King Fulke will want to see me before he leaves. He has a near obsession with me that he doesn't try to hide anymore.

Bright side? His enthrallment makes Midas pay more attention to me. It's like when children are fighting over a single toy. When Fulke is around, Midas hoards me, making sure Fulke doesn't get a chance to play.

If Midas notices my discomfort, he doesn't say anything about it. "You'll come to the breakfast room in the morning while we dine," he says, and I nod. "Now go to your room and get some rest so you can be fresh. I'll send for you when it's time."

I bow my head. "Yes, my king."

With another smile, Midas walks out of the atrium

with a flap of his robe, and I'm left alone, the atrium suddenly feeling cavernous.

I sigh and look at the expanse of gold bars that curve out into the room, silently hating them. If only I *were* strong enough to pull the bars apart and slip out. It's not even that I'd run away, because I wouldn't. I *do* know how good I have it here. But to just be allowed to roam on my own within the castle, to follow Midas to his bedroom...that's all the freedom I long for.

Just for fun, I grip two of the bars and pull with all of my might. "Come on, you little gilded prick sticks," I mutter as my arms strain.

Admittedly, I don't have much to boast about in the muscles department. I probably should use some of my free time to exercise. It's not as if I'm too busy. I could do sprints from one end of the floor to the other, or I could climb up the rungs of the cage and do pull-ups, or I could...

A snort of laughter escapes me, and my hands drop back to my sides. I'm bored, but I'm not *that* bored. That male saddle with the abs is obviously much more motivated than me.

I look past my bars to the birdcage that's hanging from a pedestal a few feet away. Inside, there's a solid gold bird sitting frozen on her perch. She used to be a snow finch, I think. A belly marked to match the white snow she would've flown over, wings outstretched to glide through icy swept wind. Now, her soft feather down is all hard metallic lines, her wings forever tucked against her small form, her throat clogged into silence.

"Don't look at me like that, Coin," I tell her. She stares unblinkingly back at me.

"I know," I say with a sigh. "I know it's important to Midas that I'm kept safe inside my cage, just like you," I say with a tilt of my head before I glance at all the luxuries I have within reach.

The food, the pillows, the expensive clothing. Some people would kill for these things, and I don't just mean that as a figure of speech. They would *actually* kill for it. Poverty is a vicious motivator. I know that all too well.

"It's not like he hasn't tried to make me more comfortable. I shouldn't be so greedy or thankless. Things could be a lot worse, right?"

The bird just continues to stare at me, and I tell myself to stop talking to the thing. It took its last breath a long time ago. I don't even remember the sound of its song anymore. I imagine it was beautiful, though, before it solidified into a gleaming, silent specter.

Is that going to be me?

Fifty years from now, will my body go completely solid like the bird? Will my organs fuse, my voice silence, tongue weighted? Will the whites of my eyes bleed out, lids stuck forever open, unseeing? Maybe it'll be me on my perch in here, stuck immobile forever, while people look in, talking to me through the bars when I can't talk back.

It's a fear I have, though I've never voiced it. Who knows if this power will change? Maybe one day, I really will be a statue.

For now, all I can do is keep singing, keep ruffling my proverbial feathers. Keep breathing with a chest that still rises and falls like the sun. Coin and I aren't the same. At least not yet.

Turning, I run my hand down the bars before letting my arm drop to my side. *Bright side, Auren. You have to look on the bright side.*

Like the fact that my cage isn't small. Midas has slowly expanded it over the years to reach throughout the entire top floor of the palace. He had workers construct extra doorways at the backs of the rooms to be fitted with barred walkways that spill out into large circular cages. He did all of that for me.

On my own, I can get to the atrium, drawing room, library, and royal breakfast room, plus my personal rooms, which takes up the entire north wing. It's more space than a lot of people have in the kingdom.

My personal rooms include my bathroom suite, dressing room, and my bedroom. Lavish rooms with giant-sized bird cages built into each one, and connecting barred walkways that allow me to walk from one room to the other so that I never have to leave my cage unless Midas comes to escort me elsewhere. But even then, he usually only takes me to the throne room.

Poor favored golden girl. I know how ungrateful I

sound, and I hate it. It's like a festering slice deep under my skin. I keep scratching at it, irritating it, even though I know I shouldn't touch it, should let it heal over and scar.

But while every room is opulent and my every view elegant, the luxury of it all has long since faded away for me. I guess that's bound to happen after being here for so long. Does it really matter if your cage is solid gold when you aren't allowed to leave it? A cage is a cage, no matter how gilded.

And that's the crux of it. I begged him to keep me and protect me. He fulfilled his promise. It's me who's ruining this. It's my own mind warping me, whispering thoughts I have no right to think.

Sometimes, when I drink enough wine, I can forget I'm in a cage, I can forget the pestering scratch.

So I drink a lot of wine.

Blowing out another breath, I look up at the glass ceiling, noticing more clouds rolling in from the north, their puffy forms illuminated by a left-behind moon.

A foot of snow will probably dump over Highbell tonight. By tomorrow morning, I wouldn't be surprised if all of the atrium windows are completely covered in white powder and thick ice, the sky hidden from me once again.

Bright side? For now, I still have that single star peeking through the night.

When I was young, I remember my mother telling me that the stars were goddesses waiting to hatch from the light. A pretty story for a little girl who would lose her family and her home in one fell swoop.

At five years old, on a clear, starry night, I was ushered out of my bed. Single file we walked, me and the other kids living nearby, while the sound of fighting erupted in the air. We crept out into a warm eventide, trying to get to safety while danger surrounded us. I cried beneath my parents' kisses, but they told me to go. To be brave. That they would see me soon.

One order, one urge, one lie.

But someone must've known that we were being whisked away. Someone must've told. So while I and the others were snuck out, it wasn't safety that we reached. Instead, before we could even get out of the city, thieves attacked from the shadows, like they were just waiting for us. Blood was cut out of our escorts. Hot liquid sprayed over small, stunned faces. The memory still makes my eyes burn. That was when I knew that I was awake during a nightmare.

I tried to yell for help, to call for my parents, to tell them that this was all wrong, but a leather gag that tasted of oak bark was pressed into my mouth. I cried as we were stolen. Tears trickled. Feet shuffled. Heartbeats lurched. Home faded. There were screams, and metal clangs, and crying, but there was silence, too. The silence was the worst sound.

I kept looking up at those shells of light in the black sky, begging the goddesses to be born and come to rescue us. To return me to my bed, to my parents, to safety.

They didn't.

You'd think I might resent the stars for that, but that's not the case. Because every time I look up, I remember my mother. Or at least, a piece of her. A piece I've been desperately trying to hold onto for twenty years.

But memory and time aren't friends. They reject each other, they hurry in opposite directions, pulling the binding taut between them, threatening to snap. They fight, and we inexplicably lose. Memory and time. Always losing one as you go on with the other.

I can't recall what my mother's face looked like. I don't remember the rumble of my father's voice. I can't dig up the feel of their arms around me when they held me for the last time.

It's faded.

The single star above winks at me, the sight blurred from the water gathered in my eyes. In the next second, my star is smothered by roiling clouds that block it from view, making a pang of disappointment scrape the surface of my heart.

If those stars really are goddesses waiting to be born, I should warn them to stay where they are in the safety of their twinkling light. Because down here? Down here, life is dark and lonely, and it has noisy bells and not nearly enough wine.

CHAPTER 3

*I*n the morning, I get woken up by the damn bell, a headache bursting to life behind my eyes.

I snap open my crusty eyelids and rub away the blur. As I sit up, the wine bottle that was apparently still in my lap falls onto the gold floor and rolls away. I look around and find two of the king's guards standing watch on the other side of my bars.

My cage takes up most of the room, but there's enough space for the guards to walk through all the rooms on the outside when they're doing their rounds.

I quickly wipe the drool from my mouth and stretch, waiting for the bell toll to stop its incessant dinging, my head tender from the alcohol I consumed before I finally fell asleep last night.

"Shut up," I grumble at it, my hands swiping down my face.

"About time she woke up," I hear.

I look over at the guards and notice Digby—the older one with gray hair and a thick beard—standing sentinel by the door. He's my regular guard, and he's had this post for years. He's completely *straitlaced* and serious, always refusing to chat with me, or play any of my drinking games.

But the guard who talked? He's new. Despite my hangover, I instantly perk up. I don't get many new ones.

I study the newcomer. He looks like he's barely seventeen winters old, still with pockmarks on his face and gangly limbs. He was probably just drafted from the city. All males who come of age are immediately enlisted into King Midas's army unless they have farming rights.

"What's your name?" I ask, walking forward to grip the bars.

His eyes shoot over to look at me, and he straightens his golden armor, the bell emblem on the chest plate shining proudly. "Joq."

Digby cuts him a glare. "Don't talk to her."

Joq chews on his lip in thought. "Why not?"

"Because it's orders, that's why."

Joq shrugs, and I watch the whole exchange with budding curiosity. I wonder if *he'd* ever play a drinking game with me.

"You think she has a gold cunt?" Joq asks abruptly, tilting his head as he looks over at me.

Oookay, so he's not interested in a drinking game, then. Good to know.

"It's rude to talk about people's cunts right in front of them," I tell him pointedly, and his eyebrows shoot up in surprise at my blunt words.

"But you're a saddle," he says with a frown. "Your cunt is what you're good for."

Wow, okay. So Joq's an asshole.

I grip my gold bars as I narrow my eyes on him. "Female saddles aren't *only* good for their cunts. We usually have awesome tits too," I say dryly.

Instead of catching my scathing tone, he just looks excited. Joq is an idiot too, it seems.

Digby turns to him. "Careful, lad. The king hears you speaking about his favored's body, and he'll have your head on a gold spike faster than you can say *forged fuck*."

Joq's eyes trail over me like he isn't listening to Digby at all. "She's a fine piece, that's all I'm sayin'," he replies, clearly not wanting to shut up. "I thought it was a myth that King Midas gold-touched his favorite saddle." Joq scratches the back of his mussed up, mud-colored hair. "How do you think he did it?"

"Did *what*?" Digby asks, clearly irritated with him.

"Well...shouldn't everything he touches turn solid gold? She should be a solid statue right now, right?"

Digby looks at him like he's a fool. "Look around, boy. The king turns some things solid gold, and other things keep their form and just go golden, like the curtains and shit. I don't know how the fuck he does it, and I don't care, because it's not my duty to care. It *is* my duty to guard the top wing of the castle and his favored, though, so that's what I do. If you were wise, you'd do the same and stop yapping your damn mouth. Now go walk your rounds."

"Alright, alright." Chastised, Joq sends me one more curious look before he turns away and slips out the door to do his walking rounds of the rest of the floor.

I shake my head. "Young guards these days. Idiots, all of them, am I right, Dig?"

Digby just glances at me before looking away to stare straight ahead in his *guardy* pose. After all the years of being around him, I've learned that he takes his job very, very seriously.

"Best get ready, Miss Auren. It's late," he says gruffly.

I sigh, pressing a thumb against my sore temple before I head for the archway that leads to the barred walkway that separates my rooms. I walk through it and go into my dressing room, while Digby stays in the other room to give me privacy.

Some of the other guards like to push the boundaries and follow me in here from the other side. I'm glad to be behind my bars in those instances. Luckily, I do have a golden sheath of fabric draped down from the ceiling. It covers part of the cage so that I can undress behind it without being seen, but I'm pretty sure it still casts off the shadow of my silhouette, which is why those pricks follow.

But I don't have to worry about Digby ogling my shadow. He's never tried to be inappropriate or steal looks at me—not like some of the others. Come to think of it, that's probably why he's been my guard for so many years, while some of the others haven't lasted. I wonder if King Midas put *their* heads on golden spikes.

This morning, it's dark and dreary in my dressing room. I only have one skylight in the ceiling above, but the window is usually covered in snow, and today is no different. My only other light source is the lantern on the table. I quickly refill it and turn up the flame, and then get started with my morning routine in the soft light. Midas is going to summon me this morning, so I have to be ready on time.

I look around at all the racks of gowns hanging up in the room, my eyes searching through them. They're all made with gold thread and fabric of course. As Midas's favored, I'm never seen in anything less.

Walking over to the back, I pick one with an empire waist and a non-existent back. *All* of my dresses have no backs. It's necessary because of my ribbons.

I call them ribbons for lack of a better word. I have two dozen long golden ribbons that sprout out on both sides of my spine, spanning the entire length, from my shoulders to my tailbone. They're long too, so they drape to the floor like a train on a gown, dragging behind me as I walk.

That's what most people think they are—just extra

fabric from my dresses. They have no idea that they're actually attached to me. And honestly, it was a surprise to me as well. I grew them right before Midas saved me. It wasn't painless, either. I went through weeks of night sweats and burning pain as they grew from my back, slowly lengthening each day until they finally stopped.

As far as I know, I'm the only person in Orea with ribbons. All the royals have magic, of course. They can't take the crown without it. Some commoners have magic too. I once saw a jester who could make the flares of light emit from his fingers every time he snapped or clapped. A nice little night show for shadow puppets on the wall.

But as far as my ribbons, they aren't just pretty or unusual. They aren't just a throne room trick. They're prehensile. I can control them like I can control my own limbs. Usually, I just let them drape behind me like supple fabric, but I can also move each one when I want to, and they're stronger than they look.

Lifting off my night dress, I leave the wrinkled fabric in the pile near the bars where the maids can come to pick it up later for washing. I pull on the new gown, adjusting the drapery to lay just right and cover everything that should be covered.

Sitting down at the vanity table, I look into the mirrored glass. My ribbons raise behind me, threading through my hair and braiding it into intricate weaving plaits until it looks like I have a net of braids resting against the crown of my head, and then every long golden strand that was hanging down my back gets woven up at the nape of my neck.

It's a lot of hair, but since the king is possessive of me, he doesn't let anyone near me. Not even the barber. Which means I always have to give myself haircuts, and I suck at it.

After one particularly tragic haircut incident, I had lopsided bangs for two months before they finally grew out long enough to tuck behind my ears. It was not cute. I've tried to avoid the scissors as much as possible since that debacle and just trim my dead ends because I learned my lesson.

Though, to be fair, I'm not sure even straight bangs would've been a good thing. One should never decide something as serious as bangs when they have a bottle of wine in their stomachs.

Once my hair is tightly woven against my scalp, I get up from the table and walk back into my bedroom, just in time for a servant to walk in. She addresses Digby, slightly out of breath from her climb upstairs. "King Midas has summoned the favored to the breakfast room."

Digby nods at her, and the woman scurries away, a fleeting glance over at me before she disappears through the door. "Ready?" Digby asks me.

I look around and tap a finger to my lip. "I actually need to run a few errands before I head over. See some people, do some things. I'm *very* busy, you know," I tell him, my lips curling up in amusement.

Digby doesn't fall into banter with me though. The man doesn't even smile. All I get back is a patient stare.

I sigh. "Are you ever going to start laughing at my jokes, Dig?"

A slow shake of his head. "No."

"One of these days. I'm going to finally crack that gruff guard façade. Just you wait."

"If you say so, Lady Auren. Are you ready? We shouldn't keep His Majesty waiting."

I blow out a breath, wishing my headache would subside a little bit more before I have to face King Fulke. "Fine. Yes, I'm ready. But you really need to work on your cageside manner. A little small talk would be nice. And would a friendly quip every now and then kill you?"

He just stares back at me with his brown eyes, totally expressionless.

"Alright, alright. I'm going," I grumble. "See you in eighty-two seconds," I add with a hint of snark and a blown kiss. "I'll miss you."

Turning, I walk out of my bedroom to the other side of the cage, which leads down a hallway specifically added for me. I walk over the gold floor in my silk slippers, my ribbons and the hem of my dress trailing behind me.

It's dark down here, but the narrow hallway is only ten feet or so, and then I'm spilling into the library, which is massive, but smells of musty parchment and stagnant air, despite the fact that the servants come up here to clean.

I go through the caged-in portion of the library, down another dark hallway, past the atrium, and then I make it to the hallway that leads to the breakfast room. Once I reach the archway, I pause to listen for a moment, giving my sore temple another rub. I can hear King Midas speaking to a servant, and the sound of plates being placed onto the table.

Taking a breath, I head through the doorways and into the small cage that spills out into the room. On the other side of the bars lies a long dining table, filled with exactly six platters of food, six pitchers of drink, and six bouquets of solid gold flowers to match the plates and goblets, Midas's numeral and gold fetish are ever present.

My stomach churns sourly at the sight of the food, and I'm glad that I won't be expected to dine with them. I expect it would be a bit off-putting to vomit all over their place settings.

Gray, snowy light from the windows streaks into the room, somehow making all of the opulence seem a bit dimmed. The fireplace roars with flame, but no matter how many fires are lit, it never quite gets warm enough. The fires are always just chasing away the perpetual chill.

My eyes immediately find King Midas at the head of the table, dressed in a handsome tunic, his spiked gold crown sitting perfectly atop his combed blond hair.

King Fulke is sitting at his left, a gluttonous belly hanging over the edge of his waistband. And as is consistent with Fifth Kingdom's fashion, he's wearing velvet leggings. He also has on a dark purple tunic—his kingdom's color—to match. His own golden crown is skewed on his bald head, a careless reminder of his rule, purple gemstones set into it that are the size of my fist.

I have no idea if Fulke used to be a handsome man when he was younger. All I see now is creased skin and an over-plumped body. But the yellowing of his teeth from too much pipe smoking is what makes me cringe. That, and the leer in his dark eyes every time he glances at me. It's a tie between the two, really.

Right now, it's not just velvet leggings that are wrapped around his legs. He has two blonde, scantily dressed saddles straddling each of his thighs, the women feeding him bits of pastries and fruit as part of their all-in-clusive duties.

Polly sits on one thigh while Rissa straddles the other, giggling as she feeds him berries between her own lips and he gropes their breasts. I guess it's *that* kind of breakfast.

When the women see me come in, both of them shoot me irritated glares and then pointedly ignore me. They don't like me much. Not only because I'm the king's *favored*, but because I'm also Fulke's favorite thing to covet when he comes to visit.

To them, I suppose I'm just competition. Everyone knows what happens to royal saddles who become obsolete. They get tossed aside for newer, firmer, prettier saddles.

Although, I'm convinced that if they actually spent any length of time with me, they'd really enjoy me. I'm ridiculously fun. You kind of have to be when the only person you hang out with is you. I wouldn't want to bore myself.

Maybe I'll wait until Midas is in a good mood and then ask if some of the girls can come up to hang out with me one night. I could really use company that doesn't include silent, stalwart Digby.

Speaking of Digby, he and five other of the king's guards are standing at attention alongside the back wall, and they don't even blink at the display of the erotic breakfast. So professional.

The other men dining at the table with the kings are their advisors, and there are two more saddles standing by, one of them massaging the shoulders of one of Fulke's men, while the other keeps shooting flirtatious looks down the table.

"Ah, Precious," King Midas purrs from his seat when he notices me approach. "You've joined us for breakfast."

Of course I have, because you ordered me to.

Instead of saying that aloud, I smile demurely with a nod and then take a seat at the pillowed stool that's placed in front of my harp. I start plucking the strings gently, because I know it's what my king wants. I'm here to put on a show.

It's always the same thing. Whenever foreign representatives from other kingdoms come here, King Midas likes to flaunt me. I sit in the breakfast room, safe inside my cage, where the visitors can ogle me and be amazed at the extent of Midas's power while they eat their eggs and fruit tarts.

"Mmm," King Fulke says from around the bite he's chewing as he looks over at me. "I do enjoy looking upon your gold-touched whore."

I bristle at the term, but I keep my spine straight. You know what's way worse than being called a saddle? Being called a whore. I should be used to it by now, but I'm not. It makes me want to lash out at him with my ribbons and hit him in the dangles. Instead, I change up the tune on the harp and play one of my personal favorites, "Cock Him in the Cuckoo." I think it's the perfect song for my current mood.

King Midas chuckles after taking a bite of fruit. "I'm aware."

Fulke eyes me thoughtfully. "You sure you won't change your mind and gold-touch one of my saddles for me?" he asks, even as he kneads Polly's ass where she sits atop his thigh.

Midas shakes his head. "No. That honor is only bestowed on my Auren," he replies smoothly. "I like setting her apart."

Fulke makes a grunt of disappointed amusement, while I bite my lip in pleasure at Midas claiming me. Polly and Rissa both share a look of clear displeasure and start fondling each other at the table, like they want to draw attention back to themselves. "I can see why you chose her," Fulke says, ignoring Rissa when her hand runs over his crotch. "Her beauty is unparalleled."

My skin prickles with his roving gaze and with the daggers that Rissa's and Polly's eyes are throwing at me. But based on the gleam in Midas's eyes, I can see how pleased he is. He gets great satisfaction when people envy what he has.

"Of course she's beautiful," my king says smugly. "She's mine."

My face heats, his possessive tone making my insides go warm. I steal a glance at him through the strings of the harp, my fingers plucking the tune out like an offering.

Fulke turns his gaze over to Midas. "One night, Midas. I'll pay you handsomely for *one* night with her."

My fingers slip on the strings. A sour note clangs through the air, ruining my favorite crescendo. My gold eyes shoot over to my king. Midas will say no of course, but holy Divine, I can't believe Fulke dared. Is Midas about to smite King Fulke for saying such a thing? Right here at the dining table?

My stomach twists as the room goes completely silent. Once, one of Midas's financial ambassadors said something very similar, and my king had all of his toes and fingers cut off one by one before he threw them in a vat of melted gold and hung them on the man's door. Harsh? Definitely. But it was a message to everyone who leered a little too long, who became a little too bold.

The guards and saddles go tense and alert, all of us waiting with bated breath. The kings' advisors look between the monarchs anxiously, and my fingers stay paused on the strings, the silence a different kind of song.

King Midas carefully sets down his fork and then looks up at Fulke steadily. A long pause stretches through the air. My heart thumps in my chest as I wait to see how he'll reprimand Fulke, how he'll dress him down.

Midas braces an elbow on the arm of his chair, setting his face into his hand as he regards the other king, and now my stomach churns for an entirely new reason. Because there's a gleam in my king's eye, an inkling of contemplation.

Oh Divine, is he actually *considering* it?

CHAPTER 4

No. No way.

I refuse to believe that my king is considering giving me to another man to use. Midas would *never* let anyone have me. He's far too possessive of me, loves me, prizes me. He has ever since he rode in and rescued me.

But every second that passes and he doesn't say anything makes my gut churn.

"Well? What do you say?" Fulke presses. "Name an amount."

Bile burns the back of my throat at Midas's cocked head. *What the hell is happening?*

Finally, Midas lifts his hand and gestures around the room like he's reminding Fulke of his surroundings. Gold walls, gold ceilings, gold floors. Gold fireplace and portraits and window frames. Gold, gold, gold. "In case you haven't noticed, I don't need to be paid anything. I have more wealth than all of the other five kingdoms combined, including yours. I'm the richest person alive."

Thank Divine.

Instead of getting offended, Fulke just waves him off. "Bah. Not money. Something else you desire."

My eyes bounce between them, my headache coming back full force. It pulses at my temple like an aching war drum. A beat of threat. A rhythm of dread.

How is this happening?

Usually, King Fulke just makes lewd comments about what he'd like to "do to me," but Midas never entertains him, and it never moves past that, because my king always shuts it down. But this has gone much further than ever before. Fulke is getting bolder, and Midas...Midas is looking at Fulke with that cunning look in his eye that I know all too well. The look that tells me he's thinking.

Unease swirls in my stomach like a dark tidepool.

One of Fulke's advisors chances to lean forward, his face anxious. "Your Majesty—"

"Quiet," Fulke snaps, not even looking at him.

The man promptly shuts his mouth, sharing a look with the others.

When Midas leans forward, my bated breath leans with him.

Midas holds up a single finger, his expression like a hook to a fish. "One night with her, and you give me your army for the attack I'm launching next week. I want them mobilized today so they can catch up with my own armies at Fourth's borders."

What?

Shock courses through me. My breath stutters to a stop, and my fingers curl around the strings of the harp like I'm trying to grab hold of reality and pull it apart. I grip them so tightly that the taut threads slice into the pads of my fingers, sending droplets of golden blood dripping down. I don't even feel the pain.

Fulke scoffs, pushing the saddles off his lap so he can lean forward, while Polly and Rissa hurry to stand behind him. "There isn't time for that, Midas. My army couldn't possibly catch up to yours. And I've told you my stance on the matter."

"There is if you send word today and I have my army change course," Midas counters, as if he already had the cogs turning. My mind churns with the direction of their spin.

He's going to make me fuck another king so that he can use an army?

"It's against the Orean Covenant," Fulke replies.

"Don't pretend that you haven't sent soldiers to weaken Fourth's border."

Fulke's nostrils flare. "Fourth was pushing into *my* lands, spreading his rot. I'm simply defending what's mine."

Fulke's defensive temper rises, while Midas looks like the cat who got the bowl of cream. "And I'm simply being proactive. It's time to cut Fourth off before he can attempt to encroach on territory that isn't his."

I can't help but stare, appalled. He's launching an attack on Fourth Kingdom? *Nobody* launches an attack on Fourth Kingdom. King Ravinger is called King Rot for a reason. He's powerful and brutal and vicious. What the hell is Midas thinking?

The allied kings look at each other, both of them contemplating, judging, studying. Like a scholar poring over ancient texts of a dead language, trying to thumb through the pages and comprehend the passages without a key.

Seconds tick by, a whistling wind from the blizzard bolstering the moment, the noise a representation of the harrowing gale that's gusting through my insides.

The same advisor who tried to interrupt before leans forward to King Fulke, speaking quietly into his ear. Fulke's eyes dart over as he listens, the man pulling back just a moment later.

A meaty hand comes up to trace over the gold goblet in front of him as Fulke gazes contemplatively at Midas. "We're allies, Midas. I support you in your endeavor toward challenging Fourth Kingdom's breach. But one night with a whore is hardly worth the might of my army."

Midas lifts a shoulder in an unimpressed shrug. "You're wrong about that. A night with my famed favored, one who has never been touched by anyone other than myself, whose body alone is worth more than all the riches in your vault. Trading her for the use of your army is more than fair."

Fulke's eyes narrow while my own vision tunnels. My bruising head thrums with a pulse of its own, anxiety whipping it like a cruel horseman, forcing it to go faster and harder with each snap of the lash.

"One month."

The back of my throat burns with Fulke's counter offer. My fingers dig in harder to the strings.

"One night," Midas repeats, unyielding. "One night with her, and you stand with your ally. We share the victory of Fourth and split the land, or I may need to reevaluate your worth to me as an ally."

A gasp hitches in my throat. The tension in the room spikes up again to an entirely new level. If I weren't already watching Fulke, I might've missed the shocked flash that goes through his eyes, but I catch it. The thought of him not having Midas to add to his own wealth alarms him. The shock makes way for anger, but not quick enough. Midas saw it too, I know he did. He hit Fulke's mark.

"Are you threatening me?" Fulke growls.

"Not at all. But after an alliance of seven years, and with a common enemy, I'm offering you a way to solidify our collaboration. Having my favored is a gesture of my appreciation."

My headache inflates, pressure popping behind my eyes with a snap of my mouth. "No."

Everyone's eyes slide over to me at my sudden

outburst, but my heart is pounding so hard that I can't focus on anything except the pain that somehow traveled from my head to my chest.

I'm not sure when I jumped to my feet, but I'm suddenly standing, facing Midas with my sliced hands held up in front of me as if I can ward this off. "No, my king. Please…"

Midas ignores me. Fulke's eyes trail over my body, half of me cast in snowy shadow, the other in firelight.

"One night, no interruptions, to do with her as I wish?" Fulke asks in confirmation.

Midas tips his head. My whole body tips forward.

I catch myself on the bars of my cage, cut fingers curling around the metal, fusing myself to it in a shaky embrace.

"I want half of Fourth."

"Of course," Midas agrees, as if it's a done deal. As if he'd been planning this scenario of negotiation for the entire time Fulke has been here.

One more sweeping glance crawls over my body. "I'll agree to those terms, Midas."

My king lifts his chin, a victorious tilt baiting his expression. "Your army?"

Fulke shares a whispering consultation with his advisor for a moment before he nods. "I'll have them moving by tonight."

My soul goes as sour as turned grapes, my stomach crashes with tumultuous waves that lick over my organs in bitter, biting acid as denial floods me.

He doesn't ever let anyone touch me. I'm his. That's what he always says. I'm precious to him. I've been his for ten years, and in all that time, he's never let anyone near me.

Midas saved me. He pulled me from ruin and put me in a castle. I gave him my heart, and he gave me his protection. One look. He said he took one look at me, and he loved me, and I loved him right back. How could I not? He was the first man to ever treat me with kindness. How can he ruin that and give me to *Fulke* of all people?

My throat catches as I grip the bars, my vision tilting in unsteady panic. "No, Tyndall, *please*."

I hear the gasps from Polly and Rissa at my use of King Midas's first name. Nobody dares to speak so casually to him. People have been beheaded for less. But the name just flies out, unchecked. He used to let me call him Tyndall once upon a time, when I was just a girl and he was my vigilante knight in shining armor. But that was before.

My slipup is probably my mind's way of trying to call back his protector role in my life, but I can see from the hard set of his jaw that it was the wrong thing to say.

His brown eyes cut into me like the knife on his place setting. "You would do well to remember your place, Auren. You are my royal saddle to be ridden by whomever I wish."

Tears burn in my eyes. *Don't cry*, I coach myself. Don't break down.

Fulke tilts his bald head, watching me with unrestrained interest. To him, I'm already his. "I can punish her, if you like. I've been very successful at breaking in my own saddles."

The first tear slips down my cheek even though I try to keep it balanced precariously on my lid. It tracks down like a noose, a rope of remorse falling limp against my cheek.

Midas shakes his head firmly. "No punishing. She's still my favored."

I guess that's my bright side.

Fulke nods immediately, as if he's nervous Midas will change his mind. "Of course. I won't lay a hand on her. Just my cock." He laughs uproariously, his giant belly jiggling while the advisors laugh nervously.

King Midas doesn't join in, because his attention is locked on me. I'm stuck under his gaze, feeling a mix of hurt, fear, and subservience. I could kick myself for whining last night about how lonely I was. This is what I get for not being thankful for my cage.

"My king…" My voice is quiet, pleading. A last-ditch effort to speak to the core of him, instead of this staunch monarch who'd do anything to strengthen his rule.

Midas's brown eyes hold no warmth. Just cold bark of a log forcibly cut from its roots. "I didn't say you could stop playing."

I blink at his words, my lips parting in pain as I drop

my hands from the bars. He's doing this. He's truly doing this.

"Now sit pretty on your stool and play your silly music. Leave the men to speak, Auren."

I flinch at his words as if he'd come forward and slapped me. My ribbons shudder on either side of my spine, as if they want to hide from his view. Slowly, I turn and walk back to the stool. My legs shake as I sit down, like a rock settling at the bottom of a pond, sediment billowing up, the depth of water keeping me oppressed from the sun.

I feel detached from my body as I see my bloodied hands lift up to the harp once more. The skin over the vein in my temple twitches, and my back goes ramrod straight, as if the hard lines of my shoulders can be a shield from piercing eyes.

The song "Shudder Serendipity" falls from the notes unbidden.

Each pluck of string is another incision that slices into more than just my skin, but into my heart. Every note is a lament, every movement a misery, every cadence a reverberating pang. Tiny drops of blood drip down the chords in sweet sacrifice.

I play it for my king. My protector. My savior. For the man I've loved since I was just a fifteen-year-old girl. I play it, remembering the first time I learned it, when he so sweetly sang along to the pretty rhymes, his voice an accompaniment to the campfire and crickets.

In time between times
In dawnlight we danced
Sipping from shine
Your lips like romance

Another tear falls from my eye, the haunting sound of his voice a long ago memory so far away.

The man who promised to always keep me safe is giving me to another, and there's nothing I can do about it.

CHAPTER 5

K *ing Fulke doesn't leave as* originally planned. Not now that he mobilized his army and agreed to help Midas on a secret attack on Fourth Kingdom. Not now that he has a night with Midas's favored to look forward to.

Every day that his soldiers march closer to meet up with Midas's army, it feels like an attack is closer to being launched on *me*.

My hands curl over the book I have in my lap. Even though my eyes are on the page, I'm not reading any of the words. I'm too busy eavesdropping.

I'm acting as a pretty centerpiece where I'm sitting in the center of my cage inside the library. Back straight, ribbons draped across the chaise, I listen to everything that's being said with rapt attention.

King Midas and King Fulke have been meeting with their advisors for the past six days in here, poring over maps and strategizing the attack and the following victory.

Apparently, Fulke's men should be getting to Midas's army tomorrow morning. They'll breach Fourth Kingdom's borders together, essentially destroying the peace pact of the six kingdoms of Orea.

Now sit pretty on your stool and play your silly music. Leave the men to speak, Auren.

Maybe Midas didn't expect me to take his advice so thoroughly. He'd said it to put me in my place, but all week, I've sat and I've played while the men have talked.

They've talked, but I've listened. Watched. Pieced together their plans against Fourth. It's almost funny how much people will say in front of a woman they only view as a possession.

Since Midas decided to have their war meetings in the top floor library for more privacy, that means that I've been able to hear everything. It's been enlightening, to say the least.

It became very clear very quickly that Midas had been planning this breach on Fourth's borders for weeks, if not months. And with his ready answer to Fulke's bargain concerning me? It makes me think that Midas planned ahead for that too.

Which means...he had me come to that breakfast for the purpose of a lure. I was the shiny coin that Midas placed on the ground at Fulke's feet. King Fulke couldn't resist picking me up and slipping me into his pocket, not when he'd been coveting me for so long.

In his eyes, Fulke not only gets me, but gets the

chance at owning half of Fourth's lands and wealth. I admit, I don't know a lot about the inner workings of a king's mind. I don't know how their advisors advise them. But I do know this: All men, whether they're a king or a peasant, covet what they do not have. And these two men covet Fourth Kingdom.

"You're sure?" King Fulke asks as they sit around the map of Orea carved into the table, gold-touched so that it gleams on every mountain range and river ridge. "Because it must be made clear that Fourth Kingdom was the one in breach. The last thing we want is for the other kingdoms to declare war on us."

"It won't happen," Midas replies, confident and precise. "They want to be rid of *King Rot* just as much as the rest of us. The only difference is they're too timid. They fear him."

"Shouldn't they?" Fulke counters. "You've seen his power, as I have. King Rot," he repeats with a grumble. "The moniker is a true one. My border soldiers speak of the smell that wafts in. They plug their noses with leather stubs soaked in oils. And even so, they say their eyes burn from the smell of decay."

A shudder taps up my spine like a chilled fingertip, making my ribbons twitch ever so slightly. King Rot's reputation precedes him. Tales of how he rots the land to keep his people in line, how he's vile and cruel. They say he doesn't act with honor even on a battlefield—that he uses his power to make people fester and decompose, leaving their bodies in his fields for the flies to hatch maggots in.

"He's purposely instilled fear to become untouchable," Midas argues, my head turning ever so slightly to point my ear in his direction. "But he's not. We're going to prove that and take back the land he's edged into."

Fulke's eyes dart up at him from across the table, a meaty hand skimming over burnished summits. "And the Blackroot Mines?"

And there it is.

After the shock at the breakfast when I heard Midas declare that he was launching an attack on Fourth, I'd been flabbergasted. Completely confused as to why *anyone* would want to take the risk of attacking Fourth. I knew it wasn't just about the fact that Fourth was slowly edging past his boundaries. It couldn't be. It just didn't feel right.

So I did a little sleuthing of my own at night, sneaking into the library and climbing the rungs of my cage, reaching as far as I could to some of the shelves to snatch books in the history and geography section. I couldn't reach many, but I did luck out and find one with a resources map of Orea on a front page spread.

And that's when I spotted the mines. Right smack in the middle of Fourth Kingdom.

Midas smiles slyly. "The mines will be ours."

Even from all the way over at the back of the room, I can see the glint in their eyes. The excited straightening of their shoulders. I don't know what's in those mines, but whatever it is, they want it. Badly.

Fulke nods, appeased, while his advisors look on with matching expressions, like they're already anticipating the royal coffers growing, rather than the lives and deaths they're directing. But then, it must be easier to sit in a castle and move cavalry pieces on a map, rather than facing a sword on the battlefield.

"I want the north side," Fulke declares, his pale purple leggings and matching tunic only embellished with the leather belt wrapped around his sagging middle.

Midas arches a brow at him, and his own advisor frowns uneasily, but instead of countering like I expect, Midas tips his head. "Very well. The north side of Blackroot will be yours."

Fulke beams and claps his hands together once. "Ah, then we are agreed! Now all we must do is wait for our armies to meet tonight, and win ourselves a kingdom."

"Indeed," Midas says with amusement.

"What's next on the agenda?" Fulke asks, turning to his advisor.

The gangly man in similar purple leggings pulls out a scroll and launches into a list of the things they still need to discuss today, but my mind stays behind, wheels turning over what could be in those mines that has these men so worked up, so willing to breach a peace pact and risk the defeat of their armies. And why now? They're either very confident, very desperate, or there's something else I'm not seeing.

Movement catches my eye, pulling me from my spinning thoughts, and I look over at Rissa who's dancing by the window.

In true King Fulke fashion, he brought her and Polly along today. He's had at least one saddle with him up here every single day during their council. Rissa and Polly must be his favorites, because it's usually one or both of them. Sometimes he has them massage his back or serve him food, always at his beck and call.

Today, the women both have their light blonde hair coiled in thick ringlets and they're wearing matching dresses that are slitted at the sides from their feet to their hips, with plunging necklines all the way down to their belly buttons.

Polly has been making sure to refill the wine goblets in the room, earning handsy touches from the men as she does. But Rissa was ordered to dance almost as soon as she arrived. Right now, she's still swaying over by the window with seductive gracefulness, moving her body to soundless music.

Fulke gave her the order to dance over three hours ago and hasn't let her stop yet. Hell, he's barely even looked at her, aside from the passing glances. All her effort for nothing.

As I watch her, I notice what the others don't. Although she dances as if it's effortless, I can see that it's not. Every so often, she'll wince a little, like she's sore from the nonstop movement. And there beneath her pretty blue eyes, I can see dark circles, revealing her lack of sleep. King Fulke probably keeps her busy all night, and then doesn't let her rest during the day.

I hear the men begin to talk about what routes they'll have their armies take back to their kingdoms after the attack, completely distracted by the sounds of their own voices. I close my book quietly, looking down at it in my lap. The binding is such shiny gold that it could be used as a mirror, and I swipe over it with my hand, feeling its smoothness, looking into my reflection for a moment before my eyes are drawn back up to Rissa.

I get to my feet, hefting the book in my hand as I stretch slightly, acting as nonchalant as I can. I meander across my cage, heading over to Rissa at the other end.

When I get closer to the window that she's dancing in front of, I lean against the bars, holding my book in front of me again to feign reading before I turn my head in her direction. "You know, if you drop to the ground, you can just pretend that you've fainted from exhaustion. I'll back you up," I tell her, my voice barely above a whisper.

Rissa's hip-swaying falters for a half-second before she shoots me a glare. "Don't talk to me, Gilded Cunt," she replies coolly. "I'm working."

"What is it with people's obsession over my cunt?" I mumble.

Rissa rolls her eyes and speaks under her breath. "Exactly what I've always wondered."

I shoot her a scowl, but a weary sigh escapes her lips, and I feel bad for her all over again.

"Look, I know you must be tired. I can make a distraction somehow," I offer lamely, looking around my cage. I don't have much in here. Just some accessible bookshelves both inside and outside of my bars that I can reach, my chaise lounge, and some silk blankets and pillows strewn around.

"I don't need help from you," she says between clenched teeth, keeping her eyes firmly on a point in the room nowhere near me. But she stumbles, nearly losing her footing, and my lips press into a hard line.

She's obviously determined to hate me, but I'm so tired of it. She's weary of dancing, but I'm weary of always being looked at like a hated rival. I want to help her, and I'm going to, with or without her permission.

Glancing down at the gold-plated book still clutched in my grasp, I make a split-second decision. No forethought, no planning. I simply thrust my hand through the bars, and then I chuck it at her.

Bam!

It hits Rissa right in the face.

Shit.

Rissa's head snaps back, and she goes down with a yelp. It's not the usual way I see her *going down*, but still, she somehow manages to make it look pretty.

She falls, landing on her ass, her sheer dress tangling up in her long legs as she screeches and clamps her hands over her lips.

GILD

I stare in wide-eyed shock, really wishing I'd thought that through more. Or at the very least, I should've aimed. Rissa looks mutinous.

I give her an awkward thumbs up, my face in a tight smile. "Distraction complete," I whisper, as if I meant to do that. I mean, I did. But I didn't mean to hit the poor girl in the face. I thought it would just bounce off her chest, and she could act like her boobs needed a lie down. Midas likes them, so it seemed like a sure thing.

She shoves her waylaid hair out of her face, and I see the first drops of blood dripping down her chin and coating her fingers, her mouth bleeding. Great. Not only did I hit her in the mouth, I also didn't account for how damn heavy that gold-plated book was.

"What the hell are you doing, Auren?"

I snap my head over to look at a furious Midas as he glares at me from the table where the men are all circled around. Ten pairs of eyes are locked on me, and I fidget under the frowns.

I blink at my king, opting for innocence. "My hand jerked, and the book just slipped out of my grasp, Your Majesty."

His jaw grinds. "It *slipped*," he repeats evenly, his brown eyes like rusted nails.

I dip my head, though my heart is pounding. "Yes, Your Majesty."

I can hear Rissa crying beside me, and I try not to cringe. I really didn't mean to hit her so damn hard.

Where was all of that arm strength when I was trying to break out of my damn cage last week? Useless muscles.

Polly is glaring at me with hot hatred, but King Fulke chuckles. "A little saddle contention, eh, Midas?" he jokes.

"It would appear so," Midas says flatly.

I worry my lip as my king continues to stare at me until he finally looks away. "Take the saddle back to the harem wing," Midas barks out to one of the guards before he turns away from me again.

Two of the guards quickly rush forward, a little *too* eager to head to the saddle wing, if you ask me.

"See? It worked," I whisper, trying to show her the bright side. "No more dancing." She shoots me a furious glare, blood still gushing from her lip. If I had to make a wager, I'd say she's not quite ready to look at the bright side yet.

"Auren?" King Midas calls, his voice deceptively even.

I turn my head to look at him as Rissa is escorted away. "Yes, my king?" I ask, watching his back where he's leaned over the map.

"Since you've divested King Fulke of his dancer, *you* will take up the saddle's duties."

Divines be damned.

I stare at him for a beat, wondering if I could chuck a book at myself and get out of dancing too. But one look from King Fulke and the tension in Midas's shoulders tell me that they'd probably make me dance even with a bloody mouth.

No good deed goes unpunished.

Quirking my jaw in frustration, I make my way to the center of the cage and then slowly start moving my hips and swaying my arms up above my head. King Fulke licks his lips, watching me with a smirk, and my stomach bubbles with acid. The days are counting down until Midas will give me to that man. Every time Fulke looks at me, I can see the sand in the hourglass getting lower in his grainy eyes.

I'm not nearly as graceful as Rissa, but I take a breath and play a slowed-down version of "Cock Him in the Cuckoo" in my head, using the tune to guide my movements.

What I wouldn't give to cock King Fulke in his cuckoo right about now.

Fulke watches me as I move, while I try my hardest to pointedly ignore him and watch the spot on the wall over his head. Despite my best efforts to pretend he's not there, he saunters over, his velvet-covered thighs chafing together until he stops directly in front of me. There's a good eight feet or so between us, but he's still too close for my liking.

"You're mine tomorrow night, pet," he says with a grin, his plump fingers wrapping around one of my bars and stroking the gold up and down suggestively.

That bubbling acid in my stomach begins to boil up.

His eyes glitter with something hungry and excited, but I stay in my head, forcing myself to hear the music, to keep dancing, to pretend he's not here. He must not like my efforts to ignore him, because he moves to step into my line of vision.

"I'm going to mark you with so much cum your skin won't even look gold anymore," he says before rasping out a dark smoker's laugh.

Shocked at his crass words, my movements come to a jerky, awkward stop, and my gaze latches onto him.

His lips curl up, satisfied that he won. "Oh yes, how I'm going to play with you."

My ribbons curl against my spine like a snake arching up to hiss. I trade my gaze from one king to another, only to find King Midas already looking at me.

My stomach does a flip. Has Fulke finally just pushed Midas too far? Is my king coming to his senses about what a horrible, degrading thing this is, and he'll change his mind right now and put a stop to this?

But Midas says nothing. Does nothing. He just stands there, watching Fulke speak to me like this, as if it doesn't bother him at all.

I swallow hard, my stinging eyes moving away from Midas's betrayal to settle back on the disgusting man in front of me.

Fulke licks his yellowed teeth. "Mmm, yes. I'll have you bathed in my spend and unable to walk for a week straight," he promises, and it takes everything inside of me to keep my mouth shut and not to turn and get the hell out of this room. Midas would no doubt just force me to come right back.

"Auren?" King Midas says, capturing my attention, and my heart leaps with hope. *Put a stop to this. Protect me. Call the whole thing off and—*

"You're not dancing."

The words are an order. Lashed out like a stick across knuckles, abrading my skin and making me flinch. Fulke grins with an arrogant look before he returns to the map table with the others, done taunting me for now.

Sadness wells in my eyes as I shakily raise my arms, humiliation heating my skin and making me sweat as I dance.

Sit pretty.

Play your silly music.

Leave the men to speak.

I move to the sound of their resumed talks, their arguments an accompaniment to the rhythmic beat of my heart. With each sway of my hips and curl of my arms, I can almost feel the strings pulling me like a puppet on a stage. All I want to do is run to my bedroom and bury myself beneath the covers, away from lecherous sneers and betraying eyes. But I can't.

Bright side? At least things couldn't get any worse.

The door to the library suddenly opens, and inside sweeps a beautiful white-haired woman with high cheekbones and a golden crown.

Queen Malina.

I stand corrected. It just got worse.

The saddles? Yeah, they don't like me. But the queen? She fucking *hates* me.

CHAPTER 6

Malina, I wasn't expecting you this morning," King Midas says, turning to greet his wife with a tight smile.

Polly quickly backs away from the table with wine pitcher in hand, eyes immediately downcast. It's almost comforting to know that the queen freaks out the other saddles too.

The queen looks around the room, her lip and nose curling up slightly. "I can see that," she says breezily, her shoulders back and her neck poised, appearing royal as ever as the other advisors bow in her presence. She looks like a beautiful peacock with her emerald gown and sapphire jewelry dripping off her ears and neck. A display of power and poise, meant to draw the eye and intimidate.

She flicks her eyes to Polly, eyeing the woman's revealing dress before moving her gaze back to her husband. "Really? During strategizing, Tyndall? How uncouth," she says in high and mighty reproach.

Poor Polly's freckled cheeks go red with embarrassment as she dips her head further, letting her blonde hair hide her face. Midas is always careful to keep his wife separated from his saddles. It's clear that today, she's ruined those careful lines he's drawn.

The group of advisors look between the married couple, no one daring to say a word. Even Fulke keeps his mouth closed.

King Midas's lips curl up in a fake display of casual amusement, but a flash of irritation crosses his eyes that I don't miss. There's no love lost between these two.

They've been married for nearly ten years. He resents her because she's never been able to give him an heir, and she resents him because the crown should've passed onto her by birth. But because Malina wasn't born with power, she wasn't able to rule on her own—according to the law of Orea. She was forced to take a husband with power or would've had to step aside entirely, letting someone else sit on the throne.

At least by marrying Midas, she's still queen, even if her husband is the true ruler.

Highbell Kingdom is split when it comes to these two. Some remain loyal to her. After all, Highbell was ruled by her family for generations. Her father passed away just after Midas married her, so in a lot of ways, Midas is still considered the outsider.

The people sympathize with her. They still remember the pretty princess who had the rug pulled out from under her. They pitied her when no power manifested. Now, they also pity her for having a barren womb.

The others in Highbell, particularly the nobles, are loyal to Midas. They'd kiss his feet if they could, since he's brought them so much wealth. After all, Highbell was nearly broke before Midas came. He swooped in to save the desolate Sixth Kingdom with a marriage proposal. He enamored them all, boasting his power of endless riches. Of course, with an offer like that, Malina's father agreed to the arrangement. But I wonder if Malina regrets it.

I watch as the two of them have something like a silent standoff. The tension between them is heavy, but there's *always* tension. I don't think I've ever seen the two of them do more than tolerate each other.

I hold myself still, my ribbons crinkling against my back. Side by side, the two of them always look like a beautiful couple. I hate that. Where Midas has natural charisma, Malina is poised. Perfect. Her skin is so pale that I can see lines of blue from her veins at her hands and neck and temples, but she makes her severe paleness look elegant. She even manages to pull off her sleek white hair. I'm told she was born with it. White hair is a Colier family trait.

My eyes flick back and forth between them, my stomach turning in knots the way it always does when she's around. Since Midas brought me to Highbell, she's been very vocal of her hatred for me. In the beginning, I didn't blame her for it.

Finally, Midas tips his head, like he's deigning to give her this win.

"You heard the queen," he says to Polly, flicking a hand at the saddle. "Your presence is *uncouth*. You are dismissed."

Polly doesn't have to be told twice. She turns and hurries out of the room as fast as her bare feet can take her, not even stopping to leave the wine pitcher behind.

Now that Malina has gotten rid of Polly, her gaze moves to me. The glare she bestows on me is cold enough to rival our winters. And that's saying something, because we once had a blizzard that lasted twenty-seven days.

"You shouldn't leave your shiny toy out during the war meetings, husband," Queen Malina says with a scathing look.

I purse my lips, forcing myself to stay quiet.

She turns back to her husband, ignoring the rest of the men in the room. "May I speak with you?"

His gaze glints with irritation, but it's clear she isn't going to leave without talking to him. "Excuse me," Midas says to the others before turning to walk out of the room with the queen on his heels.

King Fulke claps him on the back as he walks by. "Females, eh, Midas?" he says with a condescending chuckle.

The queen's hands fist into the skirt of her dress, but she says nothing as they leave to speak in the hall.

Well, now's my chance. No way am I going to hang around here and give Fulke a chance to mess with me. On silent steps, I turn and hurry out of the room, slipping through the archway and rushing down the dark hall.

"Where'd she go?"

Fulke's annoyed words just make me go faster. I'm an idiot, though, because in my hurry to get the hell out of there, I went for the closest archway, which means I'm heading toward the atrium instead of my personal rooms. Oh, well. I can hide out there until Midas is back or Fulke is gone.

Reaching the atrium, I breathe a small sigh of relief as I walk through the archway, greeted by the bars of my confinement in the large, dim space.

With a quick glance up, I see that the dome ceiling is completely covered in snow today, just as I knew it would be, making everything seem more claustrophobic. Every single window is weighed down with frigid gray light that does nothing to lessen the tangles in my stomach. I was hoping for just a glimpse of the sky, but I'm out of luck.

Bright side? At least the bed that Midas used last night has long since been removed. One less thing to sour my mood.

I trail my fingers along the gilded ivy vines lying against the glass walls, my slippered feet padding across gleaming floors. All around are plants and statues of solid gold on display. It's a mass of weighty wealth all in one spot.

Gold is *everywhere* throughout the entire palace, but for some reason, it seems obscene in this room. Maybe it's all the blocked windows, making it feel vulnerable to the desolate outdoors. Or maybe it's just that not even the plants were left untouched. Midas might look around and see riches, but I look around and see a graveyard.

I head to the other end of my cage, aiming for the pile of pillows and blankets on the floor. With the ceilings being as high as they are, and the room itself being so massive, it's *freezing* in here. Even with the two huge fireplaces taking up either end of the room, it's not enough to leak out much warmth.

I kick a couple of the pillows to get them where I want them and then sit down, grabbing one of the blankets to pull across my lap. I might as well—

The door at the front of the room suddenly swings open, making me jolt in place.

"And you thought it was so important that you had to interrupt my meeting, Malina?"

I freeze for a half second, realizing that the king and queen came in *here* to talk.

"Your *meeting*?" Malina snaps. "Tyndall, how could you launch an attack against Fourth Kingdom without telling me?"

Divine shit.

If they catch me… I shudder, and it has nothing to do with the cold. I need to get out of here *now*.

CHAPTER 7

T*he king and queen come* farther into the atrium, their footsteps echoing like tiny snaps of a whip. There's no way I can get back through the doorway without them seeing me. They're coming closer, and it's only the few potted plants that are keeping me hidden.

At least I blend in with the decor. Bright side.

Slumping down, I lie on my stomach and cover myself in the blanket, doing my best to look lumpy and less person-y as I try to hold perfectly still.

"I don't answer to you, Malina. I'm the king, and I rule as I see fit."

"You deliberately left me out of this. You told me the army was moving out to run offense tactics," she spits.

"They are," Midas replies with a blasé tone.

I hear her scoff. "If we're going to war, I should be consulted. Highbell is *my* kingdom, Tyndall. The Coliers have ruled it for generations," she snaps back with vehemence. My brows rise in surprise at her daring.

"And yet, you're the first child in the Colier family bloodline that inherited no power," Midas retorts, his strong baritone echoing throughout the space. "Not only did you not develop any power, your family also dried up every last drop of coin in your coffers. This land was bankrupt before I came. You'd still be a ragged princess with a mountain of debts and no prospects if it weren't for me. So don't try to tout that Highbell is yours. You lost it the moment I walked up to your gates."

My heart pounds in my chest. This is...very private. Not meant for my ears at all. Malina would want to cut mine off if she knew I was hearing this.

I shouldn't, but I can't stop myself from carefully hooking my finger under the blanket near my eyes and slowly lifting it up to peek. Through the small gap, I see the king and queen facing off about ten feet away, their expressions hot with fury and their eyes cold with hate.

Even though it's no secret that the queen has no power, it's never so openly thrown in her face like this. Or maybe it is. Maybe this is usual for them behind closed doors.

"That has nothing to do with it," Queen Malina hisses at him. "The point is, you're breaking peace treaties that the six kingdoms have held for centuries! And you did it without even discussing it with me!"

"I know what I'm doing," he replies coolly in front

of her. "And you'd do well to remember what it is *you're* supposed to be doing, wife."

She narrows her icy blue eyes. "What? Sit up in my rooms with my ladies-in-waiting, knitting and walking around the ice garden?" She shakes her head with a humorless laugh. "I'm not one of your saddles to be kept, Tyndall."

"No, you're definitely *not* one of my saddles," he says, casting a look of contempt at her.

An angry blush stains her pale cheeks, and her hands fist into her skirts again. "And whose fault is it that you don't visit my bed anymore?"

I cringe, my ears almost burning. I thought their talk was private before? This just got so much worse.

Midas scoffs. "You're barren," he tells her, and I don't miss the way her head flinches back, as if he'd struck her with an open palm. "I'd rather not waste my time. Which is what this is," he says, gesturing between them. "Wasted time. Now, if you're done with your feminine fit, I have work to do."

He starts to stalk away, but before he can take three steps, her voice stops him dead. "I know the truth, Tyndall."

My eyes bounce between the two of them, wondering what truth she's talking about.

Seconds pass. Midas's shoulders are stiff as a board when he finally turns back around to face her. The look in his brown eyes is so vitriolic that the queen even takes a step back. Seems like she overplayed her hand. I just don't know which cards she's holding.

"I'd be very, *very* careful if I were you," Midas tells her with quiet harshness.

A threat, plain and simple. The cruelty in his tone is enough to make the hairs on the back of my neck sit up. Malina watches him, and I'm riveted, barely even letting myself blink.

"Go back to your rooms," he finishes coldly.

The queen swallows hard, but despite the tremble in her hands that she hides in her skirts, she tips her chin up before striding out of the room, letting the door slam shut behind her. She's not a wilting flower, I'll give her that.

Me, I'm too scared to breathe in the silence, and my heart is pounding against my chest like drums. I wait precious seconds, my cheeks puffed out with all the air I'm not letting out.

Midas takes a breath and tugs at his golden tunic to straighten it before running a hand over his hair to make sure not a single strand is out of place. After another moment, he turns to leave, exiting my line of sight. Only when I hear the door shut behind him, his footsteps receding, do I let out my breath.

I push back the blanket and sit up, knowing I need to get past the library undetected and back to my bedroom before Midas returns to the library. If he calls for me, and I'm not in my room, he'll know I'm here and that I overheard the two of them, and that...that probably won't go well for me.

Getting to my feet, I rush out of the atrium, down my private hallway, and then skid to a stop just outside the archway into the back of the library.

I can hear the advisors' voices mumbling and King Fulke eating loudly as he breathes through his mouth. Chew, breathe, chew, breathe. It's obnoxious. Daring to peek around the doorway, I find that everyone is thankfully facing the table, no one giving my caged portion any mind, and Midas isn't back yet.

The sun is going down, taking the dim gray lighting with it, but the men won't be finishing any time soon. The advisors will no doubt work through the night like they have for the past several days, and I don't want to get stuck in here with them.

The only way I might be able to hide in my rooms for the rest of the night is if I can make it there before Midas comes back. Out of sight, out of mind. Or so I hope. He'll probably be in a foul mood after his talk with Malina, and I don't want to be caught in the crosshairs.

To get to my personal rooms, I have to get across this library. Midas made sure the entire top level of the castle was remodeled so that I could roam freely. Since my cages built into each room aren't confined, they all lead into small hallways he had made for me that connect from one room to the other, all the way to the other end of the palace. But that means that there's only one way to get from one end to the other—I have to go through each room.

I do another visual sweep to make sure no one is looking, and then start tiptoeing across the caged-in portion of the library, my eyes focused on the archway at the other end, my steps hurried but careful. I can't go too fast, or the movement will catch attention from their peripherals, but I have to hurry before Midas comes back.

I'm three steps away when I hear, "Ah, you're back."

I freeze, but when my gaze darts over, no one is looking at me, but at Midas who's striding through the doorway.

Gathering my skirts in my hands, I leap for the archway and sprint down the hallway. Right before Midas's eyes can find me. I don't stop running until I pass my bathroom and dressing chambers. I duck into my room, blowing out a breath as I slump against the wall.

I rest my head back for a minute, basking in my successful retreat, while my mind spins. I'm lucky I wasn't caught.

I stay propped here for a while, my brain soaking in everything I've learned. Not just from the spied conversation, but from the bits and pieces I've picked up all week during Midas's war council. It seems even Queen Malina is wary of Midas's bold attack.

I'm not surprised he didn't discuss his decisions with her, though. That's how he operates. Purely by his own agenda and plans. It's one of the things I've always admired about him actually—the confidence he possesses. He wasn't born royal like Malina. He wasn't groomed to be a monarch. And as harsh as he may be sometimes, he knows how to rule. Highbell needed money, and it needed a strong leader, and it got both the minute Midas sat on the throne.

I blink, realizing that the day has leached out and night has crept in. A shiver travels down my spine, and I rub my arms, willing the tingles away. Bright side: If Midas was going to send for me, he would've done it by now.

What little light that existed in my room has faded into shadows that quickly stained everything in darkness. Pushing myself away from the wall, I head to the far end of my room, following the way by memory, until I reach the small table that butts up against the bars.

I blindly feel for the candlestick that I know is there, but instead of my fingers wrapping around the hard base, I come into contact with something warm. Something that moves.

I flinch back in alarm, but too late. The hand flashes forward and grabs my wrist, yanking me forward. My torso tips over the top of the table, my hands shooting out to catch myself on it. The person holding my wrist releases it and instead snatches me by the hair in a fisted grip.

I reach up in a scrabbled panic, trying to tear the hold away on instinct, but whoever is holding me doesn't release me, no matter how hard I yank.

I start scratching at them mercilessly, hoping to peel their skin into bloody strips so they'll let go. As soon as I feel my nail draw blood, the person hisses in pain and then slams my head into the bars so hard that I see stars.

I buckle at the knees, my body unsteady and my head pulsing, but the hand with the vicious hold on my hair doesn't let go. My scalp screams with pain, and I cry out, but no sooner does the whimper of pain fly out of my lips than another hand slaps over my mouth to cut off the noise.

Unfortunately, the hand is also covering my nose, blocking my ability to breathe.

Dazed from the hit to the head and unable to see much with the darkening night, I panic, lashing out to try to fight, my throat constricting and my nostrils flaring with the need to breathe.

And through it all, I can't help but be shocked that someone besides Midas is touching me.

I haven't been touched by anyone for as long as I can remember. No one would dare. Aside from fleeting caresses I get from my king, I've been so starved of touch that part of me is in too much sensory overload to react.

"Hold her up."

The order is quiet but firm, completely uncaring about my plight, and my stomach plummets when I recognize the voice.

The queen.

Whoever is holding me wrenches my head forward

until my face is squished against the bars, but the palm over my mouth and nose lets go at least. I take in ragged breaths, my neck strained at an awkward angle and the edge of the table digging into my hips as I'm forced to lean over.

I blink as Queen Malina comes forward into my line of vision. With a candle in hand, her face is gripped with fiery shadows, making her pale face glow.

"You think I didn't see you hiding and listening?" she asks, bringing the candle close enough that the heat licks my cheeks in a burning threat.

I open my mouth to reply, but she snaps at me before I can even find my voice. "Quiet."

I immediately close my mouth, the hand at my hair pulling my strands again, pain blooming across my head and making my eyes water.

Malina eyes me dispassionately. "The king's *favored*," she spits, like it's the most hated word in her entire vocabulary. It probably is. "It always bothered me all these years why he chose to Gold-Touch a useless orphan girl and keep her like a trophy on a shelf," she says, looking around my cage with disdain. "But Midas always did have his obsessions."

I'm not an obsession. He loves me. She just doesn't want to admit it.

As if she can see the defiance in my face, she laughs. "You think you have his heart?" she asks, her tone a mix of mock pity as she leans down so that we're eye-to-eye.

She's so close that I can feel her breath coming from between her colorless lips. "Oh dear, you're nothing but a dog he keeps kenneled. A prize that he likes to show off to make himself seem more interesting."

It's a lie. I know this, but I'm not thick-skinned enough to face her spewing words of hate and jealousy and not be affected. So her declaration, along with the pounding sharp pain at my scalp makes even more tears build in my eyes until one dives onto my cheek.

She sighs and shakes her head, her eyes darting to the snow-covered window. "I was a foolish girl then. A powerless royal with no way to rule on my own when Tyndall showed up."

I watch her steadily, keeping very still so that my screaming scalp doesn't get more abused than it already is.

"My father said Midas was a gift from the gods. A handsome vigilante with a romantic marriage proposal on his tongue and gold in his hands? It's no wonder I happily went along with the proposal. He *did* seem serendipitous. Exactly the savior we needed. I didn't even care that he kept you."

My mind whirls as I try to think past the pain to focus on her words. I inwardly kick myself for getting caught. For not even being mindful enough of my surroundings to know that she was in here, waiting to pounce.

"All men have their vices, after all," Malina tells me, her tone making it clear what she thinks of me. "Tyndall's was making you into an heirloom. A caged orphan girl with gold-stained skin that he could show off and keep to himself. It's garish and gaudy. But you were of no consequence to me then, and you're of no consequence to me now. Do you know why?"

I clench my teeth together, anger warming the lids of my eyes so that each blink sears. My ribbons inch forward, slipping up the legs of the person holding me. I don't want anyone to know that I can move my ribbons, but right now, my priority is my safety over my secret.

Malina and I have had a few run-ins in the past, but for the most part, we do our best to avoid each other. She's never had me attacked before. This is a new reaction for her, and one I fear is the start of something more violent. I can deal with her disparaging comments and disdainful looks at my expense. But this? Having to fear that she's hiding in the shadows, ready to punish me? The thought makes me shiver.

"Why?" I ask, when it's clear she wants me to.

Malina's eyes gleam. "Because you're in there, and I'm out here."

A simple statement, but one that bites into my heart with the vicious, snapping teeth of a beast.

Whatever she sees in my expression makes her smirk in victory. Her eyes move up to look at whoever is holding me. "You can release her."

My ribbons immediately let go of the person, retreating back to the floor behind me.

My hair is released, and my face is given one more

shove into the bars before I'm let go of completely. I grip the golden spires of my cage to keep from falling, my hand tenderly cupping my scalp as my eyes find the queen's personal guard. The beefy, stern man has a jaw full of beard and eyes full of snide smugness. It takes everything in me not to let my ribbons come out and strangle him.

"Remember your place, *saddle*," Queen Malina says, drawing my gaze back to her as she begins to walk away. "You're just a pet for Midas to mount. A souvenir to show off." She pauses at the doorway to look over her shoulder at me. "The next time I catch you spying, I'll cut off your golden ears."

My hands curl into fists. *Bitch* reverberates in my head as I glare at her, though I don't dare say it.

Malina nods to her guard. "Make sure she heard what I said."

I frown at her words as she walks out, but without warning, the guard turns and knocks his fist past the gap in my bars and sends it flying into my gut.

The impact makes me fall back onto the ground. I clutch my stomach in pain, coughing and trying not to vomit. "Did you hear the queen?" he grunts out from above me.

"I—heard—" I choke out, sending him a vicious glare.

"Good."

Without another word, he turns and stomps out, the door closing quietly behind him.

Fucking Divine hell. I wish I hadn't gotten out of bed today.

It takes a couple minutes of deep breathing before I manage to pull myself off the floor, but my stomach and scalp hurt so damn badly that I don't bother lighting any candles. I stumble over to my bed. Bright side? At least the bars of my cage kept them from doing anything worse.

As soon as I lie on my bed, my ribbons curl around me, like silken sheaths that want to ward away the world. A cocoon hiding the caterpillar.

But I realize that it's not Malina or her guard that keeps me awake well into the night. It's not even my throbbing head or sore stomach. It's the fact that my time is slipping away. Because soon, the armies will reach Fourth's borders. And King Fulke will be collecting his payment.

Me.

CHAPTER 8

I dread waking up.

Usually, that's just because I'm not a morning person. I often have a wicked hangover from all the wine, so waking up bright and early is not my favorite. Plus, it's not like I have any bright sunshine to greet me. I haven't seen the sun's rays in years.

But when the last of sleep slips away from me, I dread it even more than my usual passive disdain for mornings, because today, I know my time has run out.

I don't know *how* I know this—maybe it's a charge in the air. Maybe it's the wicked wind outside my window—the Gale Widow shrieking her shrill lament. She's warning me that the last of the sand in the hourglass has settled at the bottom like a stone in the sea, and I have no more grains to count.

My eyes peel open, and I stare at the window, shivering at the blurry ice distorted over the glass. I push the ribbons from my body, but groan from how sore I am. My scalp and stomach feel like one giant bruise from the vicious attention I received last night.

I sit up carefully, looking past my bars into the rest of the room to find that Digby is already standing watch for his morning rounds. Too bad he wasn't here last night, but that's my own fault.

When I was eighteen, I argued with Midas for months to stop sending night guards. It creeped me out to have someone standing there watching me sleep. He finally relented, agreeing to let me have my privacy at night, but I can't help but regret that a little bit right now.

Even if she is the queen, I don't think Digby is the type of man to let me get assaulted on his watch. At the very least, I think he would have informed Midas. Unlike me. I have zero intention of telling Midas anything. All that would do is infuriate Malina even more, and that's the last thing I need.

Getting up is more difficult than it should be, and I wince a little at the pull on my stomach. Digby shoots me a frown, his eyes narrowing. He's way too attentive for his own good.

"Stomach's upset. Too much wine," I lie as I lightly pat my stomach to drive my point home. I don't want him to be suspicious or ask questions. Questions are dangerous.

I turn and rub the tiredness from my eyes, but out of my peripheral, I notice a gown hanging up on one of the bars of my cage. Gold and gauzy, so sheer that it's barely a gown at all.

My teeth press together as I look at it, my spine gone rigid. Midas had this dress pulled out for me. A message, plain and simple.

Tonight, I'm to be dressed as a saddle. Tonight, he's going to let me out of my cage.

I stare at the wispy fabric, at the plunging neckline, at the slits up the thin skirt. My ribbons curl at the same time that my fingers do, fists clamping onto emotions, tension contracting. The appearance of this gown goes perfectly with Queen Malina's words.

You're just a pet.

A souvenir to show off.

Turning away, I leave the dress hanging there and walk through out of my bedroom and into my dressing room, feeling Digby's eyes on my back as I go.

Once I'm in the other room alone, I pause in the darkness, letting out a calming breath. I force myself to release my fists, and my ribbons grudgingly uncurl. In the other room, I hear the outer bedroom door open and shut, signaling that Digby is walking his rounds of the rest of the rooms, but no doubt doing it to give me privacy.

Turning, I walk over to the table, my ribbons trailing on the floor behind me as I go. At the vanity table, I reach over and turn the lantern up, casting more light in the room since the window is snowed in again.

I use my ribbons to undress myself, letting the fabric

pool at my feet. Naked, I stand in front of the mirror and look over my body. My gold skin is marred on my stomach, a bruise the size of a fist with edges like a puffy cloud from where the guard's fist slammed into me. I press my fingers to it, wincing at the tender twinge. It reminds me of the gold tea set Midas has—the one that the servants always have to shine. It's a tarnished spot in need of polishing.

With a sigh, I remove my hand from my stomach and pluck a floor-length dress robe from the hook near the mirror and pull it on, tying it at my waist.

I check my scalp next, my fingers running carefully over my head, but it throbs at the lightest touch, making me suck in a breath. I'll have to be gentle when I brush my hair.

"How did you sleep?"

Midas's voice startles me so much that I whirl around with my hand over my heart. "Divine be damned, you scared me," I admonish. I didn't hear him open my cage door or his footsteps leading from my bedroom to here.

He smiles from where he's standing, leaning against the bars of my cage near the archway. "Tsk tsk, Auren. You shouldn't curse the gods."

My racing heart slows down now that I know it's just Midas who's crept up on me. He looks so good in the soft lighting. His golden tunic more like butterscotch, his hair like warm brandy.

"How can I serve you, my king?" I ask, and although my words are proper, my tone is unsure. Tenuous.

Midas reaches up and taps his chin in thought as

he studies me. I try not to fidget under his stare, the thin cover of my robe leaving me feeling like I'm naked in front of him.

"I know you're angry with me," he finally says, catching me off guard.

I study his expression, trying to discern what thoughts are spinning through his head. I don't know what to say.

He gives me a sad look at my lack of response, and just for a moment, he doesn't look like the mighty King Midas. He just looks like Tyndall. "Speak, Auren. I miss hearing your voice, spending time with you," he says quietly, and my gaze softens a little.

I'm furious at him. I'm crushed. I don't know where I stand with him or what's going on, and yet I can't say any of that because I don't know how. So instead, I clear my throat and say, "You've been busy."

He nods, but he makes no move to come closer to me, and I don't either. There's more than just the ten feet of space separating the two of us. There's a hole dug between us too. A hole of his own making. And I'm terrified that one wrong step will have me tipping right over the edge, headfirst into a fall that I can't recover from.

I stare at him, hope and fear burgeoning beneath my skin. He's been harsh with me, harsher than he's ever been before. I know he's under a lot of stress, and I know that I should never have behaved that way publicly, but I've lost my footing with him. And then there's the deal with Fulke.

My gold eyes sear into him.

You're giving me to Fulke.

But even as I silently scream at him, that nagging voice in the back of my head chirps at me. This is *Midas*. This is the man who was once a vigilante. No crown, no title. Just a strong, confident man with a purpose. The one who rescued me and took me in. Elevated me until I became renowned throughout all of Sixth Kingdom—hell, all of Orea. He made me his gold-touched prize and held me up on a pedestal. But even before that, he was my friend.

And as I look at him now, I see what others don't. What he doesn't *let* them. I see the troubled cloud that's hanging over his brows. The tightness of his shoulders. The stress that's drawn lines on either side of his eyes.

"Are you alright?" I ask quietly, my words unsure.

My question seems to startle him and he straightens up, whatever quiet thoughtfulness there was between us suddenly snapping in half like a weakened rope.

"I need you to behave tonight, Auren."

I blink at his words as they climb through the cogs and wheels of my mind, like I'm trying to interpret it in a different way, that he could mean something else, speaking in riddles or between the lines. But...there's no other way to decipher this.

My throat feels dry. "Behave?"

"Wear the gown tonight. Mind your guards. Don't speak unless addressed, and all will be well. You trust me, don't you?" he asks, his face penetrating, unyielding.

My eyes prickle. *I used to*, I want to say. *Now, I'm not so sure.*

"Shouldn't I always trust you?" I reply carefully.

Midas gives me another smile. "Of course you should, Precious."

He turns and walks out of my dressing room, his steps echoing back at me as he walks out of my bedroom, where I hear the door to my cage clinking shut. I stay still until I hear his footsteps walk away, the bedroom door closing behind him, silencing the rest of his retreat.

A giant breath whooshes out of me, and my body nearly collapses into the chair in front of my vanity. I stare into the mirror, unseeing, my fingers trembling from the rush of emotions that leaks into me.

I'm so conflicted that my stomach churns, threatening to make me sick. "Get it together, Auren," I chastise myself, pressing the heels of my palms against my eyes to force them to stop stinging.

He wants me to behave. He wants me to trust him. And hasn't he earned my trust, after all these years?

Hasn't he?

The answer should be a resounding yes. The answer should be easy. The problem is, it isn't.

Gritting my teeth, I shoot to my feet in a rush, and before I know what I'm doing, my hand has grabbed the glass lantern and I've hurled it with all my might against the mirror in a wave of anger.

A crash resonates through the room, and I relish in

the shatter. Chest heaving, I stare at the cracked glass of the mirror, my body distorted, broken off into three reflections.

"My lady?"

I turn my head numbly and see Digby on the other side of my cage, peering at me through the bars with a troubled look on his face. With the lantern now extinguished and lying broken on the floor, the room is cast in shadows, save for the candle in his hand. He says something, but my ears are ringing, my breaths coming in too fast to hear.

I shake my head to clear it. "What?"

His head tips, his brown eyes flicking down. In a daze, I follow his line of sight and look at my hand, turning my palm up. As soon as I look at it, it's as if my brain connects with my nerves, and I realize I've burned my palm when I grabbed the lantern.

I touch it lightly, frowning at the slight twinge. It's not too bad, just slightly discolored and sore. "I'm okay," I tell him.

Digby grunts but says nothing.

I drop my hand to my side and look over at him. "I know how this must look to you," I say with a shake of my head. "Poor favored girl throwing a fit in her room, surrounded by all her golden things," I say with a self-deprecating scoff.

"Didn't say that."

His gruff words surprise me. They're oddly...nice.

Like the gruff old guy is trying to make me feel better. He turns and walks out of the room before I can reply, leaving me to stare at the place he left with a small smile on my face.

He comes back less than a minute later, holding a new lantern. It's bigger, one that he must've taken from the library, but he feeds it through the bars and places it on the floor.

"Thanks," I say quietly before I go pick it up and put it on the table. Now that there's adequate light, I cringe a bit at the mess I've made. The servants who come in here to clean probably won't be happy.

I kneel down to start to pick up the broken glass from the lantern, but Digby raps his knuckle against the cage to get my attention. "Leave it."

My hand pauses over the glass. "But—"

"Leave. It."

I arch a brow and sigh. "You know, for someone who barely talks, you sure are bossy."

He just looks steadily back at me.

I sigh and stand up, relenting. "Okay, okay. No need to glare at me."

Digby nods and scratches his scruffy gray beard, satisfied that he's won. My trusty guard is very serious about my protection. Even when he's protecting me from myself, apparently.

"I knew you were my friend, Dig," I tease him, even though the smile doesn't quite reach my eyes, it's nice to pretend. I latch onto these emotions with him, and forcibly shove away everything else with Midas so that I can breathe right again. "Hey, how about a drinking game?" I ask hopefully.

Digby rolls his eyes. "No." He turns on his heel, walking away, clearly satisfied that I'm not going to throw another hissy fit and break something else.

"Oh come on, just one?" I call after him, but he keeps going, just like I knew he would. It makes me smile a little bit wider.

When I'm alone again, I sit down and sigh into the broken mirror, the distracting playfulness with Digby leaking out of me all too soon. I study the three images of myself for a moment, and then I get to work, letting my ribbons carefully comb through my tender scalp so I can plait my hair. I imagine it's a lot like a soldier putting on armor.

At least for now, while daylight burns, I know I'm safe. For now, I still have time.

But tonight, as soon as dusk descends and the stars burn, I'll be expected to play the part of King Midas's favored pet. I'll be expected to *behave*.

But one question burns in my mind for the entire day: What would happen if I *didn't*?

CHAPTER 9

I take my time brushing and braiding, doing everything slowly, as if moving at a crawling pace will prolong my fate somehow. I'm pretending that I'm not operating on borrowed time.

You can pretend a lot of things in life. You can pretend so well that you even start to believe your own deceit. We're all actors; we're all on pedestals with a spotlight shining on us, playing whatever part we need to in order to make it through the day—in order to help ourselves sleep at night.

Right now, I'm going through the motions, refusing to let my mind think of what's going to happen tonight. But my body knows. It's in the tightness of my chest, the labored inhales coming from constrictive breaths.

I try to distract myself and stay busy, but there's only so much harp a girl can play, only so much sewing one can tolerate before she goes out of her mind with boredom.

At one point, I'm so jittery with nerves that I just start walking the circle of my cage, the bars probably making me seem like an agitated tiger pacing in its enclosure.

Bright side? The burn on my hand feels better. There's only a small slash along the center of my palm, making my golden skin look more orange than its usual cool gleam. My stomach still hurts, but my scalp is fine... so long as I don't touch it.

Looking out the single window in my room shows nothing but a rabid snowstorm blowing a confetti of white against the pane. It's nearly nightfall. I wish I could string up the sun and keep it tied in the sky, but wishes are for stars, and I hardly get to see any of those anyway.

Fulke's and Midas's armies should've reached Fourth Kingdom's borders by now. I could go into the library to find out for sure, but that's the last place I want to be today.

I still think they're crazy for attacking King Ravinger's land. Not only is Midas breaking a centuries-old peace pact, but Ravinger isn't exactly known for his magnanimous kindness. They call him King Rot for a reason, and it's not just because of his power of decay and death. It's said that his viciousness makes everyone near him cringe.

His land is one of withering corrosion, but it's also a place where he lets wickedness flourish. His power allows him to deteriorate anything he wishes. Crops, animals, land, people...but I think his cruelty might be the worse evil.

I hope Midas knows what he's doing, because making an enemy of someone like Ravinger is dangerous. If Midas fails, I'm not sure any amount of wealth could buy him out of the consequences, and that scares me. Sometimes I wish he wouldn't be so confident in the ability to solve all his problems with gold.

Midas takes wealth for granted—and why wouldn't he? One look around, every surface, every possession, it's all gold. He knows that he'll forever be as rich as he wishes.

Queen Malina believes that *I'm* garish and gaudy, but what about this entire castle and everything in it? The soles of her shoes are golden silk—for only her sweaty feet to ever appreciate. The structure of the dungeons beneath the palace—pure gold for the withering prisoners to die in. Even the toilets we piss in are gilded.

If there's one thing I've learned, it's that this much wealth...it becomes meaningless after a while. Empty. You can have all the gold in the world and yet lack everything of real worth.

But maybe...maybe the underlying reason for Malina's hatred of me isn't that Midas keeps me here even though he's married to her. Maybe the queen simply wishes that Midas had gold-touched *her*. Because of what it represents. Because of the way he calls me his Precious.

And just like that, I find myself feeling sorry for her. For her childless, loveless marriage. For losing the kingdom before she could even take it. For having to compete against a gilded orphan girl.

As I contemplate all of this, I lean against the gold bars to stare at the snowfall outside. That jealousy, if that's what it is, has festered for years. There's no way for me to do anything about it now. What's done is done. The queen will never look at me with anything other than hatred. That's simply the way it is.

But if she's jealous that Midas hasn't gold-touched her, she doesn't understand at all. I won't deny the fact that there are benefits of being gold-touched...but there are disadvantages too.

No one sees me for anything but the metallic glimmer of my skin. No one looks past the pure gold threads of my hair. Aside from the whites of my eyes and teeth, I'm just a golden statue to everyone. A fixture to be seen and not heard.

A commodity to be bought for a night.

My bedroom door opens suddenly, making me flinch away from the window. I turn to see a maid come inside and walk over to Digby where he's still standing at attention at his spot near the wall. She delivers hushed words to him, while I stand by, watching warily.

As soon as she leaves, I walk over to the other end of my cage to face him. "What's going on?"

Digby gestures up at the gown that's still hanging up. "It's time."

My stomach breaks apart in cold, brittle pieces, falling down through my feet.

"Already?" I ask, and I barely recognize my voice.

It's timid and quiet like a skittish mouse, and I can't afford to be a mouse tonight. I have to be strong.

Digby nods, and I blow out a breath, sending a tendril of hair to shift up and out of my face. I force myself to swallow hard, as if I can internalize my nerves and drink them down, bury them into a chasm inside of me.

Turning away, I pluck the sheer dress off its hanger with a pounding heart, and head into my dressing room with wooden steps. In front of my broken mirror, I take off the simple gown I dressed myself in and slip into the sheer one. My ribbons do all the work while my arms move robotically, my face expressionless.

When I have it all the way on, I take in the gauze drapery hanging over my body, and I will myself not to flinch. Just like I knew it would be, it's so sheer that it shows every trace of my curves, even a veiled glimpse of the burnished tips of my nipples.

The dress has see-through sleeves of swirling gold lace, clasps at each shoulder holding it in place. It drapes over my breasts with a loose, plunging neckline that shows the edge of my bruised stomach in the front.

At the skirt, there are slits on each side that reach from my toes to my hips, so that no matter which direction someone is standing beside me, they'll get an eyeful of flesh. The whole thing flows loosely over my curves, easy access for anyone to slip their hand in and touch an intimate part of me.

Midas has never dressed me like this before. Sure, I

wear sensual dresses that accentuate my body, but nothing as provocative as this. My body, for the most part, is private. For him to enjoy. But for the first time in my life, I'm dressed like a true royal saddle, ready to be ridden.

I know the moment the last of daylight recedes, because a chill fills the air. I look up at my skylight, seeing darkness descending already. A dejected emptiness pulls at me, a shiver scattering goose bumps over my arms as night starts to rise.

Behave tonight.

A souvenir to show off.

Sit pretty.

Leave the men to speak.

Gritting my teeth, my spirit rebels. Midas wants me to wear this? Fine. But he never said I couldn't embellish it.

My ribbons rise up alongside my resolve, and I get to work.

It takes a few minutes of wrapping and tucking and tying, but after some adjusting, I finally feel satisfied with the outcome. My golden ribbons are now wrapped around the bodice in elaborate braided designs, swooping over my breasts before cinching at my waist, the rest of the strips hanging down around the entire circumference of my skirt.

I'm still way more exposed than I'd like, but it's much, much better, holding everything in and covering my most intimate parts. I'll still have to be careful when

I walk, because even with some of my ribbons wrapped around my waist, my sides are still somewhat exposed from the gaping fabric, but at least I don't feel naked anymore.

My hair is already braided with a few pieces hanging down my back, so I leave my scalp alone. I hear voices carry in from my bedroom, and I know that more guards have arrived to escort me downstairs.

I should be starving by now since I haven't eaten all day, but I wouldn't be able to tolerate food right now even if I wanted to. When I hear Digby call my name, I slip my feet into satiny slippers and then straighten my spine.

Don't be a mouse, Auren.

I walk into my bedroom, facing the group of guards standing on the other side of the bars who have come to escort me downstairs. I haven't been let out of my rooms for months. It's not often that Midas allows me to leave my cage, his possession over me so intense. When he does on those rare occasions, it's usually just to have dinner with him because he misses my company or stand behind him in the throne room, showing off to visiting dignitaries.

A skeleton key is passed to Digby as I approach. Solid iron, as black as coal, is fitted into the lock. Ironic that the key is the one thing that isn't made of gold.

The metal creak of the key turning is so loud that it infests my eardrums and hatches into a hundred fluttering fireflies zapping against my skull.

Digby pulls open the door and the other guards step

aside, careful to keep their distance under my faithful guard's watchful eye. They know that one overstep on their part will have Digby telling the king, and that's not something any of them want.

I walk through, the cage door swung open wide, like a rigid rib cage peeled back on a hinge, allowing its heart to spill out.

My ribbons don't trail behind me as usual, but I take comfort in the feel of them bound around my torso like an extra set of strengthening bones as I begin to make my way out of the bedroom, sandwiched by the guards on both sides.

My footsteps feel alone, despite the fact that four pairs of feet accompany me as I walk. The sound of dread is in the soft swipes of my slippers over the polished floors, in the suck of air that pulls my lip in between teeth.

You trust me, don't you?

Shouldn't I always?

Of course.

That answer is all that I have. I just have to trust him. But I'm not going to be a mouse.

CHAPTER 10

I remember the first time I walked through this castle ten years ago. Walking into a palace, after the places I'd been... Surreal. It had been surreal.

I was fifteen years old, but a girl in only one sense of the word. *My innocence was lost*—that's how some people would put it. But not me.

I never misplaced my innocence. It wasn't my own doing from a forgetful lack of care. It was taken from me, one cruel exploit at a time. I remember each piece of it as it broke away from me, until I was raw and bare, exposed to the harsh elements of the world with a chip gouged deep in my shoulder and a bitter taste always at the back of my tongue.

No, I wasn't innocent anymore when I walked into Highbell with Midas for the first time, but he brought back something I thought I'd never have again.

Trust.

He wasn't a king yet then, and the castle wasn't made of gold. It's difficult, even in my own head, to reconcile what it looks like now with what it looked like then. The walls were the mottled gray stone cut from the frozen mountains that the palace is perched on. It was gloomy even as it was luxuriant, this ashen gray fortress buried in the snow.

And despite the opulence of my surroundings, when I first came here, I was gloomy too, because I knew that our short few months alone together were coming to an end.

"I'm going to offer my hand in marriage to the princess of Sixth Kingdom."

He'd startled me with his words. There was no mention of any of this before. He had plans and ideas, I knew he did, but I wasn't interested in hearing them. I was too enraptured with soaking in the peaceful reprieve, the safety, the friendship. But I always knew the other shoe was going to drop.

I looked up at Midas, my handsome nomad with snow-flakes in his blond hair. We were camped beside a frozen fissure, icicles formed around its mouth like a geode, diamonds for teeth that glittered beneath a waning moon.

"Why?"

If he heard the heartbreak in my voice, he didn't say so, but his brown eyes softened as he looked over at me, the campfire crackling between us like tension.

"The kingdom is broke."

I scrunched up my nose. "How can a kingdom be broke?"

Midas smiled over at me, swiping grease-stained fingers down his pants as he tossed the last of the bones from our meal that he'd caught. "Kingdoms can go broke quite easily, actually. But in this instance, Highbell has struggled for years. They're little more than a frozen wasteland at the tip of the world. No farming to speak of, no mining lucrative enough to sustain them. They're crumbling without the proper allied ties and trade. It's a wonder the other monarchs haven't struck already."

I curled my toes inside my fur-lined boots, trying to leap from his words to his intentions. He had the advantage of age over me, being seven years older, but I wasn't naive.

"What about me?" I asked him. I wasn't sure how I was able to talk with the lump in my throat.

Midas came in front of me, snow reaching the laces of his boots. "You stay with me. I made a promise, didn't I?" he asked, and my relief was instant and warm, almost enough to ward away the chill of the night.

"With you by my side, we'll save Sixth Kingdom from ruin."

I smiled up at him, appreciating his smooth face that he insisted on shaving every morning, despite the fact that we were weary travelers, oftentimes with no one to look upon but each other. He was meticulous about himself just as he was about everything else.

He didn't have to spell it all out to me, but he did anyway. He trusted me with his vulnerabilities, his hopes, his dreams. A man with no important bloodline, with no family, no land. He wanted to save a kingdom. To bring back glory to a place that was dying in a frozen tomb.

We talked long into the night as he laid everything out, all his plans, his intentions, my role in his life. It was a brilliant plan, one he'd clearly thought through right down to the smallest of details. I was in awe of him.

Midas pulled me up to my feet, his hands warm, steady. "I'll put you in a palace, Auren. You'll be safe. With me."

"But you'll marry her."

He petted my cheek with the edge of his thumb, and I leaned into the touch. The first man I'd ever done that with. It felt like petals opening to soak up the sun.

"Yes, if all goes well, she'll have my name. But you have my love, Precious."

And what's a ring when you have a heart?

He made love to me there, over a puff of snow that somehow felt like clouds, beneath a thick tent made of leather that brined in the salt of our sweat, soaked in the heat of our murmurs. He held me until the last of the stars winked out.

My eyes slowly adjust to the brighter light of the hallway as I begin to walk downstairs with the guards on either side of me. Gone are the weathered browns of wooden floorboards. No more are the walls a solemn weathered gray stone. Scratches are buffed into the gold floors, thousands of footsteps worn into the malleable metal. The walls gleam with a servant's touch, the banister to the stairs smelling slightly of vinegar and salt, the abrasive varnish used to polish its every surface.

My rooms are on the very top floor, so that means we have six grand staircases to walk down. My legs begin to burn by the second, telling me I've been confined for too long.

Painted portraits of long-dead royals watch me as I pass by, the number of sconces growing in number with every level we descend to banish the night away with their flames. My pulse pounds in my ears as I'm led down to the first floor, where I hear music drifting out of the ballroom.

My escorts stop outside a pair of carved doors. The guard standing beside it opens it, stepping aside for us. "You may go inside."

"Yeah, I just don't really want to," I mutter back.

Digby clears his throat, and I inhale a tight breath as I take in the flood of light, heat, and sound coming from the room.

I can't scurry off to hide, because I'm not a mouse.

My ribbons squeeze around me, just slightly, a prompt to brace myself as I walk inside. The moment I step through the threshold, my eyes sweep around the space.

Musicians are playing in the very center of the room,

instruments a lull of pretty composition. They're surrounded by people dancing, the notes encouraging sensuality, the tune dipping into a heated croon. It's a collection of fabric and skin, of limbs weaving through an impalpable melody.

The whole space is lit up with three huge chandeliers that cast sparkles against the floor. There must be at least two hundred people here, all of them basking in King Midas's ostentatious wealth, their clothes a splash of lavish color.

The scent of their collective sweat and perfume is enough to overwhelm me. Despite the blizzard raging outside and the massive size of the room, the collective heat from all of these bodies makes the back of my neck prickle with beads of perspiration. Or maybe it's from nerves.

Along both sides of the walls, there's more reverie. Long tables are set up where guests are drinking, alcohol-faces gone ruddy and open. There are saddles everywhere, making the party far more licentious than it already is, which tells me that this gathering started a while ago.

I can see two groups slaking their desires against the wall, pretending that they have privacy inside shallow alcoves. Two men are even sharing a female saddle right in the middle of the dance floor, the woman held between them, hands sweeping inside a loosened bodice and up a draping skirt. She's moaning loud enough that her throaty vocals mix with the music like it's her own version of a serenade.

And past it all, on the very far end of the room on the raised dais, is my king.

Right now, he looks every inch the notorious Golden King that the people dubbed him. From his shined boots to his sparkling crown, everyone looks at him and knows that he's the marvel of riches, the master of fortune, the ruler of wealth.

And the moment I move further into the room, his russet eyes find me.

He's sitting on his throne, the queen noticeably absent, but that's not surprising given the type of celebration this seems to be. He has three royal saddles draped around him; two of them sitting on the armrests of his throne, and one at his feet, her head resting against his knee in adoring submission.

All of them are topless, wearing sheer skirts similar to mine, though theirs are black. Behind Midas are several of his guards and King Fulke's guards standing watch together, two kingdoms' crests, gold and purple, standing together in a show of alliance.

King Fulke sits on his own throne set beside Midas's, with Rissa straddling his lap. I can't help but imagine that it's me up there, forced to let his bony hands touch me and his yellowed teeth to nip at my flesh.

Behave tonight.

My eyes flick back to Midas as he leans in toward

one of his guards, speaking words I'm much too far away to hear. In a moment, the music cuts off, the dancers coming to a dizzying halt, while everyone in the entire room turns to look at the monarch, who sends his saddles scurrying away as he gets to his feet.

"People of Highbell," Midas announces, his strong voice carrying to every ear. "Tonight we celebrate the strength of Sixth Kingdom."

People cheer in the crowd, shouting incomprehensible words, but I can't help the way my lips press together in a thin line, the way my brow furrows. They did it. They attacked Fourth Kingdom, and they were victorious enough to warrant this party.

"Yet none of it would have been possible if it weren't for King Fulke and our alliance with Fifth," Midas goes on, gesturing magnanimously to the king beside him.

Fulke's crown is slightly askew on his bald head, and his cheeks are ruddy and pulled into a grin, but at least he had Rissa get up from his lap.

"King Fulke, as promised, I gift you this night with my gold-touched favored." Midas looks at me, pinning me in place despite the distance between us, those brown eyes like soil burying me with suffocating weight. "Auren, come forward."

Two hundred pairs of eyes swivel to me. Frenzied whispers pass from one to another as bodies shift to leave an empty path from where I stand, all the way to where the king awaits.

Midas isn't just giving me to Fulke tonight. He's also making it a public spectacle.

"Go on."

Digby murmurs the words quietly, but loud enough to get me moving. Swallowing hard, I force my feet to take their first steps, my body moving forward despite the fact that I want to turn and run away in the other direction. The other guards hang back, but Digby sticks with me, his stern expression in place as I match his stride.

My eyes skate around the gaping crowd, my ears assaulted with their murmured observations. They talk about everything from the shine of my skin to how much they think my fingernails are worth.

The way they look at me, I can tell that I'm not a woman to them. I'm a trinket that the king usually keeps hidden away. Everyone wants to take advantage of this rare sighting like I'm a nearly extinct animal.

The walk through that room feels miles long.

By the time I stop in front of the dais, everyone has gone quiet. All I hear is my own thudding heart and the howling wind outside.

I curtsy in front of him, knees bending, neck curving down with learned poise.

"Rise, Precious."

I do, my eyes meeting his as his hand extends. I walk up the steps of the dais, stopping beside him. He's so handsome that it makes my heart hurt just to look at him.

Instead of looking back at me, he addresses the assembled crowd again. "Continue your celebrations."

As soon as he finishes saying the words, the musicians strike up their instruments again, dancers slowly begin to move, and the crowd converges once more.

"Hmm, you've made some adjustments," King Midas says, his eyes flicking over every place where my ribbons are wrapped around my dress.

There's no use in denying it. "Yes, my king."

He clicks his tongue in disapproval but runs a knuckle against my cheek. My entire body reacts, fluttering with the desire to curl against his chest and be wrapped in his arms. To pull me from this madness, to be the dreaming wanderer in the snow drift once more, when we could just talk for hours, lying in each other's arms.

As if he knows the direction of my nostalgic thoughts, Midas's knuckle settles beneath my chin and tilts it up so he can look me in the eye. "You're spectacular, you know that?"

I don't answer, my tongue tied to the knots in my stomach.

He taps my chin affectionately before dropping his hold. "Be a good girl?"

Behave tonight.

Sit pretty.

A hard swallow pushes bitterness past the tangles of my throat. "Yes, my king."

He smiles, transforming his face to easygoing

handsomeness that makes my heart clench. "Go and sit with King Fulke," he murmurs. "We owe him a debt that needs to be paid."

I've never felt like a walking coin so much in my entire life as I do right now.

Midas gives me a reassuring nod and then turns away from me, grabbing more wine from a servant as two new saddles surround him with sultry giggles as he takes his place on his throne and is immediately approached by a pair of nobles. I'm officially on my own.

Turning, I walk over to King Fulke with my chin held high. I won't let him see how much I'm dreading this. I have a feeling that would only amuse him more, when what I really want is for him to lose interest entirely.

When I was tossing and turning last night in my bed, I told myself that no matter what happened tonight, I would handle it. Saddles are forced to give away their bodies to people they don't like every single day. I've endured far worse than this before.

Besides, King Midas is growing his empire, ridding Orea of a rotten king. And he was able to do that because a single night with me was worth an entire army of soldiers.

King Fulke grins at me, showing off his yellowed, rotting teeth. His eyes run over my form greedily with carnal hunger. Despite the way my ribbons are giving me extra coverage, one look seems like he's peeling away the layers in his head, imagining what lies beneath the wrapping.

"You're mine for the night, gilded pet. Let's celebrate."

The music lifts into a crescendo.

My spirit drops into my shoes.

CHAPTER 11

He makes me feed him.

Platters of food are brought out and placed on a table between the thrones, and Midas and Fulke enjoy the spread, the saddles around me indulging too.

Meats, cheeses, chocolates, fruit, bread. Sweet-smelling cakes and vinegar dips. I feed him everything as I sit on the armrest of the throne, my body twisted toward him as much as I have to without allowing any part of me to touch him.

But no matter how careful I am to hold as little of the food as I can without dropping it, he still sucks my fingers into his mouth, licking the pads of my fingers, scraping my nails with his teeth.

The piece of chocolate in my hand is quickly nabbed, his mouth sucking my fingers in before I can pull away. He laughs as he chews, the confectionary staining his teeth as he licks them. "Your gold skin makes the food taste so much *richer*."

I feel the eyes of the other saddles look over at me, assessing, judging, calculating, sizing me up as a threat, as if I *want* his attention.

Midas is speaking to more nobles again, the spot beside his throne filled one after another, as people occupy his time and borrow his ear. He hasn't glanced my way at all since I was traded off to Fulke.

"Open."

My eyes flick up to Fulke's hand that's hovering in front of my face. A slice of meat is caught between his fingers, sauce dripping off the bottom and landing on his black velvet leggings.

When I start to shake my head, horrified at the thought of having his fingers anywhere near my mouth or touching my food, Fulke raises a bushy brow. A question. A demand.

Behave tonight.

My lips part, barely, and Fulke presses the meat into my mouth, more forceful than he needs to. When he tries to push his fingers inside, I turn my head and snap my mouth closed.

He smirks. "What a naughty thing you are."

I feel Midas's gaze fall over me, and my shoulders stiffen.

"No matter. It marks for a titillating evening, doesn't it?"

Bread is pushed past my lips next. Cheese. Grapes. I chew mindlessly, staying silent, my eyes watchful, my ribbons tight.

With an outstretched index finger, he does a double tap against his goblet, his power flaring as he duplicates the cup and hands one to me. With a snap of his finger, a servant hurries over, filling them both with wine.

"A toast to our night," he says before tipping it against his lips and gulping down the contents.

I take a bitter sip.

When Fulke is bored of feeding me, he takes both goblets and places them on the table, shooing away any more trays of food. I'm glad that's over at least. The food sits in my stomach, as heavy as stones, my tongue belligerent for the taste of his fingers still lingering on it.

Of course, I don't get let off that easy though, because Fulke lifts a finger to point to his plump cheek. "Kiss me."

My eyes narrow, skin tightening, fingers curling in the skirts of my dress. When I don't move, Fulke's eyes flash. His hand comes up to pinch my ear, pulling me forward until my mouth lands against his scratchy cheek. Scratchy, not smooth like Midas. A rounded jaw and pudgy cheek, smelling of wine but reeking of arousal.

My lips don't pucker, because I refuse to kiss him. My mouth presses against his skin as he holds me there, my ear squeezed between his finger and thumb.

"There, that wasn't so hard, was it?" he laughs.

The moment he releases my ear, I lurch away, nearly

tipping myself over the side of the throne, but Fulke grabs hold of my arms to catch me, holding me steady as his laugh deepens. "No need to fall down to your knees for me yet."

My cheeks burn with embarrassment, with anger. I want to get away. I want to be back upstairs, safe in my cage with only the Gale Widow's cries for company.

Fulke doesn't release me right away, and his hands that are still gripping my arms squeeze tighter, enough for me to wonder if I'll be bruised later in dots of bronze. "I don't think you're close enough yet."

He pulls me onto his lap without warning. A feat, considering my body is so rigid. It's a wonder he's able to get me to move at all. I land awkwardly, stiffly, the back of my legs hitting his thighs and my spine snapping upright so that I don't lean against his chest. I try to grab the armrests to pull myself up, but Fulke snatches one of my wrists and places my palm over his crotch.

"Here, golden pet."

My eyes flare wide. My stomach churns. I feel his flaccid length begin to grow and harden. And as much as I want to snatch my hand away, I can't, because he's holding my wrist there with surprising strength.

I live in a cage, but I've never felt so trapped.

"Your Majesty."

Fulke's eyes travel past me to where Rissa has come up in front of him. "Shall I dance for you?" she asks with a sultry smile, her blonde hair in long waves against her front, somewhat hiding her naked breasts.

King Fulke eyes her greedily and tilts his head, giving her the go-ahead. She starts to dance, her black skirts swishing against the polished floor and arcing against her ankles, her hips moving to the pulse of the music, her eyes a lure of enticement matched by the curve of her lips.

Fulke finally releases my wrist to lean back, and I'm able to snatch my hand away as he gives his attention to Rissa's performance. "Watch her," he tells me, his mouth entirely too close to my ear for my liking. "This is a saddle who knows what she's doing. You'd do well to learn from her on how to please a man."

How to please a man. As if that should be a woman's—saddle or otherwise—sole purpose for living. The edge of my lip curls with the hint of a sneer.

Rissa's smile widens at his commendation, her eyes casting over me as if to gauge whether or not I'm jealous, but of course I'm not. I'm relieved. Whether she intended to or not, she gave me a much-needed reprieve from his attention. Like I tried to give her in the library.

No one else can probably see the slight swelling of her nose or the layer of makeup beneath her eye that's more than likely covering a bruise, but I do, and the sight makes me inwardly cringe. I really didn't mean to hurt her.

"Mmm, she is a rather good dancer, wouldn't you say, pet?"

I nod obediently. He clearly has a thing for making

her dance for him. Rissa, ever the professional, continues to sway seductively.

She's beautiful. High apple cheekbones; large, round eyes; blonde hair nearly down to her waist; curves; and full pink lips. It's no wonder why Fulke likes her so much. And it's not just her beauty, either—all of Midas's saddles are beautiful—but it's her confidence, the way she can read a man and know how to seduce him. She can transform, from her walk to her words, into becoming what someone wants.

Fulke rests a hand on my hips, thick fingers digging above the bone, pressing into flesh with a clear indication of possession. Until he gets bored with this as well, and instead moves me to sit on the floor in front of his legs. I think he likes the visualization of Midas's most prized favored sitting at his feet.

My legs are tucked beneath me, the only position I can be in to keep myself covered. Some of the nobles attending the party grow bolder, no doubt bolstered by the wine. They come closer to the dais, murmuring and staring at me, and I stare right back. I don't lower my head. I don't turn my gaze away.

Let them talk.

Let them look.

Fulke gets caught up in a discussion with Midas and a few other men as they discuss new trade routes to be established from Fourth Kingdom. About new investment opportunities with the Blackroot Mines. As if standing in a solid gold ballroom isn't enough.

The longer I'm made to sit on the floor, the more my knees and calves begin to ache. I try to shift to relieve some of the pressure, allowing some of the blood to rush back into my sore, scrunched limbs.

I tense when Fulke's hand comes down on my head. A master petting his dog. "Speaking of new commodities," Fulke begins, his fingers stroking through my hair, eyes gleaming. "Just a dozen strands of her hair must be worth a month's wages for a peasant."

"Hmm," Midas says noncommittally, even as his eyes watch the way Fulke touches me. There's possessiveness in his gaze, but he doesn't step in. He doesn't stop this.

I can feel a sharp, wet crackle burn in my eyes like a spitting wick, some invisible flame flickering in the center of my irises as tears threaten to pool like liquid fire.

And there, in the corner of a ten-year-long foundation of reliance and trust, a break appears. Like a shallow, jagged chip knocked into glass, a tiny fissure like spider's silk spreads up an inch.

Rissa stops dancing long enough to perch beside Fulke, her deft fingers kneading into his shoulders, her legs draped over the arm of the throne in a graceful stretch.

While he talks, she expertly continues her sensual touches, from shoulders to chest, down to his abdomen and the waist of his pants. She brushes against his hardening length with a teasing smirk, catching the eyes of other men across the room who watch with hunger. A show for more than just the benefit of the king beneath her.

And I realize right then, that this woman, this saddle, holds power. Not the magic of kings and queens, but a different sort of power—one of control. She holds these men in the palm of her attentive hands, directing their desires, driving their emotions, feeding their fantasies.

In all my time as the *royal saddle*, I've never done anything close to that, never learned how. I haven't needed to, since I've never been shared. Next to her, I probably look like the worst saddle ever, sitting here straight-backed, my hands tucked into my lap, cringing every time Fulke's leg touches my shoulder or his hand comes down to pet me again.

"You're really good at that," I murmur, low enough that no one else can hear.

"I'm a saddle," Rissa replies, as if that answers everything. I guess it does.

"I think we'll retire now, pet," Fulke says, snagging my attention to his face, his eyes cast down into the line of my cleavage. "Up. I want to be buried in your golden cunt this hour, since Midas insists on taking you back before dawn."

I'm wrenched up by the arms, the blood in my cramped legs rushing back through my limbs as I stand. "You go on, girl," he orders Rissa. "I have no need of you tonight."

"Yes, Your Majesty," she says with a pretty dip of her

head before she turns and gracefully glides away, toward the group of men who are still watching her.

Fulke turns to Midas, one hand still on my arm. "I bid you goodnight," he says with a smirk. "I'm eager to have her to myself."

King Midas tips his head at Fulke, though his brown eyes flick to me. "Enjoy."

That's all he says. Like I'm a wine or pastry, set out for King Fulke to *enjoy*. I turn my head away from him, too hurt to look at him anymore. That spider crack spreads another inch higher.

A few of his guards close in around us as Fulke leads us down the stairs of the dais, his escorts the only separation between me and the chortling crowd as they begin to hoot and holler out lewd things to us.

"Ride the golden saddle good, sire!"

"Fuck the gold right outta her!"

My teeth snap together at the continued vulgarity. My ribbons itch to lash out at them, to sharpen their edges and slice across their sneering mouths. When King Fulke decides to egg on the audience by releasing my arm to slap my ass, the ends curl around my ribs like clenched fists.

I have to be strong.

I *have* to.

Except...just his touch on my backside is enough to make me cringe. How am I supposed to allow him to touch any other part of me? How am I supposed to go through with this?

Souvenir.
Sit pretty.
Behave.
Trust him.

And suddenly, right there in the middle of the ballroom amidst the mocking revelers, I decide that I won't.

CHAPTER 12

I don't want this man to touch me. I don't care if he is a king. I don't care if *my* king traded me to Fulke for the night, or if he won a battle because of it. I don't want this, and I'm not going to just lie down and take it. I'm not going to *behave*. This...Midas can't ask this of me. Can't demand it.

I come to a stop right before we reach the gleaming doors.

King Fulke and his guards don't even notice for a moment. They're too caught up in the celebration. In the excitement.

When they start to walk toward the doorway, the five men seem to realize I'm not moving with them anymore, and they all look behind them where I'm standing a few paces back. The king is the last to turn but the first to speak. His bushy gray brows pull together. "Come, pet."

My neck feels as stiff as stone, but I manage to shake my head. "No."

I swear, my voice echoes. Ridiculous, since there are two hundred people here and the musicians are still playing—albeit drunkenly. But my single, soft spoken word? It might as well have been the rumble of an avalanche, because it makes everyone go quiet and strain to listen, to decipher the disturbance that ripples through the air.

"What? What did you say?" King Fulke asks, all good humor gone from his face. Now, his dark eyes shine with disbelief and outrage.

I back up a step and shake my head, my resolve unwavering even as my fear grows. "I'm the king's favored," I say, lifting my chin and speaking with a strong tone that doesn't match with the fact that my hands are shaking. "Despite what I look like, I'm not a coin to be spent."

I thought there was silence before, but now it's crushing. Even the wind outside has gone quiet. I look around, though I'm not sure why. For an ally? I have none.

I don't know the hit is coming until my head snaps to the right and an explosion of red-starry pain crashes over my eyes.

The only way I'm able to stay upright from the hit across my cheek is because his hands are fisted at the back of my dress, his hold crushing some of my ribbons between his knuckles.

Fulke wrenches me to face Midas, who's already

striding this way, the crowd parting for him like he's a rushing rapid, a river to cut through the land.

"Is this how your saddles speak to royalty?" Fulke asks, spit flying from his furious mouth and hitting the side of my throbbing face as he shakes me. "I should have her head!"

"Well, I gave you her cunt, not her head," Midas replies coolly as he walks past the gawking crowd.

My own weak river flows down my cheeks, pitiful drips that move nothing at all, landing uselessly at the floor near my feet.

I know I should keep my mouth shut. I *know* this. But I can't help it, and I'm already in trouble as it is, so why not? What the hell have I got to lose?

"Aren't I worth more than this?" I ask quietly. Not to Fulke, but to Midas. Not about the gild of my skin, but the love of my heart. Isn't *that* worth more?

"*Worth*?" King Midas seethes as he stops in front of me. His tone is quiet, but the closest onlookers can still hear, and everyone is pressing closer, straining to hear what he says. "You are worth more than all the gold in this castle. But I still own you, and I will spend you any way I see fit."

I've never heard a heart shatter, but it sounds like a crack spreading up glass.

But you promised to keep me safe. You promised I'd always have your heart.

I want to say it, but I'm silent. My wet eyes scream

with the truth of those soundless words, but my king doesn't hear me.

Midas looks over at his ally. "Apologies, King Fulke. You'll have to excuse her innocence. I've always spoiled her. She will not misbehave again."

I can't tell if Fulke is assuaged, because I don't look at him. Midas's eyes flick behind me to the guards. "Escort Auren to King Fulke's rooms."

"No!"

Spurred into action, I try to wrench away, but I'm dragged forward by two of Fulke's guards, like it's not even a strain. Smashed between the guards' purple-dipped armor, I'm mindless with anger, with shock. I hurl curses at them left and right, but their holds don't loosen.

King Fulke stalks in front of us as we walk through the doorway. "Quiet!" he snaps. "Or I will belt you this night until your golden skin is welted!"

My mouth shuts, though I'm not convinced that will save me. I defied him publicly, and in my experience, defying a king never goes unpunished.

Outside of the ballroom, I'm hauled across the entry hall, my escorts turning me in the direction of the grand staircase at the other end of the room. But before we reach it, the main doors suddenly fly open, and a soldier wearing Fulke's armor comes sprinting in. Midas's guards standing watch at the door shout for him to stop, but he ignores them when he spots Fulke and starts racing toward his king.

His heavy purple cloak is covered in snow and ice, his boots muddy with frozen slosh. He slips on the floor as he runs, yet he doesn't lose his feet. "My king!"

Fulke stops with a frown. "What is the meaning of this?"

Stopping in front of us, the bedraggled soldier pants so hard he has to kneel over a bit to catch his breath before he can speak. His chest plate is crusted with frost, his face red and chapped from the wind.

"Where are you reporting from, soldier?" one of Fulke's guards asks, stepping forward in front of the king in a defensive stance.

"Fourth Kingdom's border, sir," the soldier answers.

The guard frowns. "Where's Gromes?"

He shakes his head. "The messenger was killed in action. The general attempted to send two others, but I was the only one who managed to get on the back of one of the timberwings and escape before we were shot from the sky. I flew all day and night."

Raucous laughter from the ballroom bleeds out as a few of the party-goers come stumbling into the hall, hands groping, unaware of their surroundings.

Midas comes striding toward us a second later with six of his own guards—*of course* it's six—including Digby. He takes one look at Fulke's messenger, and a grim look crosses his face.

"Come. Speak in private this way, away from the ears and eyes of revelers," Midas says, nodding his head in the direction of the letter room off to the left. I'm hoping to slip away, but the guards don't let me go. Instead, I'm hauled down a short hallway, away from the staircase, and our group files into the room.

The space holds a few scattered tables and chairs, while parchment, candles, ink bottles, wax, and quills are piled up for anyone to use to write their letters and send them off.

The door is closed behind us, shutting me in with two kings and ten guards between the two of them.

The messenger doesn't look any more composed than he was when he first burst in through the doors. If anything, he's breathing even harder now, his eyes shifting nervously around the room as he positions himself behind one of the golden tables.

"Well?" King Fulke demands. "I want to know why my messenger is dead and why you've been sent here from the border."

The messenger's hands shake slightly. Whether it's from nervousness or exhaustion, I don't know. "My king, if I could speak to you in private…"

But Fulke's dark eyes narrow on his request. "Are you a traitor, soldier? Did you defect?"

The messenger's eyes go wide. "What? No, sire!"

"Then explain yourself!" Fulke demands, crashing his fist onto the table, making both me and the messenger flinch.

Somber resolve settles in the man's face, though he grips the hilt of his sword. "As soon as your army breached Fourth's border, King Ravinger's men attacked. Your entire fleet was decimated, sire."

King Fulke's brows pull together. "You are mistaken. Our troops broke through Fourth's line earlier this morning. We took Cliffhelm. Our joined armies with Sixth's were victorious. Fourth was caught completely off guard. Our negotiations are already in place."

The messenger darts a look around the room, eyes landing on a stoic, expressionless Midas before returning to Fulke. "No, Your Majesty."

"No?" Fulke repeats, as if he's never heard the word before. "What do you mean, *no*?"

"We—we didn't take Cliffhelm. Ravinger's training outpost there was full of soldiers. We never even breached the walls before they were on us."

One of Fulke's guards curses, Fulke's fists tightening at his sides. "You're saying my entire division was taken out?"

The messenger hesitates. "Yes, Your Majesty, and..."

King Fulke picks up one of the ink bottles and sends it hurtling against the wall, the glass shattering, ink splattered and dripping. "And *what*?" Fulke fumes. "Spit it out!"

Something is wrong here. Very, very wrong. They were celebrating. Their plan was victorious. My brows pull together in a frown as my mind whirls. What happened between then and now? How could such misinformation be passed to the kings earlier? Or is this soldier lying? But if so...for what purpose?

The messenger grips the hilt of his sword tighter under the scowl of his king, and I'm not the only one who notices. "What are you doing, soldier?" King Fulke's guard asks, tone heavy with suspicion as he reaches for his own blade.

But the messenger isn't looking at him. He's not even looking at Fulke. He's looking at Midas.

My body coils with tension, my instincts blaring at me that something terrible is about to happen, but I have no idea what.

"Explain to me how we were told that we took Cliffhelm this morning, only for you to now inform me that my men were all slaughtered!" Fulke snarls. "Tell me how Ravinger's men were able to overtake both my soldiers and Midas's without us knowing!"

Fulke's guards close in on the messenger, like a pack of wolves sniffing out a traitor. A liar.

But they're closing in on the wrong man.

The messenger tilts his chin up, a proud stance widening his feet even as resignation flashes in his eyes. "They didn't overtake King Midas's men. Because Midas's army never met ours. Sixth's army never went to Fourth's border. Your soldiers were there to face King

Ravinger's men *alone*, and the earlier messages were a deceit." Accusatory eyes cut over to my king. "Midas betrayed you."

CHAPTER 13

For a span of a breath, no one moves.

Shocked silence fills the room at the messenger's declaration. Then both sets of guards tighten formations around their kings.

King Fulke frowns, confused. "You are mistaken, soldier," he says to the messenger.

"He's not."

My eyes shoot over to Midas at his bold declaration, but he only looks steadily back at Fulke with pleased arrogance. Fulke's face changes from confusion to shock and then into budding fury as the world settles in, shaking with the aftershocks of the shift.

"You *betrayed* me?" King Fulke asks, his voice like a whip.

His guards tighten their hands around their blades, purple pommels with their kingdom's sigil of jagged icicles carved through the hilt. Just minutes ago, these men were all drinking and laughing together. Now, tension radiates through them as they face each other.

Allies to enemies.

Enemies from allies.

"Let this be your last life lesson, Fulke," Midas replies calmly, not the least bit threatened despite the deadly menace hanging in the air. "True kings don't give out their armies for cunts."

I don't know who looks more shocked—Fulke or myself.

The monarch of Fifth Kingdom stares hard at Midas, like he's truly *seeing* him for the first time, like he's no longer being blinded by all the gleaming gold, the immeasurable wealth. "You were never going to take Fourth Kingdom," he says, a flat understanding braced in his tone.

Midas laughs. He actually *laughs* at the other king. "Of course not. Everyone knows you don't attack Fourth Kingdom. King Ravinger decimates anyone who dares."

All of the faces on Fulke's guards fill with bleak hate. It darkens their brows, makes their eyes flash.

Horror fills my veins as I realize the extent of what he's done. Midas has been forming a bond with Fulke for *years*. Seducing him with riches and filling his coffers, and Fulke has lapped it all up greedily. Happily.

It always made me curious—what Midas was getting out of it. But now I know. Midas was never making Fulke rich. He was treating Fifth Kingdom like his own secondary vault. Fulke was simply transporting the gold for him, while Midas bided his time.

It's brilliant. It's brutal. And I know without a doubt that there won't be two kings who walk back out of this letter room.

Fulke's lips thin, a bead of sweat collecting at his left temple as he nods—in either understanding or resignation, I don't know which. He shows no fear, only wears a cold glare as the pieces fall into place. "Your army was never going to Fourth Kingdom to attack. You lied and drew my own soldiers away to be slaughtered so that you could invade *my* kingdom."

Midas's eyes glitter with satisfaction. Fulke's harden with enmity.

Allies to enemies.

The bead of sweat starts to fall off Fulke's temple, an invisible line down, like the one Midas crossed.

I don't get a warning, and I don't know which king gives the order to attack first. I just know that all at once, a battle breaks out.

I'm dropped hard onto the floor by someone before I can blink. The breath is knocked out of me, a woven rug the only thing to break my fall.

Purple and gold clash in an explosion of metallic clangs.

Red comes next, in violent splatters.

I hear the short shouts. The swords meeting in vicious swipes. And the abruptness of it acts like a shock to the brain, dredging up memories as my past and present meet.

Fighting is too close and too loud, and I'm sprawled on the ground just like I was on a different day, during a different fight.

A fight under a yellow moon, its shape like a fingernail scratching at a dark sky. Ten years ago, when raiders came to the tiny town where I was living. Raiders doing what they do—taking. Taking everything that didn't belong to them. Money, livestock, grain—women.

The sound of swords clashing again is like a gruesome melody, the sound prompting my mind of a tavern song that I've played on my harp.

They pillaged the village,
They burned the sterns.
They hail to no king,
But they'll bow for a ring.

The silly lyrics play in my head as I slap my hands over my ears. My mind wavers from then to now, from there to here, as I start to scramble backward, aiming for the wall. If I can just stay low and get to the wall, then I can get to the door, and if I can get to the door, I can—

A body suddenly falls on top of me, making my chin slam to the ground hard enough that I see stars. With a grunt at the heavy weight pinning me, it takes me a frantic moment of shoving and rolling to get the person off, only to realize that he is very, very dead.

Before I can really take in the fact that he no longer has a head, I'm suddenly dragged up to my feet. My ears are ringing, the stupid song still playing, as a blade is shoved against my throat.

"You fucking bastard!" King Fulke shouts beside my ear, jostling me in his hold.

I whimper as his erratic movements make the dagger dig down too far, his hands unsteady as a shallow scratch is cut in. "You think you're so clever. You want to kill me?" he snarls. "Then I'm taking your gilded bitch with me."

It's a surreal feeling, to have Death breathing down your neck. In this case, Death is Fulke, and his hot exhale slithers down my spine like spilled wine, dampening my skin with slick fear. His hand clenches onto the hilt of the dagger so tightly that the blade shakes, the tremble making it dig deeper into my skin, making blood gather there.

There are eight men lying on the floor or slumped over tables, their red life pooling beneath them, falling out of gaping wounds. I blink at the puddles, like it's just paint, and all of this is just a bad dream playing out right alongside that macabre tune.

Except it's not.

All of Fulke's men, including the messenger, are dead, along with three of Midas's guards.

The other two of Midas's guards stand at his side protectively, their sharp golden blades stained crimson.

The wind howls outside, hail hurling at the glass of the window.

Midas looks at me with something indistinguishable in his eyes, while mine are probably wide with shock, shock and horror.

I squeeze my eyes tight, because I don't want to see what happens next. I don't want to watch their reactions as my throat is cut open.

Die. I'm going to die.

As soon as my eyes are closed, the blade presses in, like it's cornering me, trapping me, fulfilling Fulke's savage threat to take my life. I suck in one last breath of air and hold it in my lungs, bracing myself, willing the breath not to leave me.

But before the sharpened edge can cut any deeper, Fulke's body lurches, and I'm suddenly being wrenched to the side by a grip on my arm as the king's form slams to the ground on his side, jerking violently at my feet. I look down in shock at the sword stuck all the way through him from back to front.

Whipping my head to the right, I see Digby. Digby, who I'd forgotten was even in the room. Holding me up with his steady grip on my arm, blood splattered on his face, his sword missing from his scabbard.

At the sound of a horrible gurgle, I look back down at Fulke where he writhes. His hands come up, touching the sword where it's coming out of his chest. His mouth opens and shuts without words, blood lining his lips. He grips the blade, slicing his palms into ribbons as he holds it tight, as if he wants to strangle it into submission.

He dies like that, with both hands clenching the golden weapon, mouth sneering like a curse was left on it, one that would damn us all to hell.

Midas stands across the room with his other two guards, all eyes on King Fulke as his chest gets stuck on his last gurgling exhale. My vision tunnels on it, on the deep red blood bubbling out of the wound, slow as syrup.

The shakes hit me first. Then it's the tunnel vision.

My heart pounds against my skull with a *rap, rap, rap*—or is that still the hail against the window?

I turn and bury my face against Digby's collar. I don't even care how uncomfortable it is because of his armor. I hold on to him anyway, my whole body a tremor.

"Thank you, thank you, thank you," I repeat against his chest. He saved me. My quiet, stoic guard just killed a king to save my life.

I hear voices—Midas's, one of the guards, maybe Digby too. I can't hear what they're saying, though, can't care enough to concentrate on it.

My feet sway a bit, and my eyes pop with flares of black light. More talking. More hail pattering. That song still playing.

"Take her to her rooms," Midas says—or maybe I imagined it.

Digby's hands shift me around, and then he's picking me up, letting my face stay buried against his chest plate.

"You have blood on you. I have blood on me." My voice sounds far away, small. The blood is such an inconsequential thing compared to everything else. I don't even know why I point it out.

He carries me away, away and up.

"I need a bright side," I mumble.

Bright side. I need a bright side to ground me. To keep me from going under.

Bright side...bright side, I didn't get raped or murdered.

Great Divine, what an abysmal bright side.

Digby stays silent, not offering any suggestions, not that I expected him to. But the sure steps of his boots reassure me for some reason, even though my mind is whirling and those black flares in my vision are getting worse. "You killed a king for me, Digby," I mutter.

He just grunts.

I close my eyes just for a second, lulled by the sway of him walking. I open my eyes after what feels like just a few seconds, but I realize I'm already on the tallest level of the palace, back in my bedroom, and Digby is setting me down on my bed.

I sit up, bracing my hands on the mattress, my fingers curling into the covers. With one departing look, Digby turns and walks out on quiet footsteps, the creak of my cage door closing softly before he leaves me to my privacy, the lit candles in my room my only companion.

I was going to be raped by a king tonight.

But that king was killed, a blade shoved through his chest just inches away from me. His blood is soaked into my slippers. I can still feel his hot breath against my neck. And the night is crushing me. Crushing me on all sides, as every part of what happened presses against my mind, replaying, picking it apart. Showing me again and again what happened, from the moment I woke up to right now.

I sit here like this for a long while, thinking, listening to the hail and the wind, wondering if I did something in a past life to offend the goddesses—or if I'm so hidden here in Sixth Kingdom, beneath a cover of snow clouds that never leaves, that the stars just haven't been able to see me.

And for the next hour, that's all I do, is wonder. With the blood of a dead king still smeared on my shoes, and a shallow wound drying at my throat.

CHAPTER 14

T*he sound of a key* fitting into my door pulls me from my thoughts. Several sets of footsteps come near as servants file into my cage one after the other. They walk past me, steps determined, as they head for my bathroom, steam rising from buckets in their arms.

A minute later, they all walk right back out silently, the cage closing again, my bedroom door shutting.

I don't turn, don't move, but I wait. Listen.

I can feel him behind me, watching, but I keep my back straight, keep my eyes on the window, to the blizzard raging outside.

Finally, Midas walks over, a dark silhouette that stops in front of me a few paces away.

He waits for a beat, and although I can't see his eyes, I feel the trace of them, feel them land on the slash over my throat.

Midas takes three slow steps and then offers his hand, holding it in front of me, waiting.

I don't take it.

"Let me get you cleaned up, Precious."

My eyes lift up to his face. I still don't take his hand.

His expression fills with remorse. "I know," he says hoarsely. "I know, but let me explain. Let me—I want to hold you. Take care of you. Let me help you, Auren."

That slowly creeping crack spreading up from the gash in the glass, it halts. Waits. Wonders.

Because Midas said those words to me before—*Let me help you.*

Is that why he's using them now? To remind me?

When I was on the streets, I slept during the day and crept around at night. Hungry, often. Afraid, always. I was too scared to buy anything, to approach anyone. I did so only when it was absolutely necessary.

I wandered alone, stayed hidden. It was the only way a girl like me could stay safe. To make sure I didn't end up right back in the same situation I'd escaped from.

Bad men. The world was run by bad men.

And as much as I tried to lay low, to be invisible, I couldn't. I wasn't.

I knew better than to stay too long in one place. I knew better, but I was tired. Worn down. I slipped up. Got sloppy. I knew it was just a matter of time before something bad happened to repay me for it.

The looters came that night.

With fire and axes, they took the village I was hiding in—the one I should've left behind days before.

They took everything and anything they wanted. The farmers who lived there didn't stand a chance, didn't have any defensive training. They didn't even own weapons other than their pitchforks and shovels.

I tried to run. Too late. I was far too late.

Pulled from an alleyway, I was shoved into a cart with the other women who'd been dragged from their beds.

They screamed and cried, but I was silent. Resigned. I knew it was over for me. I knew there was no way I'd escape. Not again. The fates don't give second chances. So I steeled my spine, and I readied myself to face the life I'd tried to run from.

And that's when he came. Midas. Like the goddesses themselves had sent him, riding in on a dappled gray horse with a half dozen other men.

At first, I thought the shouts were just continued fighting from the villagers, a last-ditch effort to defend their homes. But then I saw the looters being cut down. And then the cart was opened and the women were running, sobbing again—this time, with tears of terrified relief.

But I had no family to reunite with, no one to run to. So I staggered back to that alleyway. Tense shoulders collapsed against a rough stone wall. I didn't believe it was over so quickly. Didn't trust it. But I thanked the stars, all the same.

At some point, the sounds of the fighting stopped. The

fires tossed on thatched roofs were put out, the clinging smoke in the air the only thing warming my thin, bedraggled body.

And then a lone figure appeared in the alley. I cowered against stacked crates until he stopped in front of me, and I looked up at his handsome face. He smiled at me. Not a jeer, not a cruel tilt of lips. A genuine smile. It was warm. Just looking at it stopped my ceaseless shaking.

He held out a hand while that smile stayed on his face. "You're safe now. Let me help you."

And I was. And he did.

From that moment on, he kept me safe. When I wanted to hide from the world, he gave me his cloak and hood. When I shied away from other people, he made sure we stayed separate. When I clung to him, he held me.

And when I kissed him for the first time, he kissed me right back.

You're safe now. Let me help you.

I was done being exposed and vulnerable in the world, so he made sure I didn't have to be anymore.

Swallowing hard, I look up at Midas as our past settles around me, like he's once again leading me out of that dark alley, like he's reminding me where we've come from. Of what he did for me.

He earned my trust. My love. My loyalty. I wouldn't be here, in this gilded cage, if he hadn't.

"Please," he pleads, surprising me. Midas never pleads. Not since he put a crown on his own head.

I hesitate for a moment, but the past is a powerful thing, so my hand finally lifts, slips inside his grasp, and squeezes. That smile lights up his face as I let him pull me up, let him guide me into the bathroom, and something in me warms slightly. My body stops shaking.

Inside, a golden tub is filled, tendrils of steam curling over the lip, oil poured into the water, making it smell of winterberries.

He stops us in the middle of the room, the hanging sconces already lit, casting everything in its comforting glow. The hanging mirror above the washbasin shows the two of us, shows Midas step up behind me.

I feel his fingers skim up my spine before delving into my ribbons—each silken strand still bound around me.

Carefully, he unwraps me, layer by layer.

My ribbons don't do anything to help him—but they don't stop him either, don't rip from his grasp.

He works slowly, taking his time with each pass, until the last of my long ribbons are let out, draping from my spine to the floor behind me. All the while, I watch him in the mirror, my heart beating quicker than usual.

He helps me out of the saddle gown next, his fingers never once straying, never crossing any sort of line except to simply help me undress.

When the fabric falls at my feet, Midas looks at my eyes in the reflection of the mirror for a moment, before taking my hand once more and leading me into the tub.

One leg over, then the next, and I sit down, the hot water shoulder-deep, a few scattered bubbles mingling with the oil that seeps into my skin.

I sigh.

Midas sits on a stool beside the tub with a cloth in his hand, dipping it in the water before his eyes come back up to look at me.

"May I?"

I don't answer or nod, but I tip my chin up slightly, and that's invitation enough. He reaches forward and gently begins to dab at the wound, the sting making me flinch.

"I'm sorry."

His words are gentle but steady—same as the swipes against my throat.

"For what part?" I ask, my voice croaky from disuse or emotion. Maybe both.

The cloth is dipped again and again, new warm water to wash away the dried blood, to clean the cut.

"You weren't supposed to get hurt."

My brows rise at his admission, even as indignant anger rises up, shouldering past the numbness I've felt for the last few hours.

"The slice against my throat is the least of them," I reply, and I mean it.

I pull away from his ministrations and lie all the way back, dipping my head and hair beneath the water. With eyes closed, I let it envelop me, let it press into my skin, let the warmth soothe my body like I wish it could soothe my aching heart.

When I sit back up, I take a gulping breath and rest my head against the back of the tub, my eyes landing on Midas. I don't cover up the hurt and anger there, don't mask it from him.

Midas nods, like he accepts what I'm silently telling him.

"I know," he says again, just like he did in the bedroom. "I know what you're thinking."

What I'm thinking isn't nearly as bad as what I'm feeling, but I don't say that.

"I didn't think you'd actually go through with it," I tell him, my tone accusatory. "And as nervous as I was, as gutted, some part of me thought that you'd have a plan. That you wouldn't go through with it."

My breaths come quicker, the water line rising and lowering over my chest. My ribbons swim in the water, pulling tighter around me once more, like they're trying to keep me from cracking to pieces.

"I trusted you, Midas. I trust us. After all these years, after all I've done—"

Midas grabs one of my hands, squeezing it between his, his face earnest. "I was never going to let him touch you."

I frown, my thoughts cut short. "What?"

"Just listen," he tells me. "I knew Fulke coveted you. Hell, everyone knew. He was a fool. He dared to ask for what was mine."

I blink, remembering the morning when Fulke asked for me, when they struck their deal.

"You set him up for it."

Midas tilts his head. "Did I? Is that what you think?"

My lips turn down, confusion swimming through me, making my thoughts murky. "I don't understand."

Midas hooks his foot around the leg of the stool to move it closer, his hands still holding onto mine, the water droplets collecting on his palms.

"Fulke is a flesh trader."

Shock courses through me. "What?"

Midas nods solemnly. "I heard rumors, but I found out for sure months ago. When I was able to confirm it, I knew something needed to be done."

I try to keep up with his words, try to make the connections. "So you planned how to take him out? How to kill him?"

Midas's lips press together at my damning tone. "Would you rather I let him continue to sell his own people for profit?"

"That's not what I meant."

"Auren, I'm a king, and kings have to make hard decisions. When it became clear to me that Fulke was no longer a viable ally, not even a good person, I decided to act."

"By setting him up. Tricking him. By sending his men into a meaningless slaughter," I accuse. "How many of his soldiers died, Midas?"

"As few as possible, just enough to make it work."

I scoff. "As if that makes it any better!"

"Better a man die with honor on a battlefield than a child be sold to slavery. Wouldn't you agree, Auren?"

A punch.

That's what it is. His words punch into my stomach, against my heart, up my throat. He shreds me inside with a sentence, memories threatening to come up, to spill out my eyes.

"I did it for you, Auren," Midas says, quieter now, losing the defensiveness of his voice. "To make sure they don't endure what you did."

When a tear slips past my eye, he swears and wipes it away, his face earnest. "I'm sorry. You know me, you know how I get. Once I get a plan in my head, it's all I see. I didn't stop to consider the consequences. I just knew I wanted him gone. Done. To stop him once and for all." His hand comes up to cup my cheek, his eyes boring into mine. "But listen to me when I say this: I was never going to let him have you. It was a ruse."

My throat is dry, but I clear it so I can speak. "Why not just tell me, then? Why not explain all this before so I knew?"

"I was worried that he'd find out somehow, that you wouldn't be able to pretend. I needed Fulke complacent. Distracted. You did your part beautifully."

I drop my head, shaking it. "I was so damn terrified, so *hurt*. I don't know if I can get past that."

"Like I said, I didn't think," he tells me, a stroke against my cheek before he drops his hand.

"You killed a *king*, Midas. Used him to attack another. What are you going to do?" I ask, the worry gnawing at my insides as my teeth gnaw on my lip.

"Don't worry about that," he tells me. "I have a plan."

I can't help the bitter snort that escapes me. "I suppose you're not going to tell me it, just like you didn't tell me that you were tricking Fulke about giving me to him."

Midas sighs. "I didn't dare say more. No one knows any of this, Auren. *No one* aside from you knew what I set up. And I have to play this next part just as carefully. Just as meticulously. But I need you to forgive me, Precious. I need you to understand."

Do I? Do I understand?

I'm relieved, I know that much. The coiled tension that's been inside me these past days has eased. He wasn't going to let Fulke have me. He had a plan.

It was callous and thoughtless, but it makes sense. This is how Midas is, how he's always been. That strategic, brilliant mind of his sometimes falls short on emotions. He can scheme and plan like an expert, but he often forgets the human side of it.

"I was so mad at you."

Midas chuckles, the sound breaking some of the tension between us, bringing us a step back to what we were, what we should be.

"I know. I thought you were acting. Figured you trusted me enough and you were just putting on a good show. But then in the ballroom earlier, you were furious."

A heat crawls up my cheeks. "Yeah, sorry about defying you in front of everyone."

He gives me a soft smile. "It's alright."

Midas gets up and grabs a drying cloth off a hook, holding it up for me. I stand up at the silent direction and step out of the tub, letting him wrap me up in it.

Once I'm dried and dressed in a nightgown, Midas takes me back to my bedroom. My damp ribbons splay behind me with my hair, my head resting on his chest as his hand rubs down my back.

This. This is what we've been missing. How many nights has it been since he's held me like this?

Months. I'm not sure how many.

"You used to hold me every night," I say softly against his tanned skin, his chest peeking out from the undone tie at the top of his tunic. His legs are crossed at the ankles, both of us lying atop the blankets, not needing any other warmth besides each other.

Midas smiles against my head. "I did. Probably not the best thing for a newly wedded man to do."

Probably not, but I was greedy for it anyway.

"If the queen was jealous, she had a strange way of showing it," I say, remembering that first year. "She gifted you three royal saddles for your birthday."

I remember being shocked. Shocked and jealous. His

own wife expected him to have sex with other women. Encouraged it, even. Just not with me.

The first time he slept with one of them, it had gutted me. I've grown used to it by now. Not that it doesn't still hurt, but I understand. He's a king. What did I really expect?

As if he can sense the directions of my thoughts, Midas's arm pulls me up until I'm lying on top of him, our faces in front of each other.

"It's just me and you when I'm here," he reminds me. "Nothing else exists outside of this cage."

I nod slowly. "I know."

His brown eyes fall to the mark on my neck before his hands come up to grip my waist. "You're mine."

I know that too.

His gaze flicks down my body, his grip tightening as lust simmers between us, and my breath catches. So long. It's been so long.

I've waited to see this look from him again. For him to have time to give me more than just a passing caress, a distracted smile. For him not to be a king that has to behave like one, but to just be Midas. *My* Midas.

"You're mine," he says again, and his hands move, one to hold the back of my head, the other to skim down to my ass and squeeze.

"I've missed you," he says, his lips poised at the hollow of my throat, right below the blade's mark. "You looked beautiful tonight. So damned sexy."

His fingers pull up the side of my nightgown, until his hand can dip beneath, bare palm against thigh. My breathing quickens, and I sigh into his mouth as he kisses me in quick, angled bursts.

"I missed you too," I reply.

He sits us up, keeping me on his lap, my hands coming up to his shoulders to steady myself. With hunger in his eyes, he pulls off my dress, lets me undo the laces at his pants. "So pretty, Precious. So damned pretty."

My heart beats fast, my stomach knotting and unknotting as his lips once again caress my throat, travel up my jaw. And then his hard length is pushing into me, his groan a taste in my mouth that I swallow down and try to keep.

He possesses me like this, hips pushing up, driving himself deeper, even as his arms tighten around me, squeezing, telling me he won't ever let me go. And when I moan, my eyes fluttering closed, his tongue comes in to claim me, to rule me. He takes and takes, and I give. I give it all.

My heart swells when he sucks at my tongue and plunges deeper into my core, and I move with him, my spine like a wave as I work to bring him pleasure, to give him what he needs. To make him happy.

And when he pulls from my body and spills his seed against my stomach with a groan, I lie back down against his sweat-slicked chest with a sigh and a soft smile.

But the traitorous tear that falls from my eye tells a

different story as it lands on my lip. It brines my happiness and rinses the smile away, leaving a bitter taste in my mouth.

Midas leaves before dawn with a kiss, but his lips don't take the taste away. And there in the dark, alone, I cry.

And that, that secret sob I let drain into my pillow, is an ugly truth. But it's not one I'm ready to face yet.

So I let the satin soak it up, and then I fall asleep, the candor hidden beneath my head and shoved away by the time the morning dawns.

CHAPTER 15

I *watch the guards amble* around my bedroom, carrying out the last of the trunks that I filled earlier.

My space looks emptier than usual, my dressing room with noticeable gaps from where some of the gowns and shoes have been taken and packed away. Outside, dusk has fallen.

It's nearly time to leave.

It doesn't appear to be snowing out right now, but snow never stays away for very long here, which is why I'm dressed in a heavy woolen gown, complete with fur trim and sheepskin-lined boots. Everything is shiny gold, of course, right down to my thick leather gloves.

My hair is coiled tightly against my head in countless braids so that the wind won't thrash it around, kept out of the way so that my hood can conceal both my hair and my face.

"It's time."

I turn away from the window to see Digby standing ready on the other side of my cage. He looks gruff and quiet as usual, no hint of the man who ran a sword through a foreign king. No expression of worry, like when he carried me up six flights of stairs while covered in blood. But then, I appreciate that about him. His complete unruffled manner, his steadfastness.

Unconsciously, I lift a hand and run my fingers against the newly formed scar at my throat where King Fulke tried to slit it three weeks ago. Digby notices the movement, his eyes flicking down to my fingers, and I immediately drop my hand, trying to stop myself from that nervous fidget I've developed.

Sometimes, my mind forces me to relive that moment in my nightmares, and I wake up screaming and clutching my throat, convinced that I'm suffocating on my own blood.

Other times, my mind decides it would be a good idea to imagine what would've happened if that messenger had never shown up, if Fulke had dragged me all the way to his bedroom instead, and Midas never came to stop it.

Neither nightmare lets me get much sleep. That's probably why I have circles under my eyes like bronzed bruises shaded above my cheeks.

I wish Midas were here.

Three days. He could only stay for three days after the incident, and then he had to leave—he and a regiment of soldiers to travel to Fifth Kingdom.

I stood beside him in the throne room the night after Fulke was killed. Watched Midas's plan play out as he wove a tale of what had happened. The people know about Midas's Golden Touch. But his golden tongue? To me, that's his true power.

"We were deceived."

The room was quiet, the gathered nobles watching Midas with rapt attention as the king and queen sat on their thrones with somber but determined faces, looking out over the gathered crowd.

"My ally, King Fulke, is dead."

Shock rippled through the people, wide eyes and open mouths spanning across the room.

Midas waits a beat for the news to sink in, but not long enough for the whispers to start.

"King Fulke wanted to stop rot from spreading over our borders. Wanted to ensure that our territories were safe—and he was assassinated for it."

I stood behind him, a step in front of the guards, my presence there meant to show a united front while Midas weaved his story.

"He sent his soldiers to the edge of Fifth Kingdom to do his duty to his people, but he was deceived by one of his own. One who slipped into enemy lands. King Fulke's regiment was killed in a brutal battle against Fourth's awaiting men. And as if that weren't treason enough, that same defector, that betrayer, flew back here to Highbell to deliver a message—by murdering his own unsuspecting king."

The mood in the room moved and ebbed, a tide stretching from horror to indignation.

Midas motioned to someone behind him, and a guard came up, holding something wrapped in black cloth. With a nod from Midas, the guard unwrapped it and held it up for all to see.

Gasps rang out. I couldn't even track how many. They were all repelled, and yet, and they couldn't look away.

The guard held up the decapitated head of the messenger—the one who was guilty of no crimes. His head gleamed shiny gold, his gruesome, dying expression to forever live on in this frozen state, never able to deteriorate as a body should.

The crowd gaped at the face of the messenger-made-traitor. Midas watched the crowd.

"This," Midas said, pointing a hand at the cringing face. "This is the kind of rot that is spreading from Fourth Kingdom. This is what King Fulke was trying to staunch. Not just decimation and disrespect of our lands, but of disloyalty. Distrust. Treason against one's own kingdom and monarch."

He was good. So very good at speaking. At drawing in a crowd. Like a spider spinning a web, he caught them, each one.

The head was wrapped up once more, no doubt to be forged to the front gates later, where all the gilded skulls of traitors stayed. Exposed for the public to spit at, for the icy winds to batter.

"I shall go to Fifth Kingdom," Midas told them. "I will assist them in their time of need, ensure that the land and people don't suffer with the loss of their king. I shall take King Fulke's seat, uniting our lands after his death, even as we were allies while he lived. I will continue to keep our borders secure. To make sure the rot of outside kingdoms does not touch us. Until the day his heir may come of age and take his father's seat."

It didn't take long for the news of King Fulke's death to spread like a heavy snow, drifting over the land, coating every tongue. Midas managed to come out heroic, to give the people a villain to blame, while he gained more power in one fell swoop.

And now, he's sent for me to join him—though it's a secret.

Most everyone thinks I'm already there in Fifth Kingdom, that I traveled with him. However, Midas didn't want me there until he deemed it safe, so he left me behind.

But Midas knew that leaving me alone in the castle was a risk too, so he used a decoy. A woman traveled with his caravan—not gold-touched, but painted to look like me. In the meantime, I've been guarded day and night while I've waited. Not even the servants have been allowed up to these levels. Not even the queen was told that I'm still here.

The only people I've seen these past few weeks are the small number of guards Digby apparently hand-picked to watch over me.

But now it's time to go.

Giving one last glance out the window, I turn away with mixed feelings roiling in my stomach. I head for Digby, who's holding the cage door open for me, and I try not to show the apprehension on my face.

Just as I pass through the threshold, I cast one last look at my cage, my eyes running over all of the things I've had around me every day for as long as I can remember.

It's strange, but I feel a sense of loss when I turn away and follow behind Digby and the other guards as they escort me out. My cage...I've relied on it for so many years. I resented it, too, yes, but it was still a safe haven— one I'm now leaving.

We take the stairs all the way down to the main floor, the five of us quiet, the castle itself subdued. When we make it to the bottom level, I can't help that my eyes dart to the right, seeking out the closed door to the letter room.

I wonder which servants were made to clean the blood up. I wonder if those servants are still alive or if they took those blood-soaked rags to the grave with them, because—

No. Don't think of that now. Loyal. I'm loyal.

Forcing my eyes to peel away from that room, I see that the great doors leading to the dark outside are already open, letting gusts of chilled air blow in. Past the stone steps and courtyard, I can see a procession of carriages and horses waiting to take our party to Fifth Kingdom.

Feeling the back of my neck prickling, I turn to see

GILD

Queen Malina standing on the second floor, her hand curved over the banister as she looks down at me. Her face is blank, sleek white hair coiled around her head like a crown, while her eyes watch me, watch with an intensity that makes my throat clog.

Hate. That's hate in her eyes as she glares down at me, as she realizes that Midas lied, that I've been in the castle all this time. That I'm now going to him because he sent for me.

If I were her, I'd probably hate me too.

"My lady?"

I turn back around, finding the guards waiting for me by the open door, one of them holding up a thick fur coat for me. "Thank you," I murmur, taking it from his outstretched hand before I slip it on. I don't turn back to the queen, but I can feel her stare follow me all the way out into the night.

I clutch the coat tighter.

It's heavy but soft, the fabric lined with leather and fur to keep me warm during the brutal nights. I lift the hood over my head as I walk down the front steps, feeling the last of the castle's warmth leave me. But feeling the tension start to leave, too.

My chin tips up as soon as I pass the doorway, and my face points at the sky.

Ten years.

That's how long it's been since I've stepped foot outside.

The cold wind drifts over me with a lazy current, whispering across my face like a gentle welcome. The guards share a look, their feet shifting from side to side as I stand there, not moving, but I ignore them.

Because this moment—this is mine.

When I chose to hide away, I was barely more than a girl. Vulnerable. Battered. Scared. Utterly sick of what the world had to offer.

So I hid in a cage, and I was content to do so. After the things I endured, I wanted it. I accepted the bars, embraced them, even—not to keep me in, but to keep others out.

But I missed this. The fresh air in my lungs. The smell of the breeze. The cold against my cheeks. The feel of the ground beneath my shoes.

I missed it so damn much.

"My lady," one of the guards says hesitantly. "We should go."

I let my eyes scan the dark sky above me for one more moment, the clouds glowing gray before a hidden moon. But I swear, for one fleeting second, I see a glimpse of a star winking at me.

So I wink back.

CHAPTER 16

The seat of the carriage is velvet, the wood-paneled walls lined with leather, the floor plush with woven carpet. The entire thing is luxurious and golden, though I'm sure after being stuck inside of it for the long journey, it'll start to feel cramped.

For now, I'm content looking out through the window and feeling the chilled air pass through the gap in the frame as our procession moves away from Highbell Castle.

A dozen other saddles are traveling in separate carriages, all of us called to join Midas in Fifth Kingdom, while the guards on horseback escort us down the long winding road along the rim of the frozen mountain. It's achingly slow, but I don't mind the pace right now. I relish in the peace of the night, in the steady steps of the horses as they pull me forward, away from the cage in the palace, toward something new.

As we get further away, the clouds begin to gather, the weather ending its short reprieve. Rain starts to come down like strings, the iridescent lines freezing as they fall.

But our group travels on, the guards simply pulling up their hoods, the horses long since adapted to Sixth Kingdom's cold, not even balking at being made to travel downhill on a snowy, slick road in the dead of night.

When the carriage slides from a patch of ice or jolts over a rock in the road, my heart jumps into my throat, but my escorts trek on, and I do my best not to imagine that I'm one bad step away from careening right off the side of the mountain.

Fortunately, the guards and horses slog through the snow with competence. We'll be traveling all night, just like Midas ordered. We'll sleep during the day, giving the scouts the best advantage when keeping watch.

It will be slow going, two weeks, one and a half at the very best, and that's if the weather holds—and the weather never holds. Not here. Definitely slower than Midas and his men, but our party isn't used to travel or being exposed to the elements, so the going will be slower, more cautious.

As I watch our painstaking way down the mountain, my breath fogs up the glass of the window, forcing me to wipe the condensation away with my gloved hand. Gloves that I'm going to become very familiar with, that I probably won't ever take off until I'm tucked inside Fifth

Kingdom's castle. A small concession when I'm out here in this frigid world, so exposed.

By the time our caravan makes it down the winding mountain road, it's fully dark. No hint of moon or stars behind the thick canopy of clouds, only the lanterns hanging from the carriages offering light to guide our way.

We cross Highbell's bridge, hewn from the shale hollowed out from the mountain behind us. Hooves clop over the sturdy bricks as we make our way across, the bridge built over the chasm between mountain and valley.

And at the other end of it, Highbell City. Built in front of the forest of the Pitching Pines—trees so tall that you can't see their tops when you look up, so large that it would take several men with outstretched arms to span the width of a trunk. The trees stand proud, growing pine needles of blue and white, shedding down like teeth of icicles, dripping with sap at the tips to grow longer, sharper.

But those trees, hundreds of years old—maybe even thousands—they offer the city a break from the wind that comes in down from the mountains, the branches taking on the brunt of the wintry gusts and brutal blizzards, shielding the buildings behind them.

The city itself is dwarfed by them, looking almost comical next to each other. Even in the dark, I can see the light of even the tallest buildings completely dominated by the trees at their backs.

And all at once, I'm too far, too closed off. Maybe it's just now really hitting me that I'm out, I'm truly *out* of my cage. No Midas, no expectations, no role to play. I'm out of the palace, off the mountain, and I just want to see it, see *everything*. And not behind a pane of glass like always, but in the wide open, with the outside all around me, and me on the outside with it.

The moment the carriage wheels start rolling easily over the paved city road, I rap my knuckle against the window. Digby is riding next to me, of course, and his head whips to the side when he hears my knock. But I don't wait or give him a moment to stop me. Instead, I open the carriage door while it's still moving—albeit slowly—and I jump.

Digby swears and calls for my carriage to stop, but it's too late. I've already landed on the ground with a spring in my step as my boots hit the ground. Digby pulls his horse over to me, a scowl curling down his weathered face. The sight makes me smile.

"Glaring so soon, Dig?" I tease. "This isn't a good sign for our journey, is it?"

"Back inside, my lady."

Digby doesn't look amused. Not at all. But of course, that just makes my smile stretch wider.

"Glaring it is, then," I say with a nod. "But scowl or no, I want to stretch my legs. I feel cooped up."

He narrows his eyes, giving me a look like, *Really? You've lived in a cage for the past ten years, but* now *you feel cooped up?*

I shrug at his silent challenge. "Can I ride a horse for a while?"

He shakes his head. "It's sleeting."

I wave it off. "Barely. Besides, the sky is always doing *something* here. But I have a hood, and I'm not cold," I assure him. "I want to feel the air on my face. Just for a little while."

His gray eyebrows pull together as he looks down at me from his spot on his horse, but I wave my hand ahead of us, toward the city's buildings where people are walking around. "It's safe in Highbell, isn't it?" I ask him.

Of course it is, which is why I asked.

"Fine," Digby finally says. "But if the weather gets worse, or if you get too cold, you'll have to return to the carriage."

I nod, trying not to visibly gloat.

"You know how to ride?" he presses, looking unconvinced.

Another quick nod. "Of course. I'm an excellent horse rider."

He regards me dubiously, seeing right through my smile, but he doesn't question me further. Truth be told, I'm not sure that I *do* still know how to ride a horse, but I guess we're all about to find out.

Digby whistles, and a pure white horse is brought forward by another guard holding the reins. I walk over to it, running my eyes over the animal, noting the long, shaggy hair all over his body.

Sixth Kingdom horses were specifically bred to withstand the cold. They have long, thick hair all over their bodies, the longest at their chests and right above their hooves. But even so, they've still been equipped with heavy woolen blankets draped over their backs beneath their saddles, along with thick leg warmers.

I walk up to the horse, crooning a soft hello as he blinks at me. I lift a gloved hand to his nose and pet him slowly, noting how his braided tail flicks. The Highbell emblem on the front leather harness hanging around his neck sits proudly against his chest, gleaming in gold.

When he nudges my hand for daring to slow my strokes, I smile and continue to rub his nose affectionately. "What's his name?"

"Crisp," the other guard answers me, hood over his head, matching cloak and gloves to keep the cold out.

I hum and look again into the horse's eye. "Help me out here, okay, Crisp?" I murmur to him before I circle around to the saddle.

Luckily, he's not too tall, so I easily slip my foot into the stirrup and then stand, praying that I don't embarrass myself and go falling on my ass.

Gritting my teeth, I swing my leg over the other side, my grasp slipping slightly on the saddle before I manage to hoist myself up. I beam as soon as I get settled on top of Crisp, shooting a pleased look at Digby, only to find all of the guards staring openly at me with something akin to horror.

My smile drops. "What?"

Digby scowls at the others. "Move out!" His words snap everyone to attention, and the other riders face forward before the procession starts moving once more.

I look over at Digby as I fix the hood over my head to keep the icy rain off my face.

Digby nudges his horse forward, staying to my right, and clearly not going to tell me what that was all about. Looking over, I meet the eye of another guard who comes up to ride on my left. "Why were they looking at me like that?" I ask.

The guard looks at me sheepishly, a blush crawling over his pale cheeks that I can see even beneath his hood. "Well...it's just that ladies don't normally sit astride."

I look down at my legs straddling the horse. "Oh." I forgot that. I always rode this way before, but I wasn't worried about propriety then.

Behind me, in one of the carriages holding the other saddles, I hear feminine snickers at my expense. "So she *does* like to spread her legs after all," I hear one of them say—Polly. That's Polly's voice.

My cheeks heat. "Should I..."

But the guard shakes his head. "You'll be more secure this way, and it's better for long distances. Don't worry about them," he says, tipping his head at the carriage.

Nodding, I gently tug the right reins while pressing my left leg against Crisp to get him to turn a bit, to get him to move ahead, where I don't have to hear the saddles' taunts.

My horse maneuvers us with ease, and I breathe a

sigh of relief that I seem to remember what the hell I'm doing. The longer I ride, the more relaxed I become, not even caring if the other saddles have anything more to say.

As we move steadily forward, I bask in the open air, glad to be out of the carriage. The rain, while light, is still cold and wet, but I'm too excited about being out in the open to care.

Crisp moves steadily beneath me, his hair helping to keep my bottom half warm. I'm glad that I'm wearing such thick stockings beneath my dress and that my boots are so well insulated.

Highbell City is pretty at night, though, and that distracts me from the dropping temperature. Most of the buildings are three stories tall, all made of the same gray rock that the mountain is made of.

The streets are cobbled and slightly uneven in places, but I like the sound of the horses' hooves clomping over them. The street lamps create a flickering path for us along the winding road, and it's all so picturesque that it brings a smile to my face.

People come out to view us, eyeing the royal procession with avid interest, but I'm careful to keep my hood up so that it covers most of my face and all of my golden hair. Even the saddles in the brothel pop out of the windows, waving topless at the guards and blowing kisses as we go.

The guard to my left clears his throat and snaps his

head forward when one of the women purrs out a rather generous offer to him. I don't blame them. He's handsome, with an open, friendly face. The sort of face that probably always looks kind, even when he's angry. He has ashy blond hair and deep sea blue eyes, a patchy line of hair across his jaw that tells me he can't quite grow in a full beard.

"What's your name?"

He looks over at me, and I notice how young he looks. Maybe only twenty years or so. "My name's Sail, miss."

"Well, Sail, you seem to be popular with the ladies," I note, nodding to the saddles hanging out the windows who are still beckoning to him more than any other.

That pink hue on his cheeks deepens, and it's not from the brisk air. "My mum would wallop me if I ever disrespected a woman enough to force her to sleep with me for a few coins."

I decide I like Sail right then and there.

"You know, some could argue that it's one of the few jobs we women can have to earn a decent wage and manage to stay independent," I tell him.

Sail blanches, like he just realized what he'd said— just remembered who I am. "I didn't—I...I didn't mean to imply that being a saddle isn't respectable. I'm sure plenty of saddles are respectable. Or, I mean, I just—"

"Relax," I say, cutting through his stuttering. His eyes nervously look back at the royal saddles' carriages, as if they might be listening in. "So long as you don't look down on saddles, I have no issue."

"Of course not," he insists. "The saddles in this city are probably tougher than the whole of the army, for all they have to put up with."

I eye some of the sneering people on the streets who are openly staring up at the brothel, their faces not filled with lust, but with violent, carnal hunger and bitter jealousy. I nod slowly before I can look away. "On that, we can agree."

CHAPTER 17

W*ord spread quickly about our* group passing through the city. Soon, more people start lining the street until they're five and six people deep, waving and calling to us with excitement, wondering who travels in the group, what important person they might catch a glimpse of. I keep my head down, my gloved hands on the reins, not daring to look up or let my hood fall back.

The guards in front keep the way clear, our procession going even slower as they constantly have to urge people aside to make way for our carriages.

After a while, we turn off the cobbled road, away from the gathered crowd, heading deeper into the heart of Highbell. I sigh a bit when we're no longer being watched under the scrutiny of dozens of people, my hands relaxing on the reins, but that relief is short-lived.

The further we go, the poorer our surroundings become.

Right before my eyes, Highbell goes from a beautiful and pristine city proper into a dismal, back-alley slum.

I eye the change warily, noting that even the noise seems insulated here, not carrying any of the joviality that existed on the main road. Here there's only the sound of babies crying, men shouting, doors slamming.

"Normally, we'd stay on the main street, but since we're heading for Fifth Kingdom, the south road is the quickest way out of the city," Sail murmurs, riding much closer to me now—he and Digby both—since the hard-packed road is even narrower.

No longer are the buildings on either side of us made of thick stone, but of wood instead. The structures aren't well made, some crooked and crumbling, others sagging with age, like the snow and wind has been trying to weigh them down for years, nature winning against the man.

Even the Pitching Pines seem rougher here, their bark craggy and splintered, branches half empty of needles.

The lamps along the road become fewer and further between, until they finally stop completely. The road, no longer cobbled, turns to sodden, icy mud that kicks up with the horses' hooves.

And the stench...the air no longer smells crisp and fresh and free. Instead, it's held captive, a stagnancy that seems to cling to the sagging faces of the buildings, piss and sweat so overwhelming that it makes my eyes water.

"What is this?" I ask as I look all around the broken and depressed part of the city.

"The shanties," Sail answers.

More babies wail, more people argue, shadows scuffle down alleys, and stray dogs sniff around corners, their ribs visible through mangy, ice-ridden fur.

Highbell doesn't feel so picturesque anymore.

"How long has it been like this?" I ask, unable to look away.

"Always," Sail replies with a shrug. "I'm from the east side, myself. Little more space, but...not much different than this," he admits.

I shake my head, eyeing the puddles on the ground, knowing they aren't from rain but from the filth buckets people pour out their windows.

"But...Midas has all that gold," I say with confusion.

Call me naive, but I assumed since Midas was crowned, since the palace turned from stone to pure gold, that the entirety of Highbell became a wealthy city too.

I didn't even consider that some of Midas's people would be poor, right here in the city. Why would they be? He has all the means to pay them handsomely, no matter the job. Gold is no hardship for him, so why are his people living in squalor like this?

"I'm sure he uses his gold for other things, my lady," Sail says, though I don't miss the way he darts a look down to his gold-plated armor over his chest, or the guilt that seems to crawl into his blue eyes as he scans our surroundings.

He's on high alert, all of the guards are, like they

half expect bandits to come out and attack us. Given the scenery, I don't doubt the possibility of that. Some of the people look desperate enough to do it.

But when some of the guards unsheathe their swords, an open threat at the bedraggled people we pass...something in my chest presses against my heart, hard and persistent, making it bruise.

And when I see children start to peek out from behind empty crates of garbage or follow us with wide eyes, their clothes little more than threadbare scraps, their faces gaunt with missing meals, cold dirt caked against their cheeks...that press against me digs deeper, bruises harder.

Pulling on the reins, I steer Crisp to cut off Sail, pulling up against the carriage. "My lady!" Sail calls, and I hear Digby curse again as I stop Crisp and jump down, landing harder than I mean to. I nearly slip on the icy mud, but the carriage blocks my fall. It's still rolling when I wrench open the door, but it jolts to a stop just as I lift myself up.

"My lady, we cannot linger here!" Sail says behind me, but I ignore him as I lift up the velvet seat inside the carriage, my hands digging through my things.

"Get back on your horse." Digby growls, and I search frantically, shoving aside scarves and extra mittens, looking, looking...

"Got it."

I back out of the carriage and step down, but our stop

in the middle of the street has brought those peering eyes closer, those dark silhouettes converging.

"Get back on your horse," Digby orders again.

"One second." I don't look at him, too busy scanning, searching.

There. Across the street, a group of them are huddled beside a water well, broken buckets and snapped strings littered around the sad-looking water source.

I make my way over, and I hear some of the guards grumbling, some of the saddles in the other carriages asking why we've stopped. Then the unmistakable sound of someone jumping off their horse, long, sure strides heading after me.

But I keep going, right for that group of kids. They're skittish. As soon as they see me coming—or maybe see the guard stalking behind me, two of them dart away, slick steps disappearing into the shadows. But the smallest one, a little girl, maybe four years old, doesn't run. She stays there in front of the others, watching me as I kneel in front of her.

Twelve in total now, not counting the others that ran, all of them too skinny, too dirty. And their eyes, their eyes are too old for their ages. Their shoulders drooping with a weariness no children should ever hold.

"What's your name?"

She doesn't answer me, but her gaze scans over my face, as if she can see the glimmer of my skin beneath the hood.

"Are you a princess?" an older girl asks, but I smile and shake my head. "No. Are you?"

The children all scoff together, trading looks. "You think princesses live in the shanties like street urchins?"

I lower my hood and give her a conspiratorial smile. "Maybe hidden princesses do."

Several of them gape. "You're the golden girl! The one the king keeps."

I open my mouth to answer, but Digby steps in front of me, body tense. "Time to go."

I nod and stand up, but not before I dip into the velvet pouch. "Alright, you secret princes and princesses. Hold out your hands."

Sensing what I'm going to do, they all eagerly push their open palms in front of me, shoving each other aside. "None of that," I reprimand.

One by one, I place a coin in each hand, and they race away as soon as their dirty fingers curl around it. I'm not offended or surprised. When you're on the streets, you don't linger. Especially with money or food in your hands. All it takes is a second for someone bigger and meaner to come along to take it from you.

When I reach the quiet, small girl in the front, I press the pouch in her hand, three coins still inside. Her eyes widen at it, and like her body knows what this could mean, her stomach growls loud enough to rival the stray dogs.

I hold a finger to my lips. "Use one, hide one, and give one away," I whisper. A risk—it's a risk to give her this much gold. Hell, it's a risk to give them any at all, but I have to hope she's savvy enough, smart enough to be safe. The girl nods solemnly at me and then turns and sprints away as fast as her little feet can carry her. Good girl.

"Carriage. Now."

I straighten up and turn to my guard. Digby wears his anger on his face like some people wear a coat—heavy and dark. I open my mouth to tease him or say something smart, but snap it closed when I notice that *all* the guards have their swords out, facing the people who have come out onto the streets. Who witnessed me giving out gold coins right out in the open, enough money to fight for. To kill for.

The ragged, hungry, desperate looking men and women dare to step closer, roving eyes on the gilded edges of the carriages, the fine armor of the guards, probably tallying how much they could buy with just a single piece.

But then their eyes fall to me. To my hair, my face. I realize too late that I didn't put my hood back on.

"The king's favored."

"That's the gold-touched woman."

"She's Midas's gilded pet!"

They keep edging nearer, despite the halting warnings of the guards, and guilt and worry curls in my stomach. Stupid. This was stupid.

The tension is thick in the air, like the people are just a second away from snapping, from deciding to take their chances and attack the armed soldiers for a chance at some of Midas's gold.

RAVEN KENNEDY

Digby's hand lands on my arm, spurring me into action. "Go."

I quickly follow Digby's order and hurry toward the carriage as the people's voices get louder, their steps closer.

And then, right before I make it to the carriage step, one of them launches forward, racing right for me. I scream as he snarls at me, screaming about taking some of my golden hair, hands curled like the talons of a hawk, ready to snatch its prey.

Digby is there in a heartbeat, between me and the crazed man. Digby sends a well-aimed shoulder into his gut, sending the man sprawling, splashing into a half-frozen puddle.

"Get back!" Digby growls, holding his sword, pointing it at the crowd like a warning. The creeping, gathering crowd pauses, but they don't back down, they don't leave.

The moment I scramble into the carriage, Digby is there, slamming the door shut behind me, and we're lurching forward, the sound of guards shouting orders and threats ringing out.

A nearby fight makes me jump, the sound of fists against fists, people hurling insults at me as we go, spitting on the carriages, cursing the king.

I'm too afraid to look out the window as we go, so I sit ramrod straight on the cushion, cursing myself for my stupidity.

I know better than to flash wealth around in the poor

parts of a city. But seeing those kids...it was like looking in a mirror of my past. I wasn't thinking straight.

When the shouting grows louder, the horses move faster, as fast as they dare in the slogged and muddy street. I pray that no one attacks, over and over again, I beg the starry goddesses to hold them at bay.

Not because I fear for myself, certainly not because of what they could steal. But because I don't want the guards to be forced to hurt them. These people have been hurt enough.

Poverty like this is a wound. A wound that King Midas has let fester and infect. It's not their fault, this desperation, this weighed decision of whether or not to attack for the chance at a meal, at a blanket, at medicine. It's survival. And all of us, every single one, would do the same in their position, would battle with that burdensome "what if."

But luckily, no one attacks. Luckily, the guards sheathe their swords. But relief doesn't find me. Only guilt. Guilt that I dangled that carrot in front of the starving and then snatched it so callously away.

The gold castle sitting on the mountain in the distance must be like a thorn in their sides. A constant reminder of a horizon they can't reach.

I wish the sun would come up sooner. I wish that my pouch had held more coins. That I could've bathed the street in gold. But under the chilling cover of night, helplessness weighs on my spirit as our party moves on without further incident, until the last of the decrepit buildings are past, the last haunting face disappearing from view.

And it's a sad, bitter realization that settles in my bones. Because if even the city ruled by a golden king is as impoverished as this, then what hope does the rest of Orea have?

CHAPTER 18

I *thought that after the* ramshackle shanties, the view outside couldn't get any worse.

I was wrong.

As we make our way to the edge of the city's boundaries, my eyes squint, trying to see in the distance, past the outpost's burning torches.

"What…" My question is unheard and unfinished, but the carriage comes to a halt, the sound of voices calling out.

I see Digby get off his horse and go stalking forward, and I waste no time opening the carriage door and getting out, my eyes still locked on the view ahead that I can't quite make out.

I pass by the other carriages holding Midas's royal saddles, and the handsome male—Rosh—is looking out the window, frowning. "You smell that?" he asks someone inside. I don't hear the answer.

Sail steps up to me as I continue forward, where I see a large group of the guards all gathered, speaking to soldiers at the outpost. The outpost itself is just a simple stone watchtower and wall that runs up into the side of the mountains at our back, a checkpoint for those who want to enter the city.

I step closer, but Sail moves to stop me. "We should wait here."

"What...what *is* that?" I ask, trying to look past the soldiers, at the figures I can see just beyond the torches. I can't make it out from this far away, but something tugs me forward, urges me to see.

Skirting close to the line of the horses, I make my way forward, Sail sticking by my side. And although I can tell he wants to insist I turn back, I can't, not even when a sick feeling enters my stomach, like a premonition.

When I'm twenty feet away, the smell hits me. Hits Sail too, because his steps falter, a gagging noise crawling up his throat.

I bite down on my tongue and rush on, and as soon as I make it to the gathered soldiers, I'm finally able to see, my mind able to piece together what my eyes and nose are telling me.

There, in front of Highbell's wall, hang a dozen bodies, strung up on a row of gnarly, weather-beaten branches.

The bodies are...wrong. Abhorrent.

They aren't just corpses. They aren't gilded heads

on spikes, warning people of Midas's wrath if one should break the law. No, these...these are...

"Rotted," Sail says grimly beside me, as if he were hearing my thoughts. "That's what the smell is. We've been getting these little *gifts* from King Rot all week."

My mouth is dry, moisture wicked away with the sight of their spoiled skin. The bodies are molding in some places, like King Ravinger used his power to make them decay like a piece of fruit. Green, white, and black tufts of furry mold clusters over their mortal wounds like a macabre plumage.

Other parts of them are browned and shriveled, like a husk left out too long in the sun. And the rest of them... just *gone*. Like those parts of their bodies rotted away completely, disintegrating into the air as nothing more than peeled scraps of skin and powder of bones.

Bile curls in the pit of my stomach, and I cover my mouth and nose with my hand. I don't need to ask Sail who they are. I can see the purple-plated emblems on their still-visible armor. They're King Fulke's soldiers.

"He's sent them here and to Fifth Kingdom as well," Sail explains morosely as Digby and the others still speak, several paces away from the putrid bodies.

"Why?"

Sail shrugs. "To send a message, I guess. So King Rot can show us that he's pissed. And that Fulke's men didn't stand a chance."

"But why send them here?" I ask. "It wasn't King

Midas's army that attacked," I point out, a betrayal of course, but the fact remains.

Sail shrugs. "He must know King Midas was Fulke's ally, that he's now sitting on Fifth's throne. I don't think King Rot is happy about it."

Unease fills me. I don't ever want to know what it would be like to meet King Ravinger's wrath firsthand. If he's angry enough to send these rotten corpses here when it wasn't even Sixth's army that attacked his border…I don't want to know what he would do if he ever found out that it was Midas's plotting and scheming that initiated it.

Ahead, Digby seems to issue an order, and then some of the soldiers break off, a group going to the bodies, while the watchmen return to their posts.

Sail and I stand together and watch as the guards cut down the rotten bodies, leather wraps tied around their faces to keep out the stench. A larger group begins to dig one large hole in the snow, and then one by one, the bodies are dragged in, until the last soldier is placed inside, like seeds being buried in a grisly garden.

The guards work together, piling the snow over the dead, until all that's left is a shallow mound of snow to mark their grave.

Once it's done, the last of the lingering scent of their demise clears from the air. I shiver and hunker down inside my coat, just as Digby turns to see me standing there.

He makes a beeline for me, and I tense. "Brace yourself," I mutter to Sail.

Digby stops right in front of me, sweat on his brow despite the cold. He looks at me for a long time without saying anything, and I have to try not to fidget beneath his stare as I wait for the lecture.

I know I put myself and everyone else in danger back in the city. I know it was a stupid, reckless thing to do. I know that my impulsive decision to give out money could very well have set off a bad chain of events, but I wasn't thinking of any of that at the time. I just wanted to help. I just wanted to make those kids' lives not quite so bleak, even if for only a moment.

Digby's eyes flick over my face, and then his glare slips away as he sighs. "Stay in the carriage next time."

That's all he says, and then he turns and walks away, stomping toward the men. He barks out orders, indicating to everyone that it's time to move out again.

I let out a puff of breath that coalesces in front of me like a starved cloud. Sail nudges me. "That wasn't so bad, was it?"

I let out a chuckle and shake my head, following him as we start to make our way back toward my carriage. "No. I got let off easy."

Midas would've raged at me for doing something so dangerous.

When we reach my carriage, Sail opens the door for me, stepping aside. "Well, if it means anything, I like what you did back there."

I look at him with surprise, but he shrugs shyly,

embarrassed either by his words or my attention. "It was risky and rash, but it showed you cared. That you saw, that you *looked*. Nobody else would've ever stopped for them," he tells me, and the tone of his voice tells me everything I need to know about who he is and where he's come from.

Sadness fills my cheeks, holding them up into a makeshift smile. "You would've, Sail," I tell him. "You would've stopped too."

And even though I just met him, I know this down to my bones. Because this soldier from the slums, he's not so different from me.

Sail dips his head, and I offer him a smile before I climb into the carriage, the door closing quietly behind me. At least I know that for every King Rot that exists, there's someone like Sail in the world to balance it out.

We travel for a couple more hours until Digby finally calls everyone to halt, just an hour before dawn. We're well outside the city walls now, with nothing but a plain white canvas of snow surrounding us and a mountain range at our backs, the golden castle out of view.

Nearest to the fire, a thick canvas and leather tent is erected for me, fur rugs rolled out on the floor. Sail gives me a wink where he stands watch outside, and I climb in, barely shoveling down travel rations before I crawl onto my bedroll.

By the time night eases away and the dawning sun comes, I'm snuggled deep under golden covers with my ribbons wrapped around me. My legs and back are sore from riding, though it's nothing compared to the aching sight of those molded men roped up, or the crushing poverty in Highbell.

But...I'm outside. I'm moving rather than stagnant. I'm out in the world, and I'm embracing it rather than hiding from it. So that's something, at least.

I don't know what I'm going to do once I reach Fifth Kingdom. I don't know what to expect. It's been one night, and I've already had to face heartbreaking destitution and rancid cruelty. But I'm okay. Despite not having the security of my cage, the world isn't crushing me. Isn't breaking me.

For now, I'm okay.

CHAPTER 19

"D ammit all to Divine's hell," I hiss under my breath as I grip the reins, forcing myself to stay seated in the saddle.

I haven't even been riding for very long yet—thirty minutes, tops. The night is thick and misted, like the air is holding up frozen patches of fog, forcing it to cling to our bodies as we travel over the frozen landscape.

I slept like the dead all day, so I should be well-rested and ready to go, but instead, I feel tired and sodden, like a towel wrung out.

I grit my teeth when my thighs begin to shake. My legs feel like one giant bruise from the inside out, though I have plenty of bruises on the outside too. Every time Crisp takes a step, I wince from the strain, my entire body sore.

The past seven days have been grueling. Even though the weather has held for the most part, it's still not easy to journey all night every night in the dead, stark cold of Sixth Kingdom.

Each night, I've slogged my way through re-learning how to ride a horse, and my muscles hate me for it. I'm only able to ride for a few hours until I practically fall off Crisp and have to stumble back into my carriage.

But I don't like to be cooped up in there, so I try to press on. I force myself to sit, to ride, to handle the strain, because the trade-off is that I get to be out in the open and enjoy the fresh air. I get to talk to Sail, who's always ready to ride at my side with an easy smile and a story.

It's nice, nicer than I can even express, to have a friend, to be without the constraints of a cage. Even if I do freeze my ass off.

Tonight though, my thighs and back are screaming at me earlier than usual, threatening to revolt. Unfortunately, my stomach isn't satisfied either. The dried meat I ate as soon as I woke up didn't do the trick, and I'm already hungry again. Tonight is going to be long.

"Alright there?" Sail asks, shooting me a smirk. His pale facial hair is longer now that we've been on the road for over a week, but it's still growing in uneven patches. Though somehow, he manages to make it look charming.

"Fine," I lie through gritted teeth as I try once again to shift on the saddle and relieve the ache in my back and legs. It does nothing other than irritate Crisp. I reach down and let my gloved fingers stroke over his white fur. "Sorry, boy."

"Took me months to stay seated on a saddle," Sail tells me as he rides beside me. His own horse is a beautiful, calm mare, her white hair dappled with brown streaks.

"Yeah? I'm sure your sergeants loved that," I say, shooting him a smirk.

Sail gives me a crooked grin. "Every time I fell off the damn things, they'd make me muck the stalls. And shoveling horse shit out of a frozen stable is just about as bad as it sounds."

"Lucky you."

"Well, we didn't have horses in the shanties," he replies, and there's no bitterness there, just an open, honest fact.

"I imagine not."

"But once I stopped being so afraid of the damn things, I stopped panicking and getting thrown off." He runs a stroke down his horse's neck, a friendly touch that makes her chuff. "I sit a horse right proper-like, don't I, beauty?" he croons to her.

I snort out a laugh. "If only your sergeant could see you now."

Sail shoots me a grin and sits up straight again. "What about you?" he asks, tipping his head at me. "Ever been tossed off or muck a stall?"

"Thankfully, no. But never say never, right?"

"I don't think the king's favored will be having to hold a shovel any time soon," he says, shooting me a grin.

He'd be surprised about the things I've done in my life, the things I've had to do. But I don't say that, for the same reasons I don't say how I actually learned to ride when I was younger. Or who taught me.

As we ride, I steal looks at Sail when he isn't looking.

It's strange to have a friend.

More than the desire to go outside, more than the craving for change, I realize how much I've wished for *this*, this connection with another person. Not an alliance for similar goals, not anything driven by politics or society or even lust. But a simple friendship. Just two people who enjoy talking to each other, who can share stories and meet in laughter, conspiring only for one another's amusement.

I wonder what it would be like if I loved someone like Sail. I imagine it would be easy, to fall into his air, to be caught up in something as kind and straightforward as he is. Another life, perhaps. Another body.

"Colder tonight," Sail muses, his observation pulling me from my thoughts as I take in the landscape.

"It is," I agree, feeling the chill just as he says it.

Traveling at night has taken some getting used to. At first, every shadow in the distance seemed eerie and haunting, but I've learned to just focus on the trail of the guards in front of me, the carriage lanterns bobbing left and right as we go.

The scenery hasn't changed too much since leaving Highbell. As far as the eye can see, there are snowy hills and jutting rocks. We left behind the last of the outlying villagers days ago, and for the most part, the weather really has held for us, only sputtering out a light snow or occasional sleet.

Below, Crisp jolts me slightly to the side as he goes around a rock, and when I clamp my thighs down to keep from sliding over, I suck in a painful breath. Sore. My thighs are so damned sore.

"Carriage."

I look over at the gruff voice, finding that Digby has come up to ride beside me. He moves around throughout the night, heading to the front, the back, and all throughout the middle. He's attentive, constantly mobile within our procession, checking on everyone and everything, making sure our pace is good, our direction correct, that everyone is riding well and keeping alert.

"Not yet," I say, offering a smile to cover my grimace.

He shakes his head, muttering something under his breath.

"Storm's rolling in," Sail says, drawing my attention back to him.

"You think?" I ask, looking up at the sky. All I can see are clouds moving across a darkly illuminated sky, as if the moon wants to come out, but she can't break through. It looks no different than all the other nights, to be honest.

Sail taps his nose. "I can smell a good storm. It's a gift."

I hum. "And what does a good storm smell like?"

"Like frozen hell."

I snort. "That sounds a bit ominous, don't you think? And besides, the clouds always look like that."

But Sail shakes his head. "Just you wait. I think it's going to be a bad one."

"Should we make a bet?"

Sail nods enthusiastically, but Digby cuts in. "No."

I swing my head to look over at him. "What? Why not?"

"No betting with the king's favored," Digby says, looking over my head to Sail.

I frown. "That's no fun."

Digby shrugs. "No having fun with the king's favored, either."

My eyes narrow. "Well, now you're just being mean."

He shoots me a long-suffering look before he clicks his tongue, making his horse pick up the pace to move past us.

"Don't worry, my lady," Sail cuts in. "In this instance, he did you favor, because you would've lost the bet."

I laugh, tipping my head back at the brooding sky. "Now you're just baiting me."

He wags his light brows. "Shall we make the wager, then?"

I open my mouth to answer when another woman's voice cuts in. "A bit juvenile, don't you think?"

My back straightens at the sound of Polly's voice. The saddles' carriage rolls slightly in front of us, Polly's arm is currently hanging out of the window, her blonde head resting on the crook of her elbow as she watches me with disdain.

I thought that traveling with the other royal saddles might warm them up toward me, might soften the edges of the gulf between us, but it hasn't. For the most part, we stay separated. I haven't had more than a passing glance at the others. They stay in their carriages or shared tents, and I stay in mine, and none of them make any attempt to talk to me.

Except Polly.

But it's not so much talking as it is showing off her clear dislike for me.

"I'm fairly sure that making bets is the second-favorite pastime of men in this kingdom, and they wouldn't call it juvenile," I reply.

"Second favorite?" Sail repeats. "Then what's the first?"

I shoot him a smirk. "Buying time with a saddle."

Sail laughs shyly, but Polly ruins it by snorting. "And what would *you* know about it? The king never rides you when he calls for us. You aren't even a proper royal saddle. He only lets you watch. It's quite sad, really. You're just a trophy. Hot-blooded males don't want a cold metallic bitch in their beds."

Embarrassment flares into me, all traces of my

earlier amusement burned and shriveled away with an ugly flare of degradation. It's one thing to have to endure watching Midas sleep with others, but for her to throw it in my face, and with Sail and the other guards nearby to hear...

Polly smiles at me, clearly pleased with herself. "Don't worry. I'll keep King Midas satisfied."

Sail shoots me a sympathetic look, but that somehow just makes this all so much worse. Notching my heels against Crisp's sides, I urge the horse forward. I don't offer Sail a fake explanation for fleeing as I dart past him and the carriage, there's no point.

I pass by Polly's carriage without a look, my teeth gritted and my cheeks searing. Clenching my fingers on the reins, I direct Crisp between the guards in front of us, squeezing my way past them, not caring when their own horses are forced to move over.

Distance. I just need distance.

I veer around horse after horse, not slowing down until I've nearly made it to the front of the caravan, far away from Polly and her hateful tongue. As if I could run away from my own disappointments. As if I could avoid my hurts, my shame, my dark thoughts that creep out every time I close my eyes for sleep.

One day, I suspect those plaguing thoughts will want to stop being ignored. They'll catch up. They'll slink past me, refusing to be hidden in a tear-soaked pillow or between the cracks of a mirror.

Sooner or later, every troubled thought and aching bitterness is going to come pouring out and demand I face them.

But not tonight.

Not yet.

CHAPTER 20

I let Crisp fall back into a slower canter, the last of my hope of bonding with the other saddles sparking out, like the wet wick of a candle.

Time to accept it, to be glad that at least I have one friend in this travel party. One friend, and one gruff, protective guard who killed a king to save me. That's much more than I ever expected to have.

After a few short minutes of brooding alone in silence, Sail comes trotting up beside me, just like I knew he would. "Ignore Polly. She's just jealous."

I give him a wry look, pretending not to be hurt, not to care. "Ignore her. Just like *you* ignored Frilly yesterday?"

The tops of his cheeks redden, and he whips his face forward. "What? No, nothing happened. She just needed an extra blanket, that was all."

"Relax. I'm just teasing."

Sail glances around, as if worried someone might

hear and believe anything other than the innocent truth. I understand the worry though, since the royal saddles are just that—for royalty. They're not permitted to be with anyone else. And even gossip could destroy Frilly and Sail both—something I won't let happen.

"You have any girls pining for you back at home?" I ask, curious about his life outside of the army, when he's not wearing armor or carrying a sword.

Sail flashes that boyish charm of his again as he leans toward me. "Just a few," he jokes. "Three or four, but they don't pine nearly as much as I want them to."

I snicker. "Is that so? Well, I hope you treat them kindly."

"I treat them *very* kindly. This boy from the shanties has got a few tricks up his sleeve."

Another laugh spills from my mouth. "Care to share these tricks?"

Sail enthusiastically opens his mouth to answer, but Digby appears at my other side again, cutting in with a scowl. "No sharing tricks with the king's favored," he snaps in exasperation. "Do you *want* King Midas to cut off your head and cast it in gold, boy?"

Sail goes pale and shakes his head. "No, sir."

I sigh and look over at my stoic, ever-grumpy guard. "Don't be such a killjoy, Dig."

"Carriage," he replies gruffly.

"No, thank you," I reply sweetly.

He sighs at my stubbornness, and I smile at his

aggravation. It's not a drinking game by any means, but it's still the most fun I've had with Digby, and he's talking to me now more than ever. I count it as a major victory.

While our group carries on, one after the other, Sail entertains me with stories of growing up with four older brothers, distracting me enough that I barely notice the ache in my legs.

The clouds roil over us like a curled surf of a moody sea, tossing arctic mist in the air. The horses in front create the snow breaks for the rest of us to walk, but trudging through thick snow to cut a path is tiring and difficult, even for our hardy horses, so Digby constantly rotates out the leads.

As the night wears on, the temperature seems to plummet, so cold that it even numbs my aching thighs. When the wind picks up, it's so brutal that Sail doesn't once brag about being right about the storm.

Soon, everyone is bracing against it, bodies hunched over on their horses and fabric wrapped around faces and heads to keep the ripping chill from tearing through us.

Digby comes galloping back to my side, his heavy cloak billowing around him. "Carriage," he says, and this time, it's an order.

I nod, finally relenting, because I'd be an idiot not to take advantage of the fact that I can get out of the frigid and windy cold. The skies are warning us, giving us time to prepare before the clouds unleash whatever they have held in their bellies, and as much as I like to ride out in the open, I'd rather not be out in a blizzard.

With Sail beside me, I quickly maneuver Crisp to head for my carriage. I jump down, giving him a pat on his furry rump as I go.

I shoot Sail a guilty look and gesture toward the carriage. "You sure you can't…"

But he shakes his head. "I'm alright. Us Sixth soldiers are a hardy lot. The cold doesn't even touch us," he lies with a wink, even as breath plumes in front of him like cloying smoke. "Go on in before you catch a chill."

My driver stops just long enough for me to step into my carriage and close the door with a shiver. It lurches forward, and I sit back, rubbing my legs and shaking out my hands, soothing sore muscles, trying to bring a frictional warmth back into my limbs.

I watch out the window as the weather grows steadily worse, my light limited to the bobbing lanterns and masked moonlight.

Within the hour, the storm is fully upon us. The winds howl, becoming so strong that the windows rattle and the carriage wobbles, like a threat to tip. I move over, making sure to sit on the right side to help brace against the wind.

Then the hail starts to rain down, balls of ice clacking against the roof like a thousand knuckled raps. It's so loud that it drowns out the horses' hooves and the scraping of the carriage wheels, until all that exists is just a downpour of frozen pellets that funnel from the sky.

I chew on my nails as I look outside, hating that the

guards and horses have to endure this. The hail must be punishing and painful every time it lands.

Luckily, I see us diverting off the path, heading for a copse of trees in the distance. They're not the giant Pitching Pines, but they're enough to offer us some cover from the storm, thank Divine.

But if I thought we were slow-moving before, it's ten times worse now. With the hail and the wind battering us, it takes us nearly an hour to reach the line of trees.

The leaders of our group are just crossing beneath the first of the trees when my carriage is jolted. With a lurch, I'm flung onto the floor, my body hitting the opposite seat and the back of my head slamming against the wall.

"Shit," I curse, rubbing the back of my head as I struggle to get back into the seat. The carriage gives another violent bounce, nearly sending me right back off the cushion again, but I brace myself against the walls, managing to stay upright.

It lurches to a stop, either on purpose or because of the thick snow, and then Digby is there, wrenching the door open, eyes scanning over me to check that I'm okay.

"I'm fine," I assure him.

"Carriage is stuck," he explains, holding the door open.

I climb out, my feet sinking into the deep snow that nearly reaches my knees.

"Alright?" Sail hollers as he brings Crisp forward.

All I can do is nod, because the howling wind would

only rip my voice away. I use the stirrup to haul myself up, and as soon as I'm seated, Sail grasps both the reins and leads our horses through the thick snow, their heavy hooves forcing a path through the white.

Squinting past the wind, I look back to see that the other carriages are stuck too, the snow an easy three feet deep, holding the wheels hostage.

Guards are scrambling and shouting at each other, trying to free the horses and help the saddles, while leading everyone toward cover.

As soon as Sail and I reach the trees, we get instant relief from the hail. A few pellets still manage to hit us through the branches but not nearly as much.

The guards are chopping and stacking wood, making quick work to build a fire. When they try to light it, it spits and smokes, the stubborn, wet pieces refusing to light. Until Digby marches over, stern as ever. One cast of his flint sends sparks flying, catching onto the kindling like it doesn't dare disobey him.

Sail leads me where the other horses are gathered, the snow cleared away so they have a spot to rest, a bale of hay already there waiting for them.

I jump down, ready to help with Crisp, but Sail insists that I go sit and get warm while he tends to the horses. He directs me to one of the downed logs in front of the growing fire, and I take a seat, feeling exhausted and shivering all the way through, even the marrow in my bones feeling brittle with cold. The other saddles slowly filter in too, sitting on other logs surrounding the flames, huddling next to each other for extra warmth.

I watch as the guards stack wood, set up tents, haul trunks, and shovel snow out of the way to build up a windbreak, not one of them idle while I shiver beside the weak fire, holding out my shaking, gloved hands to the flames.

The guards pile lightweight bricks near it, and I know each and every one will be gone as soon as they're hot, to be stuffed into sleeping bags, helping to warm our feet while we rest.

The guards work efficiently and quickly, amazing me at how fast they get everything done. Soon, everyone is gathered near the fire, tents scattered everywhere a gap in the trees allows it.

The hail falls. Pebbles of ice peppering down, ricocheting off bark and branches alike, leaving splintered wood in its wake. It clacks against the trees like small explosions, while the branches overhead groan from the push of the wind.

It was just a matter of time before a storm rolled in. We're lucky that we had mild nights for as long as we did.

I spot Sail off to the left setting up my tent, and I walk over to him where he's busy staking the tarp into the ground and pulling the fabric taut.

"Want help?" I ask, my voice raised so I can be heard over the hail.

But Digby walks by with my rolled-up furs in his arms. "No. You don't help."

"We serve you, Miss Auren. Not the other way around," Sail tells me.

"That's good, because I don't actually know how to put up a tent," I joke, making Sail laugh.

After he gets the whole thing together, he and Digby quickly pile furs inside, along with my own lantern to give off both light and a little bit of heat, even though my tent is nearest to the fire.

I feel a little guilty at the special treatment, especially knowing that the guards and other saddles have to share a tent with five or six others, while I get one all to myself. Though, at least they get to share the body heat.

I practically inhale my portion of travel rations and boiled water, and then head for my tent early. There are a few more hours of night left, but we won't be able to get back on the road for hours yet, based on the strength of the storm.

When he sees me coming, Sail gets up from his spot on the stump next to my tent, the spot he'll be keeping watch while I rest. He holds the flap open for me to get in. "Looks like you lost that bet, hmm?"

"Ah, but I didn't actually get to *take* the bet, did I?"

Sail laughs and shakes his head. The fact that he can always be in such good humor, regardless of what's going on around him, is a testament to his character. "You got lucky this time. I won't let you off the hook so easily next time."

"Thanks for the warning. Good night."

"Night, my lady."

I duck inside, tying the flaps closed before I quickly strip and get dressed into a thick woolen nightgown and burrow myself beneath the covers of my furs, while I leave my boots to dry beside the lantern.

The hot brick at my feet feels like heaven, but I know its warmth won't last for long. Not with the hail pelting the tent, not with the wind that seems to cut through every layer around me, slicing straight through.

The weather held for seven days, but now it's broken into a million powerful pieces, sending shards raining down from the sky.

Outside, the storm seethes like a warning.

I'll realize too late that I should've heeded it.

CHAPTER 21

The storm rages and rages.

Not like the Gale Widow blowing with the wail of her despair, but a scorned woman, raining down a frozen hell of vengeance, just as Sail predicted.

Three long days and even longer nights. Hail and snow and then a horrible downpour of rain that comes in biting rivulets, soaking our entire encampment, freezing wherever it lands.

Everyone, even good-natured Sail, is miserable. I think poor Crisp is even ready to revolt. The fire keeps going out too, no matter how many wooden lean-tos the guards build, trying to keep the wind and wet away.

They finally have to hack up one of the tent tarps and tie it tight between the trees high up to keep the pouring rain from falling directly onto the flames. It's good for shelter, not so good for the men who have to bunk up in increasingly cramped sleeping conditions.

No one can hunt, and there aren't any animals out in this weather anyway, which means all we have to eat is the dried meat and nuts. Nothing hot, nothing fresh, aside from the boiled water of endless melted snow. Everyone mostly just stays inside their tents, bored, cold, and cross, cursing at an indifferent sky.

Until finally, on the fourth day, the storm breaks.

I wake up to the sound of fire-crackling flame instead of wind or hail or rain. Peeking out of my tent for the first time in hours, I find that the muddy sludge is gone, and in its place is a new foot of snow glittering in the gray, waning light. Flakes fall gently from the sky in a lazy, peaceful dance.

"Thank Divine."

Judging by the position of the sun, I'd say there's only about an hour or so left of daylight.

I glance around, noting that most of the men are either out scouting or dealing with the still stuck carriages, while the rest are sharpening their weapons or eating. But I can tell that the mood is no longer bleak, several of the guards good-naturedly ribbing each other and talking with relaxed faces.

Most of them are used to me now that we've been traveling for days on end together, but I still get curious looks and stolen glances now and then. However, none of them attempt to talk to me or come near me, aside from Digby and Sail. Either Midas warned them off or Digby did. Probably both.

I clean myself up in my tent, waiting for nightfall, knowing that we'll be getting back on the road as quickly as we can break camp.

I wash out of a water pitcher, with a cold, damp rag. Traveling isn't glamorous, and I sorely miss the things I've gotten spoiled by like my bed, my pillows, my bath.

Just thinking about soaking in hot water makes me want to groan. Instead, I have to settle for this hurried rag-wash, going as quickly as I can with goose bumps pebbling over my skin, teeth chattering.

It takes some grit to force myself to pour the pitcher over my hair, and I nearly squeal at just how cold it is, but I manage to keep it in and scrub my scalp and strands hastily before my fingertips go numb.

I dress with my skin still slightly damp, using my ribbons to help re-braid my hair before they wrap around me, another layer to help insulate.

Just as I yank on my fleece-lined leggings beneath my heavy gown, a tray of food is shoved into my tent— probably Digby making sure I eat before we get back on the road.

I grab the tray and sit on my bedroll, dragging my furs over my lap while I eat. There's an entire leg of roasted meat, and even though it doesn't have any spices or seasoning, I devour it in seconds. It's blessedly hot and fresh, leaps and bounds better than that chewy, dried stuff I've been choking down.

When I've eaten everything off the plate short of

licking it, I help pack up the tent, rolling my furs, putting away my clothes in the trunk, dimming the lantern.

By the time I step out of my tent, the camp has already been broken down, the men suiting up in their armor and shoveling snow over the banked fire. The horses have already been led away too, strapped to the unstuck and mended carriages, while the shadow of night begins to curl over the horizon, ready to bathe the world dark.

"Ready, Miss Auren?" Sail asks, coming up from behind me.

I dash away the snowflake that lands on my cheek. "More than ready to get moving. I thought that storm would never end."

"We lost a few days, and the ground turned to ice, but the new snow will help, and we're not so far off from Fifth Kingdom."

"Good," I say, as I begin to follow him away from the trees to where the horses are already lined up.

Digby stops me, a scowl ready on his face. "Your hair is wet."

"Excellent observational skills, Diggy," I tease before bringing up my hood.

But even Sail frowns over at me. "He's right. You'll catch a chill."

"I'll be fine."

"You'll ride in the carriage until it's dry," Digby states.

Now it's my turn to scowl. I don't want to be cooped up in the carriage after being cooped up in the tent for three days. "I'd prefer to ride." Digby shakes his head.

"I'll wear my hood," I insist.

He doesn't reply, just walks me over to my carriage and pops the door open, eyeing me. He's obviously not going to be talked out of it, and I don't see Crisp anyway.

I sigh in defeat. "Fine," I grumble. "But as soon as it's dry, I'm riding next to you, and I'm going to talk for hours," I warn him.

I can't be sure, but I think the corner of his mouth tilts up, just a bit. I point at it. "Ha! You almost smiled," I say victoriously before turning to Sail. "You saw it too, right?"

He nods with a grin. "Definitely."

Digby rolls his eyes and hikes a thumb toward the inside of the carriage. "In."

"Yeah, yeah," I say before climbing into the carriage. Sail gives me a smile before shutting the door, and I lean back, settling against the cushioned seat as our group begins to move forward once more. At least my legs and back had a nice reprieve from riding, my muscles no longer sore.

I loosen my hair out of the braid, hoping that it'll help to dry it quicker. I'm already bored out of my mind, and I've only been in here for a few minutes. I lean against the carriage wall and close my eyes, wondering how many days we still have of travel before we reach Fifth Kingdom. I know the storm set us back, but I'm not sure by how much.

The steady rocking of the carriage must make me fall asleep, because the next thing I know, my eyes are flying open. I look around the carriage, noting that the small lantern inside has died out.

My ribbons are curled up around me beneath my coat, offering me some extra warmth, and my hair is dry, the golden strands hanging behind my shoulders.

I'm disoriented as I look around the dark carriage, troubled as I try to pinpoint what woke me up. But then I realize, the carriage has stopped.

It's still dark out, so I know we can't have been traveling for very long. The carriage probably got stuck again, and the jolt woke me. I wipe the condensation off the window and look out, but all I can see is a thick veil of darkness.

I rap my knuckles against the glass. "Digby? Sail?"

I don't get a response, and I don't hear any of the men outside. A corrosive edge of panic threatens to slice into me, and my hand lifts up to the scar on my throat—something I haven't done in days.

Scooting closer to the door, I press my face against the glass, attempting to see something, anything, out the window, but all that's visible is the dimmest glow of snow on the ground. Everything else is bathed in darkness.

I grip the handle to go outside and investigate, but the door wrenches open, making me flinch back in surprise as Sail's head pops in.

"Great Divine, you scared me. What's happening?"

"Sorry, Miss Auren," he says, his eyes flicking down to where my hand is holding my throat. I quickly drop it as he clears his throat. "Digby called a halt. The leads saw some disturbance in the snow, so he's sent out some scouts."

"What kind of disturbance?"

"Not sure yet."

I move to get out, but Sail doesn't step aside and instead gives me a sheepish look. "Digby wants you to stay in the carriage."

I'm sure he does, but I can't bear being stuck in here. That trapped feeling...

The second I stepped foot outside of the Highbell Castle, something changed. Like a plug pulled out of its drain, a decade's worth of water, water that's engulfed me completely, began to lower. Gone was the strain of holding my head above it. There was no sucking in breaths, counting them, reminding myself I had air, that the crushing flood wouldn't suffocate me as I treaded water.

I can't go back to that. Mentally, emotionally, even physically, the thought makes beaded sweat begin to gather against my skin, and I know, I just know that I can't bear it.

Which is why, even though I've been ordered to

remain, even though there might be danger outside, I can't stay in here. It's too cooped up, too reminiscent of that perpetual fight to float instead of sink.

So I shove past Sail and jump out into the dark.

CHAPTER 22

My boots land nimbly on the snow as I jump down from the carriage. Sail gives a soft curse behind me, but he doesn't argue, doesn't try to get me to go back. I like that about him.

"Where are the other guards?"

He points. "Up ahead on the hill where they can get a better vantage point."

I nod swiftly as we make our way through the snow. As we pass by the saddles' carriages, women's heads pop out the windows, straining to see what's going on. The drivers wait steadfastly on their benches, keeping the horses from becoming too anxious as their hooves paw at the snow.

Rissa is one of the women leaning out, but she surprises me when she calls my name. She hasn't spoken a word to me since I saw her in the throne room that night, when King Fulke demanded our attention. "What's going on?"

"I'm not sure yet," I tell her honestly.

Her blue eyes flicker around the dark landscape, though their lanterns bloom light from inside the carriage.

"If you find anything out, let us know." She pulls her head back inside without waiting for my reply, conversation between Rosh and Polly immediately striking up in quiet murmurs.

I blink at the window for a moment before moving on. I don't know whether to be glad that Rissa was willing to talk to me or offended at her brashness.

Sail looks over at me and smirks, though he says nothing. "What?" I ask.

He gives an easy shrug. "Nothing. I'm surprised you didn't ask for a book, is all."

I frown. "A book?"

"Yeah, to chuck at her head." Sail barks a laugh at his words, and my mouth pops open before a grudging, embarrassed laugh escapes me. "I was trying to help her!"

Sail laughs so hard that he loses his breath. "Remind me not to ever ask for your help, Miss Auren."

My lips pull up into a smile from his teasing. "Ass."

"It's my favorite story of yours."

I groan and wipe a hand down my face. "You guards are a gossipy bunch. Does everyone know?"

Sail grins. "Yep."

I shake my head. "Great Divine."

His chuckle tapers off. "Don't be embarrassed. I like that story."

I give him a glare, but he holds up his hands. "Not just for the reasons you think," he explains. "To be honest, I wasn't sure I wanted this position—to help escort you to Fifth Kingdom. Sure, back at home, I was just on outside wall watch. Boring as hell and cold enough to freeze your ba—er, I mean, to freeze," he corrects with an embarrassed grin shot my way.

"You *can* say balls, you know," I tease. "You don't have to be careful or censure yourself. I'm just a saddle, after all."

But Sail shakes his head. "You're definitely more than just *that*, my lady. And you should make sure people treat you as such."

Sail's words startle me, my smile slipping off as the conviction of his words put something serious between us. Something heavier than the lightness we usually keep.

"As I was saying," he goes on, filling the awkward silence. "I wasn't sure I wanted this placement, even though it was going to be a huge advancement for my rank. But then, this lot that Digby chose, we started talking. Trading stories. And that was when I heard about you tossing that book at poor Miss Rissa's face." He shakes his head with a snicker. "Some of them thought you were just being a…"

"Bitch?" I offer.

A sheepish look is sent my way. "Right. But a few of us reckoned what you were really up to, how tired Miss Rissa was. We figured it out."

"Pleased with yourselves, hmm?"

"Immensely. But that was how I knew I made the right decision to guard you. Because you aren't what some people say—you aren't some stuck-up, spoiled snob of a saddle, sitting in her tower and sneering down your nose at everyone while you polish your gold skin."

I grimace at his visual.

"No, you cared enough about getting Miss Rissa out of a tight spot, so much so that you risked looking like the villain. You did something, a little rough, sure, and probably not the most well thought out plan, but you acted. You didn't just stand by."

"I gave her a bloody nose," I deadpan.

Sail just shrugs. "You also made it so she got to retire for the rest of the night."

I look away. "Well, that was my goal. Though, like you said, the execution was a little rough."

"See?" he challenges, as if I just proved a point. "You're different. And you don't deserve to have such a rough time of it."

I eye him as we trudge through the snow, tucking my hair behind my ears. I'm touched, to be honest. For the things he's saying, for the way he sees me. But I don't know how to respond. I'm not good at opening up, at speaking any kind of truths. Why would I be, when for my entire life, I've worked to suppress everything?

Sail must see my struggle, know that I'm getting trapped beneath the weight of his observations, so he does what I've come to love about him. He lightens the mood once again, managing to put a smile back on my face and settle us back on easy, even ground.

"Word of advice, though? Maybe no more book chucking."

My lips curl. "I'll keep that in mind."

The two of us finally reach a crest of a small hill where I see everyone gathered ahead, their shadowed silhouettes lit up by the lanterns they're holding. My hair whips around from the wind, trying to escape my hood, so I quickly stuff it back under as we approach everyone.

Most of the guards are still on their horses, but a few of them are on the ground talking, though most everyone is looking straight out at the horizon in the distance. I find Digby with a cluster of guards at the very front of the group, his face trained forward.

"What are you looking at?" I ask, sidling up next to him.

A slow, heavy sigh escapes Digby before he turns to Sail. "What is the king's favored doing out of her carriage?"

Sail scratches the back of his neck nervously. "Well, see, what happened was...umm, she—"

I cut him off so he doesn't get into trouble. "It's not his fault, I insisted. What's going on?"

Digby sighs again, but surprisingly, he answers. "Scouts told us they saw a disturbance in the snow."

"Like...footprints?"

He shakes his head. "Like movement, far ahead. Snow shifting."

"What would cause that?"

The men share a look, and one of them says, "Avalanche."

My eyes widen.

"That mountain there," another guard explains, this one with a thick beard the color of caramel. He raises his hand up so he can point in the direction he's referring to. "Though we've been watching it and haven't seen anything. Another scout went ahead to where the movement was noted to see if they could hear anything, find any warning that the mountain is going to cut loose."

I squint where he indicated, but all I see are the black-lined crests of mountains ahead. And before us, all around us, are the Barrens. The wide open, frozen grounds between Sixth and Fifth Kingdoms, nothing but an iced wasteland stretching miles and miles.

"Could an avalanche reach us?"

"Yes," Digby answers grimly.

Caramel beard explains, "We got a lot of extra snow and movement from the storm. An avalanche from that mountain would come clear across the Barrens. The flat ground is slick, nothing around to block or make it slow. If anything, it would help it gain speed. It would reach us easily."

I swallow hard, a cold lump to land in my stomach.

"What if we wait here and monitor things?" Sail asks.

"We wait, we risk more exposure, more use of supplies," Digby begins. "Sitting ducks for the snow to swallow."

Caramel beard speaks up again. "And we have to go through that valley. It's the only way to cross into Fifth Kingdom."

I rub my hands up and down my arms as more of the cold seeps in, exposed as we are on top of this hill. "When will the scout be back?"

The guards share a loaded look. "That's the thing. He should've been back already."

CHAPTER 23

T he guards' faces are shuttered. Uneasy. Their stances, as they all keep sentry on top of the hill, hold tension, from the line of their shoulders to the poise of their feet.

On top of the unnamed hill over the last stretch of plain in Sixth Kingdom, I suddenly feel exposed, like a tree stripped of its bark.

For a moment, no one speaks. All faces are turned toward the mountain in the distance, to where the scout ventured off. Lone footprints leading away from the group, snowfall already starting to cover them.

Long minutes pass, and though we wait, all eyes peeled, no sign of the scout comes. Beside me, Digby's lips press together in a firm line, as if making up his mind. He looks over a few of the men. "You three with me to track the scout. The rest of you, stay with the carriages. Be ready to move."

The three men nod and walk off to mount their horses, while Digby turns to Sail. "Guard her," he says gruffly.

Sail salutes him by hitting his right fist against his left shoulder plate. "Yes, sir."

Digby gives me a look that says, *Behave yourself.*

To reassure him, I attempt to mimic the same salute motion that Sail gave him, except I overshoot and end up punching myself in the arm *way* too hard. "Ouch," I mutter, rubbing the spot on my shoulder with a wince.

Digby sighs at me and looks at Sail again. "Guard her *a lot.*"

"Hey!" I say indignantly.

Sail barely stops his snort of amusement. "Will do, sir."

Digby places his foot in the stirrup of his horse and hauls himself into the saddle while I clutch my coat tightly around me.

With a whistle, he and the three others go galloping down the hill in the same direction that the missing scout went. One of them carries a lantern pole, leading the way.

I don't know how in the Divine hell they're going to be able to see anything out there to find the scout, but I hope they find him and return quickly. Waiting here leaves an uneasy seed to fester beneath the ground I'm standing on, filling me with trepidation. Staying here, dormant, like stagnant water left to spoil.

"You think they'll find him?"

Sail nods with confidence. "They'll pick up his trail."

"Even in the dark?" I ask dubiously.

"Don't worry." Sail sends me a comforting look. "Digby is the best guard I've ever met. He's smart and he's got good instincts. I'm sure the Scout just got turned around. It's easy to do out here."

I nod, swallowing down the rest of my worries so they don't creep off my tongue and find voice.

"Come on, Miss Auren, let's get you back to the carriage. You'll be out of the cold at least," Sail tells me.

I hesitate, still watching the bobbing lantern of the search party, the light getting smaller with the distance. Soon, it's the only thing I can see, the riders' shadows totally swallowed up with the night.

I watch that light like it's one of the fireflies of southern Orea, where it's rumored that they appear on dark, lonely roads to lead the lost back home with their ultraviolet glow.

Ever since that night, when a blade was pressed against my neck, I've depended on Digby's steady presence. We've never spoken about it—that's not his way—but at night in my cage, I'd roll over from a nightmare and see him there, already standing watch against the wall, even though his shift wouldn't start for hours.

It was as if he knew I needed him near, like he knew I'd keep seeing that blade, that blood, that line between death and life. He knew, and he came to protect me, every night, even if it was just against phantom dreams.

It's foolish, but watching him disappear out of sight

leaves a raking claw to draw over my back, making the base of my ribbons recoil.

"Don't worry," Sail tells me again, obviously picking up on my thoughts. "They'll be back soon."

"And if the mountain breaks loose?"

Sail begins to lead me down the hill. "A little thing like an avalanche wouldn't be enough to stop him. He's too stubborn." He smiles over at me. "Too good of a soldier."

"Is he? He must hate having babysitting duty all the time, then," I reply with a dry chuckle, an attempt to pretend, to smother the worry.

Sail shakes his head. "I heard he requested it."

My eyes cut over. "Really?"

"Really."

A slow smile pulls at my cold lips. I knew he liked me. "I'll get him to play a drinking game with me yet."

Sail chuckles. "You have your work cut out for you. I've never seen him relax or let loose. But if anyone can do it, it's you."

"Did you find out why we stopped?"

I look up at Rissa and the other saddles who are now outside of their carriages, standing around in a circle in the snow.

"The scout went missing. They went to go find him."

Her pretty face pinches with worry. "Are we stopping here for the night?"

Sail shakes his head, one hand resting on the pommel

of his sword. "No, as soon as they get back, we'll need to keep moving." He turns to me. "Come on, you're shaking like a leaf. Let's get you in the carriage."

I don't argue as he leads me past the saddles. Just as we make it to my carriage, thunder cracks. I turn to the sky and groan. "Another storm?" The thought of being stuck in a torrent of wind and freezing rain again does *not* sound appealing.

Sail frowns, but he's not looking at the sky. He's looking at the mountain ahead. "I don't think that was thunder."

"Hey, what's that?" a saddle behind us asks, pointing forward.

Everyone converges, abandoning the carriages to skirt around the bottom of the hill to look into the valley. Sail and I join them, scanning the landscape, but my eyes catch onto something far away, far and glowing like a beacon.

"Is that...fire?" Polly asks.

The warm light hovers in the distance, an orange glow that streaks against the black, like a smear on glass.

"Maybe it's the lantern from the scout?" someone offers.

"No," Sail says, shaking his head. "At this distance... that's way too big to be from a lantern."

But as soon as he says it, the "way too big" glowing fire breaks off, into dozens of little fires. The blazes spread out, weaving and shifting, until they form a line far across the snow plain, stretched out so that my eyes have to flicker left and right to take them both in.

"What in Divine's hell..." I trail off.

Then there's that noise again. A boom of thunder in the distance. The kind of sound that's so low, it's barely heard, more felt. Except it's not coming from the clouds.

Behind the row of strange firelight, at the base of the mountain, snow shifts. Falls. Like smoke rising, a plume of white blooms, smothering the balls of light for a moment, as the snow at the base of the mountain *moves*.

"Oh, Divine, it's an avalanche!" one of the women shrills. Two more screams tear out from panicked throats as some of them turn to run.

But I watch, enraptured, as the shadows that I mistook for the base of the mountain break off. Break off and begin to follow the dots of flame. And those dark forms, those lights, they all move so *fast,* heading right in our direction. The noise rumbles through the air again, and my whole body tenses.

"That's not an avalanche," Sail breathes beside me.

Dread thickens, like a pinching fog, gripping the breath from my lungs.

"Holy Divine fuck," a guard curses. "Snow pirates!"

One blink. One breath. One solitary moment for the words to sink down, down, down. And then chaos erupts.

Before I can even fathom the implications of what's happening, Sail has me by the arm and he's hauling me away, my steps tripping through the thick snow, but he doesn't let me go. Doesn't let me slow. His face is blanched and pale, panicked. So, so panicked.

"Come on!"

He starts sprinting toward the carriages, pulling me along with him. My feet try to keep up, my legs pushing through shin-deep snowfall, the bottom of my skirts growing heavy and wet.

Slow, it feels like we're going too slow, though I'm moving as fast as I can.

Men are shouting orders, words barked back and forth that I can't concentrate on long enough to comprehend. Sail continues to haul me forward, while the other women run alongside us, tripping and screaming as they go.

Snow pirates. We're about to be attacked by *snow pirates*.

I've heard of them, but they were always a distant story, nothing I'd ever actually think to see for myself. They roam here in the Barrens, and they stalk the Breakwater Port, pillaging imports, stalking trade routes, stealing whatever they can.

They call themselves the Red Raids, their faces always covered in bloodred balaclavas. I've heard Midas grumble about stolen shipments, no doubt their doing. But no one ever spoke about the danger of the snow pirates tracking *us*. They go for the ships and the large hauls. Not traveling caravans.

Sail and I run as fast as we can, and by the time we

reach my carriage, more thunderous noise erupts in the air. Though this time, it's accompanied by a new sound as well. Sail and I both stop to listen, breaths panting as we crane our heads and strain our ears.

It's loud. Low. Unsteady.

"What is *that*?" a saddle asks, more of them piling into their carriages, shoving past each other as they go.

The noise builds, uneven yet constant, a collection rather than a single source. A split second later, I realize that it's *voices*. Hundreds of voices, raised together in a battle cry. And it's getting louder, louder and nearer.

"We need to go! Now!" Sail shouts at the others, the others who are already atop horses, yanking on reins or helping more saddles into the carriages, hurrying them along.

"Go, go!" Sail says, practically yanking off the door as I rush inside. He slams the door behind me, and I toss the lock over, my heart pounding in time with the battle cry that's echoing across the barren land.

"Where's the fucking driver?" I hear Sail shout. More yelling, more saddles racing by. More guards piling on their horses.

"Shit!"

Through the window, I see Sail abandon his own horse to race for my carriage instead, his body disappearing from view as he hops onto the driver's seat.

"Move out! Head for the pass! Protect the king's favored!"

A second later, the snap of the reins cracks through the air like a tree splintering down the center of its trunk. The carriage lurches forward, nearly sending me flying as it begins to barrel over the snow, Sail making the horses run as fast as they can.

I get tossed around the inside, my body careening from one side to the other. All I can hear is the pounding of the horses' hooves as we race away, but the wheels are groaning from the deep snow.

Guards on horseback converge around my carriage, racing beside us on either side to defend it—to defend *me*. Their golden cloaks billow behind them, hoods flown back, their faces fearful shadows I can barely make out. Through the window to the left, I can see one of the saddles' carriages racing right alongside us, though the others are out of view as we race on, race fast.

I strain to look ahead, to see how far the mountain pass is and if we have any hope of reaching it, but my stomach plummets at the truth of the distance. Too far. We're too far.

Shouts sound. My head whips left and right, from one window to the other, but every time I turn to look, it seems like another guard is gone, plucked from the night.

Snowflakes race past the window, making it harder to see, even worse when the carriage jolts, sending the outside lantern smashing against the wall, its flame extinguishing in the blink of an eye.

Now bathed in horrible darkness, racing at a break-neck speed, the noises of those battle cries get loud enough to drown out the hooves, the wheels, the snapped reins. It grows louder, no matter which direction Sail steers us, no matter how fast our horses race.

They're coming for us. As if they were waiting. As if they knew.

Sharp fear consumes me. My vision growing tun-neled, my breathing erratic.

I feel my ribbons unbind from around my waist. All two dozen of them loosen and slither over my lap like serpents, coiling and defensive. When my hands tremble, they slip between my fingers, threading over my palms, wrapping around my thumbs. Their silken lengths clasp and twine, like a friend squeezing my hand for comfort.

I squeeze back.

Loud. Everything is loud. Close. The entire car-riage begins to rattle from the speed, the wind, the sound. Outside, something crashes. Someone shouts. A horse screams. The wind balks.

Out the window, those balls of light are upon us. Fast—they got to us so impossibly fast.

There are hulking shadows behind them that I can barely see, but those lights burn red, a flare of warning, an omen that I can't look away from.

One of the wheels of the carriage suddenly hits some-thing hard, tossing me up into the air. It's only my ribbons lashing out, bracing my body against all four walls that keeps me from falling.

Sail shouts something that's lost to my ears, and then a second later, the carriage takes a sharp left turn. The wheels go up, the ground stays down. A shriek skids off my tongue as we hit the ground hard, and then we start to roll.

The pull of the ground disappears for a split second. A pause in the fall, where no gravity exists, where my entire body is weightless, floating, hanging by invisible threads.

And then that gentle hover, that pillowed air, it abandons me with a violent turn. The carriage flips, end over end, and this time, not even my ribbons can brace for impact.

I'm tumbling, I'm tossed, I'm rolling like a ball of snow down a slick hill, gathering weight, picking up speed, no hope of stopping softly, no chance of control. Just the grim realization that I'm in this fall's clutches, and only a crash can stop it.

Like a rag doll, I'm flung, blows landing to every part of my body. For a moment, I worry that the flipping will never stop, that I'll be trapped in the fall, forever spinning in the dark, no hope of an end.

Glass flies, wood splinters, gilded edges snap. And then with one final flip, the carriage groans and slams against a mound of snow on its side, where my head smacks against the wall in a sickening crack.

I feel an explosion of pain, a flare of that red, red fire burning behind dimming eyes. And then I black out, the sound of those voices still there, like a turbid presence infecting the air and engulfing me completely.

CHAPTER 24

S *trands of a long-forgotten* sun soothe over my eyes,
golden streaks caressing my closed lids.

I hum in my sleep, joy leaping up, nostalgia
pulling at me. I turn my face toward that shining warmth,
but I can't quite make it, can't quite feel it.

Another silken graze over my brow, and I manage to
open my eyes, only for a burst of pain to greet me. I blink
against the pulse that triggers through my skull, as two
of my ribbons fall away from my face, moving to caress
my arms instead, as if those are the next things they aim
to rouse.

Not beams of sun, then, but my persistent, protective
ribbons. The comforting glow was only in my head.

Groaning, I sit up to gain my bearings, just as everything rushes back. My entire body stiffens as I catch up to
the present, and I look around at the still, broken carriage
lying on its side.

Snow is crowding in beneath me through the broken window, already numbing my legs where I landed against it. I manage to pull my feet beneath me, my eyes adjusting to the near pitch-black as I attempt to get up. The door is above me, and I slink slowly to a stand, my fingers coming up to feel for the handle.

Grabbing hold of it, I flinch at the sound of fighting outside. There's the unmistakable clashing of swords, guttural groans of the injured, shrieks of the women. It makes me cower for a second, the noise making me want to curl up into a ball and shove my hands over my ears.

But I force myself to stay standing, despite how badly my knees shake, regardless of the dizziness that sweeps through my head. I push through it because I *can't* pass out again. I can't cower or hide.

Sail is out there. The other guards, the other saddles… So I tighten my hold on the handle to steady myself and then lift my head out of the empty window frame. Just a bit, just enough to peek over.

But all I see when my eyes lift is a man climbing onto the carriage, a heavy thump marking his ascent. I flinch back, smacking my already sore head against the window frame as I try to pull myself back into the carriage, as if I have any hope of hiding. But before I can fully scramble back, the man leans down, a pair of eyes latching onto me as I try to sink down, his hands snatching at my arms, hauling me right back up.

I shriek and struggle, but he lifts me up as if I weigh

nothing, as if my fight doesn't hinder him at all. The man pulls me out of the carriage, the hold brutal against my arms, my waist scraped against the jagged edges of the broken window pane.

I'm barely out of the carriage and standing on top of it with him before he turns and tosses me carelessly over the side.

I don't even have time to pull in a breath before my body tips headfirst, and I fall into the snow pile on the ground. I land cold and hard, on a hidden rock buried beneath the white. My shoulder and lip smack into the sharp edges, and I instantly taste blood in my mouth, wincing at the pain.

Dazed, I hear the person on the carriage jump down nimbly behind me, and then he's yanking me to a standing position by the back of my coat, the fabric pulling tightly against my throat.

By the veiled ethereal light of a hidden moon, I can just make out one of the horses dead in the snow, still attached to the broken carriage. The other one is gone, pole strap snapped free, reins abandoned.

Sail is nowhere in sight.

Fingers wrapped in thick white bandages grab my chin and turn my face, forcing me to look at the man holding me. The first thing I notice is that he's dressed head-to-toe in white fur. Blending in with the landscape around us, except for the bloodred cloth around his face—the notorious band of the Red Raids.

"What do we have here?" His voice is muffled but rough, like his voice box froze a long time ago in this frigid world, a throat iced over, words that dig out like shards of ice.

"Get the fuck away from her!"

My head snaps to the left, and I see Sail being hauled forward at knifepoint by three more pirates. Gone is his gold-plated armor and his cloak. He's even been stripped of his uniform, leaving him in just his thin tunic and trousers. His face is swollen and bruised, a crack of blood clotted against his brow—either from the carriage wreck or a struggle against the Red Raids.

The pirate holding me laughs at Sail's struggles, but the two holding him by the arms easily subdue him by punching him in the stomach and making him bow over with a cough. A pained breath pointed at a sagging snow, droplets of blood landing at his feet.

"Now, let's get a look at this one," my captor says before shoving my hood back.

The moment my hood is pushed off my head, the pirate grabs my chin again and tilts my head, pointing it up at the cloaked light. His eyes widen, flicking over my hair, my skin, my eyes. I don't know how well he can see, but it seems like it's well enough.

"Take a fuckin' look at this one."

My stomach tightens, fear tensing along with the ribbons caught in his punishing grip at my back.

"She's got paint all over her face."

I blink, but I don't dare look relieved. I don't dare speak.

The one holding Sail licks his lips. "Hmm. She's a pretty one. Cap'n Fane will want to see her."

The pirate grunts in reply and drops his hold from my chin. "You three bring 'em," he says before stuffing two fingers in his mouth, letting out a deafening whistle. "I'll make sure the carriage gets pulled in."

One of the others snorts. "Good luck. That fuckin' thing is heavy as shit. Look at all the gold on it!"

"Aye, heavy enough to fetch a pretty price," the pirate replies.

Behind me, I hear movement, and I see a group of more Red Raids coming, answering my captor's whistle. The first pirate releases me, just to hand me off to another. The brutal grip on my arm digs in as I'm dragged forward despite whatever protests I try to put up. Sail and I are led away, up a hill, leaving the broken carriage behind.

Sail keeps his eyes on me, ignoring the way the two pirates manhandle him, struggling not for himself, but to try to get closer to me, as if he wants to shield me, protect me from this. "Don't fucking try anything," one of the Pirates sneers, holding a blade against Sail's side in clear warning.

The stricken tears that blot in my eyes are cold. So, so cold.

"I'm so sorry, my lady," Sail says, defeat and anger in his gaze.

Apart from his armor, the pirates stripped him of his helmet too. With stark fear on his expression, he looks even paler than usual. Only the bruises and blood give his face any color at all. The grim terror he holds is so unlike his familiar joviality, so different from the open kindness normally worn on his face.

"It's not your fault, Sail," I say quietly, trying to ignore the way the pirate to my right grips my arm so tightly that it cuts off my circulation. My body wants to shake in terror, but I staunch the urge like a pressed hand against a flowing wound. Suppressing it. Holding it in.

"Yes, it is." Sail's voice wobbles, and my heart cracks with the sound of that trembled concession. Cracks deeper with the way his throat bobs, as if he's trying to swallow down his panic, trying to push through, despite our circumstances.

And all I can think of are the stories he's told me as we rode side-by-side these long nights. Of his four older brothers, who ran barefoot and wild down the slums of Highbell. Of his tough but fierce-loving mother, who swept them out of the house with the end of her broom and a scowl but would walk all night alone searching for them when one didn't come back in time for supper.

He doesn't deserve this. He made it from the shanties to the barracks, to a personal guard of the king's favored, all without a coin in his pocket. He's the kindest person I've ever met, and he doesn't deserve to be shoved up a hill by a pirate with no name.

Sail looks over at me, his blackened eye growing darker, puffier with every passing second. He looks tortured. Not for himself, but for me. That apple in his throat bobbing again. "I was supposed to guard you. To protect you—"

"You did," I say fiercely, cutting him off. I refuse to let him blame himself for this. "There was nothing else you could've done."

"Alright, shut the fuck up, you two, or we'll shove gags in your mouths." The pirate holding me shakes me to emphasize his words, turning me limp, despite the steel I try to hold in my spine.

Sail's blue eyes flash with anger at the sight of the pirate being so rough with me, but I shake my head at him, telling him not to react, not to fight.

We fall silent as we're shoved onward. The scar at my throat throbs, like a pained premonition. A physical pessimism, as if it knows my life is being held against a knife's edge once more.

My ribbons itch to wrap around it, wanting to protect the vulnerability there, but I keep them down, keep them wrapped around me.

Behind us, the mountain pass is a looming backdrop. Howls of wind rush out from that gap between the crests, pushing us even further away. I turn my back on its dark outline, hating the sight of its mocking mouth gaping at us, wide open, as if to laugh.

Too far. Much too far away. Our only chance at

escape, and we never had any real hope of reaching it. Even the mountains know it.

The laughing wind continues to blow.

CHAPTER 25

Sail and I are dragged uphill.

We make heavy, sloppy tracks as we go, snow shin-deep, threatening to topple us with every step. But the Red Raids carry on easily, as if buried legs and pushed steps hold no difficulty for them at all.

Just a few dozen steps, and yet with the effort it takes for each one and with the pirate's jostled hold on my arm, it's enough to leave me panting by the time we crest the top.

I'm too busy catching my breath for a moment to take in the sight. But once I manage to look at the flat land below, my eyes widen. Beside me, I hear Sail suck in a breath.

Gone is the emptiness, the flat landscape of nothing except the snow-white expanse that the Barrens are known for. Instead, it's been overrun.

There are three large pirate ships made of white

wood below us. They sit on the snow drifts like ships docked in an ocean's harbor, except they have no sails. Where waves of water and windy skies normally drive a boat out to sea, these ships are more like massive snow sleds, pulled not by wind or tide or oars, but by an entirely different force.

"Fire claws," Sail says in shock and awe beside me.

My wide eyes hook onto the snowy felines below. They're *massive*. Ten feet tall at least, with hooked fangs dripping down past their lower jaws, the ends shaped like shovels, used to scrape at snow and ice.

But the most remarkable part of them, aside from their sheer size, is the glowing flames that lick around their paws. Some are lit, some not, some have all four footsteps blazing red, while on others, only a single burns, as if they have one foot standing in the doorway to hell.

That explains the balls of fire we saw in the distance.

When one of the Red Raids raises his whip, cracking it over a line of the creatures to make them move the ship forward, a massive growl emits from the entire row of them, baring their ferocity in a unified growl. The noise cuts through the air and soaks into the ground, vibrating my very feet.

That explains the thunder.

"I thought fire claws were a myth," I say.

The pirate beside me chuckles. "More like a night-mare," he says, and even with his face covering, I can tell he's smiling. "One swipe of their paw and they can kill a man—or woman."

I look back at him, struggling not to shiver.

"You're either gonna be dead from their razor claws or burned to a bloody crisp from their flames. Not a good way to go, either way."

I don't want to go anywhere near those things. Unfortunately, the pirates begin to tug us down the other side of the sloped hill, heading closer to the beasts, heading closer to the ships and the hundreds of more pirates below.

My eyes take in as much as I can, searching for familiar faces, both hoping I'll see them and praying that I won't. As we get closer, I can see signs of struggle, more dead horses, another carriage that's being stripped bare and hacked up into pieces, every gilded inch pried away and carried onto the ships.

The pirates work methodically, pilfering everything, right down to every trunk and carriage curtain.

The surviving horses are being led onto one of the smaller ships too, their hooves clopping against the wooden ramp as they go, most of them eyeing the fire claws nervously. Crisp is one of them. I spot him by his tail, by the gold twine I braided into it.

Pirates crawl everywhere, hauling screaming saddles away, looting through all of our things. Fighting and taunting our vastly outnumbered guards. Every single one of them wears the same white fur clothes, the same red cloth wrapped around their faces and heads, leaving only their eyes exposed.

The flames from the fiery feline paws light up the scene, basking it in flickering red, somehow making all of this so much worse. My eyes sweep down from one of the ships, and I notice the blood splattered over the white snow—so dark that it looks black. And then I start to notice the unmoving guards littered on the ground.

Beside me, Sail goes still. Silent. Dread curls into my chest like acrid smoke, burning my eyes, polluting my chest.

Everywhere I look, there are dead or captured guards being stripped down to nothing but their underwear. The ones alive are battered and bloodied, shaking from the cold, even their boots stolen from them as their clothes and armor are thrown into a pile, to be distributed to the ships.

I bite my tongue so hard that the taste of copper drips against my cheek. I hold it there, crush it between my teeth, biting, biting.

When we get closer to the ships, the heat from the rows of fire claws chips away at the fierce chill of the night, but it doesn't warm me. Doesn't hold a lick of comfort.

I search the guards, seeking past the swarming pirates, but I don't see the face I'm searching for. I don't see Digby.

A gruff pirate sees us approaching and cuts over to

us. "Another saddle?" he asks, looking me over. "Bring her over there." He jerks his head to the left, and my head turns in the direction. The saddles are there, lined up, a group of pirates looking them over, leering, touching. Rosh, the male saddle, gets shoved onto his knees, the pirates mocking him, spitting on him. His blond head hangs down.

I whip my head back around. "Sail." My voice cuts off, because I'm already being dragged away, while the pirates holding him head in another direction.

"It'll be okay," he promises, but even in my state of shock, I can hear the lie tremble from his lips.

"Sail!" His name is a cry. Panic expanding, bursting all at once. "Sail!" I scream again, struggling against the man who holds me.

Nothing. My struggles do nothing. Even if it did, even if I managed to break away from him, there are hundreds more to grab hold of me.

"It's okay," Sail calls, voice tight, face agonized. "It's okay, it's okay."

His repeated reply sounds like a plea.

I'm wrenched away, Sail torn from my line of vision as I'm shoved toward the twelve other saddles. I get lined up with them in front of the largest ship, dozens of fire claws at our backs, their paws of red bringing steam from the snow, a haze turning the ground ruddy with temper.

When I'm put in line at the end of the other saddles, I face forward, my back to the ship, and I see Sail being dragged across the way, where he's shoved onto his knees in the snow, next to the other guards who are still alive.

The pirate leading him sends a crushing kick to his side, ensuring he stays down. But even as Sail coughs and clenches his arms around his middle, he keeps his head up, keeps his eyes on me. Like he wants to make sure he doesn't lose me, or that he wants to show me that I'm not alone.

At the sound of a whimper, I look to my left and realize it's Polly trembling beside me, with tears running down her freckled face. She's crying so hard that she's having trouble breathing, her dress ripped in several places, the top bodice in pieces. And though her shaking hands try to hold the scraps together, it's too ruined, her breasts nearly bare.

Anger rises in me, anger and despair. I quickly remove my coat and place it over her shoulders to help cover her. She flinches when I touch her and tries to smack my hand away, but when she sees that it's me, the fight seeps out of her. "What are you doing?" she asks, the usual mocking bite from her tone absent.

I ignore her question and instead grab her arm and shove it through the arm of my coat before helping her arm through the other side. When her arms are in, I do up the buttons, though my hands are shaking so hard that it takes me several tries just to get the top one done.

When she's covered, she looks over at me, a harsh line slashed against her cheek, clearly marking where she's been slapped. "Thanks," she mumbles.

I nod, feeling the cold air bite at me more aggressively now, but bright side? At least I still have on my heavy wool dress and leggings. One look at the mostly naked guards is enough to make me grimace for them. If they don't get out of the cold soon, they could go into hypothermic shock and be at risk of having frostbite.

"What are they going to do to us?" I ask, noting the pirates as they continue to work. A couple of them are watching over us, making sure we stay put, but aside from crying and whispering, none of the saddles dare to move.

A few people down the line from me, I can see Rissa speaking in low tones to the girl beside her. She's one of the newer and youngest saddles here, and I still haven't learned her name. She's small and waiflike, with silky black hair and almond-shaped eyes, and right now, she looks petrified. Rissa catches my gaze, but her expression is grim despite the way she holds the girl's hand, offering comfort.

Next to me, Polly gives a bitter laugh. "What do you think?" she answers. "They're *pirates*. The Red Raids are known for being savage and brutal. No one else could survive out here in the Barrens. They're going to use us up and then sell us off just like everything else they steal. And that's if we're lucky."

My whole body trembles, and my hand comes up to grip my scar. I was terrified that night with King Fulke. But this? This is an entirely new level of fear. This is a different form of captivity.

One look at these pirates, and I'm certain that none of us want to be brought onto those ships.

But with the savage fire claws behind us and the vicious pirates all around, there's nowhere to go. Nowhere to hide. A leering voice inside of me tells me that this is my fault. That I should never have wished to leave the safety of my cage.

I'm a fool.

The bleakness of our reality slowly sinks in. Sinks deep as we stand there, shuddering in the cold. The snow-fall hasn't stopped and continues to drop in a slow, delicate descent, the flakes landing on shaking shoulders. Another burden to carry on our backs.

I'm not sure how long we stand there.

The pirates work to strip down every single item we possessed. Then piles are distributed, pieces picked out, and one by one, everything is hauled onto the ships, down to the last piece of dry, salted meat.

The near-naked guards still kneeling in the snow grow weary, and two of them collapse, unable to hold themselves up any longer. The other guards try to nudge and rally them, try to encourage them to get back up. One does.

The other doesn't.

Sail's teeth started chattering a while ago, and even from several feet away, I can see that his lips have turned blue. His thin pants soaked through where he's been forced to kneel.

Frost has collected on brows and temples where nervous sweat dripped down. Despite the waves of heat coming from the fire claws at our backs, the bitter chill saps our strength, leaches our spirit.

But through it all, Sail keeps looking at me, gaze steady and unyielding. When my body shivers, he holds his in. When my lips tremble, he pulls his up into a sad smile. When a tear falls against my cold cheek, he nods, still speaking to me, even without words.

You're okay, you're okay.

He protects me, bolsters me, there in those kind blue eyes.

So I don't look away from him when another one of our guards crumples to the ground. I don't look away when a fire claw growls, so close that I swear it's about to slash a line down my back. I don't look away when one of the women wails and begs. Her cries like a shatter through brittle ice.

I don't look away.

And then, someone descends. From a ramp lowered on the largest ship, heavy boots sound against the white wood. Each step scares a heartbeat to skip, and only when I hear him right behind me do I finally let my eyes tear away from Sail's face.

The Red Raids go still as the man stops at the foot of the ramp, every single pirate stopping to face him. My eyes hover at the side, taking him in, noting the white fur on his body and the red band around his face, same as the rest—but I also note the grisly pirate hat sitting proudly on his head, the color like rusted crimson, as if the leather was soaked in blood. A single black feather sits at its plume, like a mark of death, and it's this that tells me exactly who I'm looking at.

The captain of the Red Raids.

CHAPTER 26

T*he pirate captain is met* by a man at the bottom of the ramp. "How'd we do, Quarter?"

"Best haul we've had, Cap'n. The gold on this lot? You were right—it's Midas's." Even with the red cloth over his face, I can hear every word, can see the excited glint in the man's—Quarter's—eyes.

"Hmm," the captain replies, his gaze sweeping over the snow. It lands on the guards kneeling, and he walks over to them, a black brow cocking up. "Stripped them down already?"

Quarter chuckles as he walks up from behind him. "Their armor was plated gold. Even their boots were tipped with it."

The captain rubs his hands together, but it's not to keep them warm. It's the satisfied friction of a crook. "Excellent."

"The horses are good stock, too. Already loaded 'em on the ship," Quarter continues.

The captain nods and then turns, his eyes finally deigning to land on us. "This many women?"

"Whores, by the looks of 'em."

This news piques the captain's interest. He walks over to survey our line, his boots crunching in the sodden snow, his intense eyes taking in every inch of us.

"Hmm, not just whores," he murmurs, fingering the dress of one of the women. She trembles, her gaze down, eyes buried in the snow. "They're dressed far too fine for common whores." He turns to Quarter, and even though his face is still covered, somehow, I know he's grinning. "These are Midas's royal saddles."

Quarter's eyes widen, and a low whistle escapes him. "Well, shit. Y'hear that, Reds?" he calls out to the gathered pirates. "We'll be ridin' some royal saddles tonight!"

A roar of approval rises up, like a pack of wolves howling at the moon in rabid jubilation. Beside me, Polly whimpers.

The captain walks down the line of women, eyeing each of us carefully. By the time he reaches Polly, she's shaking so hard that I worry she'll pass out. When he sees her wearing the fur coat, he flicks an impatient hand.

Quarter comes up and takes hold of it, snapping buttons right off as he rips the front open. Polly lets out a shrill scream, trying to pull it back together, but another pirate comes up and yanks her arms behind her, holding her still.

Now that she's being held, the captain pushes her

scraps of dress away to get a look at her body. "Nice tits. Midas has good taste, at least." His eyes travel lazily back up from her breasts to her face. "Look at me, girl."

But Polly has her eyes shut tight, and she shakes her head no, keeping her chin down, keeping her shoulders curled.

The captain's dark eyes narrow. "Hmm, these royal saddles are a bit stuck-up, aren't they, Quarter?" he muses.

The bulky man—probably his second-in-command—nods. "Aye. But we can teach 'em some manners, Cap'n."

Quarter takes a step forward and grips Polly roughly by her blonde hair, wrenching a cry from her as he tilts her head back, her eyes flaring wide. "You ain't a royal saddle no more, girl. If Cap'n Fane wants a look at ya, then you give it to him. Y'hear?"

Polly whimpers and then her eyes suddenly roll back, her whole body going slack as she passes out. All three of the pirates let her fall, let her delicate body crash into the snow. Not one of them bothers to lift her back up.

Captain Fane makes a tsking noise. "Weak. We'll have to train them."

Inside my dress pockets, my hands shake.

Above me, the blanket of night smothers, holds itself over us, keeps me hostage. Far behind, the mountain pass breathes, a yawning divide that would've led us to the border, would've led us to Fifth Kingdom.

Too far. We were just too far.

What will happen when our party never shows up to Fifth? How long until Midas sends scouts to search for us? Will he be able to find me? Will it be too late?

Guilt, acidic and hot, steams in my stomach, each rising tendril malignant. Is this a punishment? Do the Divine gods and goddesses scorn me for my urge to leave Midas's cage? Maybe this is a reprimand of the fates, proof that I should've been satisfied with what I had, been grateful for it.

The pirate captain steps in front of me.

My gaze lifts up, up, until it settles on his face. A cruel, callous face. White fur. Red band. Brown eyes.

I should never have looked away from Sail's eyes. I should've stayed there, in that look, where it was safe.

The captain runs the same assessing, nearly bored look over me, same as he did the others. But then he goes still. Squints. Looks harder.

My heart pounds.

He snaps his fingers without ever looking away from me. "Light."

"Light! Get the captain a light!" Quarter hollers, making me flinch.

I hear running footsteps, a shake of glass and metal. But I can't look away from the captain. I'm stuck in fear, stuck, as if he has a hand wrapped around my neck.

Someone rushes over with a torch, its yellow flame hissing from the snowfall, its center a wounded red, like they lit it from the paws of their hellish beasts.

Captain Fane snatches the torch and holds it close to me, so close that the heat is nearly painful against my frozen cheeks. He lets the light glow over my face, drags it down my gold-threaded clothes. The glimmering leather of my boots. The luster of my hair.

His brown eyes are no longer aloof or disinterested. There's surprise there, surprise, and then triumph.

It's the triumph that makes my chin quiver.

He shoves the torch over to Quarter for him to hold, the man instantly gripping it. Then the captain reaches forward, grabbing my tangled braid, and holds the strands in front of the light. He drops it after a few seconds, and then my hand is snatched up. He yanks off my glove, studying my fingers, my palm, my nails. My skin glitters in the firelight.

"It can't be," he mutters before he reaches up and yanks away the red cloth that covers his face, the fabric lying around his neck like a scarf. He's younger than I would've first guessed—maybe only in his early thirties.

To my disgust, the captain pulls my hand closer and then licks the skin below my thumb. I cringe, trying to pull away, but he holds me firmly and then rubs at the licked spot, like he wants to see if the gold will come off.

Paint. The other pirate had thought I was covered in paint. The captain just realized that I'm not.

A slow, daunting smile spreads across his face. A face laid bare for me to see, with a mouth revealing a few missing teeth that have been replaced with the same white wood as the ship. Short, dark blond facial hair growing on only his chin, the ends gathered in red beads. A thick piercing through his left ear, a plug of red-stained wood filling the hole. I don't dare wonder if it's been soaked in blood.

My mouth goes dry at that smile, at that look he gives me. It's the kind of look that tells a woman all she needs to know about what kind of man has hold of her. If I had breath in my lungs, I would scream. But I'm dried up, emptied out. The only thing inside of my chest is that steaming guilt and a cold clutch of terror.

Without warning, the captain snatches my wrist and tugs me forward. I stumble at the unexpected move, but he spins around on his heel, raising my hand high above my head like a show of victory, like a prize to show off. "Reds! Look at the treasure we unburied!"

His voice booms across the Barrens like a drum.

"We've got Midas's gilded whore!"

CHAPTER 27

A shockwave seems to pass over the pirates at Captain Fane's revelation.

First, there's stunned silence. I feel hundreds of eyes settling onto me, appraising me, before their shock gives way to something else. Something worse.

Shouts rise up, louder than even the fire claws' growls. I jump from the sound, trying to tear my hand away, but the captain's hold only tightens around my wrist.

He turns back to me, elation clear in his eyes. "Look at her. Even her dress is gold. This hair, too." He drops my wrist to snatch up some of my hair, fisting it in his grip. "The golden pet of Highbell."

The captain turns back to his men, his hold unrelenting. "We snatched Midas's favored." The pirates chuckle, pleased, so immensely pleased with themselves.

"He'll pay you," I blurt, my voice finally coming

out, though it's quiet, stretched thin. He drops his hold from my hair, my scalp pulsing in time with my hammering heart. "His guards, his saddles...me...he'll pay you whatever ransom you want. Just don't hurt us."

Captain Fane smirks. "Oh, I'm not going to ransom you. I can fetch a far higher price elsewhere."

His words hollow out a pit in my stomach, dark and bottomless.

"I'll be keeping this one 'til we sell her off to the highest bidder. Put the word out."

"Aye, Cap'n," Quarter replies with a nod. "King Midas's favored? There will be plenty who will be wanting her."

"The rest of them can be divvied up to entertain the men for their hard work," he tells his second-in-command. The pirates near enough to hear whoop out in celebration. The saddles cry.

Captain Fane's eyes look down where Polly is still unconscious in a heap in the snow. "And put 'em to work, too, to earn their way. They need toughening up."

Quarter nods. "Consider it done, Cap."

The captain nods, a wicked gleam in his gaze that flicks over me. "I'll enjoy having Midas's gold-plated prisoner kept in my cabin."

My trembling body starts shaking even harder, chin wobbling. I can already see the pain he intends to inflict, the force he aims to assault me with. It's all there, in his eyes.

His hand comes up to grope my breast, fingers

pinching, touch revolting. I try to shove him off, but he just laughs and squeezes harder. "Aye, I'll like breaking this one in. Midas's fucking *favored*," he laughs, like he can't believe his good luck. "I wish I could see the look on the bastard's face when he finds out I took her, used her, and then sold her off."

Tears fill my eyes, blurring the world, drowning my chest. I can't breathe. I can't even feel my limbs. This isn't happening. This is a nightmare. I'm going to wake up. I just need to wake up.

Captain Fane's fingers tighten, pinch, making me cry out. "Mmm, noisy too. I like that."

He starts to tug at the collar of my dress, scratching at my chest, but a voice shouts behind him. "*Don't fucking touch her!*"

Captain Fane stills. His hand drops. Slowly, he turns around. "Who said that?"

One of the pirates walks up to a still kneeling Sail. "This one, Cap'n."

My eyes fly to Sail just as the pirate sends a brutal kick at his back.

My guard goes sprawling forward, his face hitting the snow. Captain Fane stalks over to him, and dread catches, airborne and ruthless, infecting me instantly.

"What's your name?" the captain asks, stopping in front of him.

Sail struggles to raise back on his knees, his jaw clenching as he looks up, defiant and bruised. "Sail."

At his answer, Captain Fane tips his head back and laughs. "Reds, did you hear that? We finally got a Sail for our sail-less ships!" Mean amusement floods the icy plains. Red flames flicker through the black night.

"Alright, *Sail*. You have something to say? You must, since you hollered out like a cat in heat." More pirates laugh, and Sail's pale cheeks probably would've blushed if they weren't already chapped and red with cold.

But he doesn't cower. He looks up at the captain, expression soaked in hatred. The Barrens go quiet, as if watching, every eye trained on the scene.

Don't say anything. Don't say anything, Sail.

But Sail doesn't stay silent. "I said, don't touch her," he repeats, his tone livid. A band around my heart constricts.

Captain Fane chuckles as if amused. "Look, Reds. We got a brave one, here. How rare for Midas's army." The pirates laugh. The other kneeling guards hang their heads, humiliation and cruelty falling on them alongside the snow.

But Sail's fingers curl into fists in front of him, his gaze steady. "She's the king's favored. He'll pay handsomely for her if she's returned to him unharmed. Despite what you said, Midas *will* pay much more for her than anyone else. He's the only one that has the means to."

"Aye, the king with the golden-touch," Captain Fane says with a jeering, bitter edge at the mention of Midas. Hate. There's hate there in his tone. And maybe envy.

"Perhaps it's time that the king learned a lesson," the captain muses. "Time to ensure that there's something that he *can't* buy. In fact, maybe I'll even just keep her for myself, to make sure of it."

Sail starts to open his mouth, but he's silenced as the captain lowers himself, bending down until he's directly in front of Sail, eye-to-eye. Brown to blue. Cruel to kind. His fingers skim over the snow, lazily collecting some of it in his bare palm, piling it up with bored movements.

"Now listen very carefully," Captain Fane begins, his voice low but loud enough to hear. "I'm going to fuck her. Wherever and whenever I wish." He says it conversationally, easily, as if he were only talking about the weather. "I'm going to use her. *Break* her," Captain Fane goes on, completely uncaring when Sail begins to shake with fury.

A shaken sob totters through my throat, slips past my lips.

"I'm going to cut off some of her pretty hair and send it to Midas in a pretty box, because it will amuse me to taunt him. Perhaps I'll even take the hair from her golden snatch."

Captain Fane reaches up, the snow he gathered piled high in his cupped palm. He drops it onto Sail's bare head with a taunting slap, making my guard wince from the cold. Slabs of it slip over his face before dripping off, landing on his already soaked pants.

The captain gathers more snow.

"And after I'm bored with her—who knows when

that will be—I'll sell her to whoever will give me the highest price. But that won't be for weeks. Maybe even months."

Another handful of snow is dumped on Sail's head. Some flakes stick to his hair, some slip down the back of his shirt to soak against his shivering spine. All while Captain Fane drinks in Sail's expression, like a cat toying with a mouse, and the Red Raids watch, red bands like gaping, bloody grins.

"She's going to be nothing but a gold, cum-filled husk by the time I'm done with her." Sail flinches, shaking now so hard, and even his teeth can't stop their violent chatter. My heart pounds and hammers, like it wants to burrow down, to tunnel itself down into a chasm, hiding far below.

Another pile of snow is collected in the captain's palm, constant, methodical. "But you won't care about any of that. And do you know why?" he asks, dumping another heap over my guard, my friend.

Sail's head bows, as if the weight of it—this chilled humiliation—is growing too heavy.

Slowly, as if that's all he was waiting for, this forced capitulation, the captain gets to his feet. He dusts the rest of the snow off his hands. My heart continues to hammer. Beating against my ribs, begging.

"You won't care," Captain Fane goes on, looking down at him. "Because you'll be *dead*."

A battering ram against my chest. A single moment only long enough to blink. To look.

Sail's eyes are suddenly on mine again, blue depths of an ocean he's never seen. And that kind gaze of his keeps speaking. His nod keeps promising.

It's okay, it's okay.

But it's not okay. Not at all. Because before that nod is even finished, the captain has unhooked a knife from the scabbard at his waist and rammed it into Sail's chest.

Straight through to his heart.

"*No!*"

I'm running before I've made the conscious decision to do so. But I don't even make it three steps before someone grabs me, a pair of meaty arms closing around my middle.

I scream, a horrible rage tearing out of my throat, my voice an unearthly noise that rents through the air, hollowing out the night, thrashing through the mountain pass, cursing at the covered stars.

My scream makes the nervous horses whinny and the fire claws hiss. It muffles the Gale Widow's cries, and it blames the fates. Even when a hand slams over my mouth to quiet me, the sound rips out, as if I could make a tear in the world, as if I could shatter the skies.

Blood blooms over Sail's chest, soaking into his cotton tunic like a scarlet flower gaping. Hot tears roll from my eyes one after the other in uncontrollable tracks, freezing on my cheeks.

The hand falls away from me as I fall on the ground, scrabbling for him on hands and knees. I don't feel the bite of the ice as I crawl. But his name falls from my lips again and again, as time seems to stop, to inhale with a shocked breath.

His blue eyes are still on me, but blinking, blinking. They flick down to the blade. To the red.

I reach him just as his body curls forward, just as he falls.

Even with my hands landing against his shoulders, Sail still goes down. All I'm able to do is twist him up, to keep his face pointed at the sky.

Mouth dribbles red life, breath like choked water. Blue-tinged lips to match his eyes as they rain.

My heart shatters itself against my ribs. He looks at me, my teardrops landing on his. I sob. He shudders.

"It's okay, it's okay," I cry. Lying for him, as he did for me.

And with his last breath, he nods.

CHAPTER 28

My *heart stops raging. Stops* hammering. It slumps, defeated, gone as quiet and still as Sail's chest.

Blood draws a line from his parted lips, landing behind his ear, a small splatter in the snow.

Behind me, all around me, the Red Raids move, speak, laugh. I ignore them as I lay my hand on Sail's cold face.

"Get her onboard."

My palm scrapes against Sail's cheek as I'm hauled to my feet. I try to keep looking, to keep our eyes locked, but I'm pulled away. Sail's gaze doesn't follow me. It just stays still and unblinking, snow landing heavy against his blond lashes where he lies.

This time, when the sound of thunder fills the air, it really is from the clouds. I look up as I'm taken toward the ships, seeing the tremble that moves through the sky.

When I'm led to the ramp of the largest ship, the wind begins to whip, lightning buckles, and a storm opens up with a growl.

The soft, hovering snowfall is gone, and in its place is a punishing surge, frozen rain sluicing down like spikes. It crashes over us, as if the clouds went angry, as if they're lending me vengeful tears for what's been done below them.

But not even the plunging needles can pierce through the raw ache in my heart. Because my friend—my kind, teasing guard—is dead.

Sail is *dead.*

All because he was trying to protect me. To stand up for me. To bolster me.

Sharp. The sorrow is so damn *sharp.*

When I see some of the pirates kick at Sail's body, roughly, callously, I lose it. I start to fight, kicking and screaming. But Quarter comes over and places a brutal hold on my jaw, squeezing it to the point of threat. "Enough of that."

The pirate behind me gets a firmer hold of my arms, keeping me still. An enraged snarl comes out of me, a noise that doesn't sound remotely human, as I stare at Quarter with hate—so much hate for all the Red Raids, his captain in particular.

Quarter's eyes narrow on me before his hand delves into a pocket, and then he's stuffing a filthy cloth in my mouth, holding it there, so thick I can't even try to bite his fingers. "Quiet," he snaps, pushing so far back that I start to gag.

I'm shoved the last step up the incline of the ramp, sending me sprawling onto the ship's deck. My already sore body crashes into the wood, and I nearly choke on the fabric lodged in my mouth.

I snatch out the offending gag, coughing and sputtering with breaths as I toss it away. Before I can get up, the other saddles are shoved right alongside me, and we're all pushed together on the deck like we're just another pile of the pirate's plunder.

A hand appears in front of my face, and I look up to find Rissa above me. I glance warily at her palm for a moment. "Well?" she says, clear impatience in her tone.

I reach up and take her hand, and Rissa pulls me up, helping me to my feet before she lets go. I begin to mutter out a thanks, but I'm elbowed at my side.

Turning, I see one of the other saddles—Mist— sneering at me. Her black hair is in knots, her eyes red and swollen. "Watch it," she snarls, wiping her sleeve where I happened to brush up against her.

And maybe it's because I just watched my friend get murdered before my eyes, maybe it's because my nerves are frayed, or because we just became captives of notoriously brutal pirates, but red-hot rage comes galloping up in me, and I'm unable to stop it.

My ribbons, all twenty four of them from up and down my spine, unravel. Her eyes flicker with confusion

275

at their movement—confusion and then shock as they thrust forward and *shove*.

She goes flying back, toppling other saddles and even some pirates behind her. She screeches as she lands, and then she's up and on her feet in an instant, not to confront me about my ribbons and how the hell I moved them, but ready to attack.

Her fingers curled like claws, I brace myself for her, but Rissa steps between us before Mist can launch herself at me.

"No squabbling," Rissa snaps, shooting looks at both of us. "Or have you forgotten where the hell we are?"

With a ragged exhale, my ribbons go limp behind me at her words, but Mist isn't so deterred. She glares at me from over Rissa's shoulder, and the intensity of her hate-filled gaze throws me off-balance.

I thought that her flare of temper from before was just from emotions, from stressful circumstances. But this—this expression on her face isn't that. It's not distress that's making her lash out irrationally. Not when her eyes hold such personal vitriol.

"It's her fault we're here!" Mist hisses.

I frown, exasperated. "What the hell are you talking about? How is any of this my fault?"

Mist looks around at the other wide-eyed saddles huddled around us. "You heard them. *Protect the king's favored*." She scoffs with an ugly, humorless sound.

I go still. Those words—Sail's words, called out right

as the snow pirates ambushed us. I hadn't thought, hadn't even considered, how it would sound to the other saddles.

"When it came down to it, the guards weren't going to protect us. It was just *her*. Midas always keeps her safe, keeps her special. Even on this damn journey, she got special treatment, didn't she? Don't travel too long during the night, because we don't want to tire the king's favored. Don't eat more rations, because we have to make sure the king's favored has extra. Don't go too fast, because the king's favored wants to ride a bloody horse she has no business being on! It's all her! All the time!"

I feel the eyes of the other saddles swing over to me like a hook on a string.

"And then when it all went to shit, what did they do? Protected *her*. Tried to make it so she got away, because the rest of us don't matter. We're expendable. Replaceable." Mist is sobbing now, her petite shoulders shaking. "And now we're here, captured, and what do you think is going to happen to us?"

Rosh tries to gently take her arm, to shush her, but she shrugs him off, staring at me with that fire, that hate, burning me with it.

"Ruined. That's what's going to happen to us. We're going to be ruined. Until we're nothing. Slaves to be used and then merchandise to be sold. But the king will come for *her*. Bargain for *her*. Save his *favored*. But not us," Mist says with a bitter shake of her head as more tears fall. "Not us."

My earlier guilt may have felt like steam, but now it's like an open wound, torn right through my gut.

All the other saddles continue to look at me as Mist's words settle in, but I only stand there, silent, mouth dry and wound aching.

What is there to say? In her eyes, in all of their eyes, she's right. Maybe from no fault of my own, but an ugly truth all the same.

How would I have felt, hearing that order, *protect the king's favored*, if I were them?

"Alright, hush now," Rissa says, once more stepping in, once more trying to diffuse the situation. "Regardless of any of that, we can't afford to gain any more negative attention than we're already going to get."

Her normally seductive lips are pressed in a hard, firm line, her blonde tresses scattered over a dress spotted with blood that isn't her own.

Rissa looks at the saddles, her peers, her friends. "We're professionals. Not just saddles from the slums, but King Midas's select chosen. If we're going to get through this, we'll have to perform, but we know how to do that. We know how to work a room."

The saddles huddle closer together, a circle in the middle of a ship, backs turned on me, the outsider. Separate. I'm separate from them, even now, when we're in the same terrifying situation. But no wonder they've always hated me, always kept me apart. Who could blame them?

I turn away from them, away from the exclusion, my

feet taking me to the edge of the ship where I grasp the railing with white knuckles.

Right now, the one person I want to talk to, the one person I know could make me feel better, is dead in the snow with a puncture through his heart. My only friend. Dead, because of me.

My eyes scan the land below, taking in the littered bodies that the pirates left behind. Left there in the Barrens, for the clouds and winds to bury.

Beside me, the Red Raids draw up the ramp, heaving it back in place into the wall of the ship just as a horn blows, indicating that we're on the move. Below, fire claws grumble and hiss, the vibrations of their growls shaking the boards at my feet.

But my eyes stay planted on the landscape below, sweeping, looking, searching. Where is he, where is he...

I double check my vantage point, but a frown forms between my brows because I don't see him. I see the other fallen guards, but not him.

When the ship begins to move, slowly sledding over the slick iced ground, my gaze turns frantic, confused. There. He should've been *right* there.

I see the blood, I see the spot where it happened, where his heart emptied out. But no Sail.

My hands tighten on the railing as I continue to look, but I don't see him. As if he just got up and walked off. Except that's impossible. But I don't see him, he's not there, and I—

Raucous laughter of the pirates draws my eye to the stern of the ship, where it's lit up from the red, swaying lanterns. But I shouldn't have looked. I shouldn't have.

A choked cry flies out of me as I slap a hand over my mouth. The pirates are gathered around, laughter coming from behind their red cloths, but it does nothing to muffle their cruelty.

And Sail...I couldn't spot him on the ground, not because I was wrong about where he'd been, or that he'd miraculously lived, but because they dragged him onboard.

My horror-filled eyes are wide as I look at where they've hung him. They trussed up his lifeless body at the front of the ship, against a stained wooden post.

Ropes are wrapped around him, forcing his body straight against the pole. His vacant eyes are still open, looking ahead at nothing, but it was a gaze that was meant for *me*, a gaze that he offered with his last dying breath.

Someone shouts, "Our ship's finally got a Sail!"

I don't know who says it. Maybe the captain. Maybe someone else. I don't know because my ears are roaring too loudly to hear, my eyes too blurry to see.

"Think he'll flap in the wind?" someone else jokes. Mocking laughter is as loud as the thunder, as loud as the whips against the growling beasts who pull us.

The ship slides onward, cutting through the tides of the snow drifts, leaving behind dead Highbell guards in its wake.

And Sail's body hangs, degraded and scorned, like a carved figurehead at the bow, the last of his blood already frozen against his chest. But those eyes of an ocean don't shut. Though they don't see anymore, either.

I turn and vomit on the white-washed wooden planks.

CHAPTER 29

*T*hey leave us alone.

For an hour, maybe two, while they're busy at work, following some invisible navigation they seem to use that tells them where to go in this dark, frozen world.

It's a lot of shouting and rushing around as they get going, steered by the fire claws, our vessel leading the other two ships that travel behind us.

Soon, we start to fly.

Gliding across the barren ice land, the ships race onward as they catch the sweet spot of speed. Using the strength of the running beasts pulling like wolves on a sleigh, the ships use it to their advantage, whips cracking, until we're going so fast that all the ships need is the slick ground to carry their velocity.

All three snow pirate ships careen across the expanse of white as sleet continues to fall, whipping at our faces in the wind. The smooth wooden bottoms slide like an unstoppable force, snow spraying up against the sides like cresting waves.

Even with the wind tearing through my hair and the rain soaking my dress, I stay standing, stay gripping the railing, stay staring at Sail's body ahead.

And that anger, that first spark of it that lit when my ribbons uncurled to shove Mist, it comes coiling up again.

The shocked sadness of Sail's death was cold. But this, this is hot and red—as red as the band across Captain Fane's face.

My eyes settle on him, on where he stands at the bow as he shouts orders and directions below. The black feather in his hat is bent back with the open rush of the air, and there's a glint at his waist, at the knife tucked there.

It's that knife that I focus on, that I stare at as I let go of the railing at last, my fingers cramping, still missing one glove from where the captain tore it off to touch me.

I don't care that it's full night, carrying weighted shadows that suppress my soul. I don't care that the clouds unleashed a torrent. I don't care that I'm one woman against a ship load of men. I don't care that I'm vulnerable, that I'm walking toward the captain alone.

Because Sail was my friend.

And this is not okay.

My ribbons trail behind me as my steps grow surer, my spine straighter. A mantra plays in my mind as I remember Sail's last comforting gaze.

This is not okay, this is not okay.

No one stops me as I walk forward, no one even looks my way. I'm so inconsequential to them—all of the saddles left on the deck are. A fact made obvious since we've been left unguarded. Left to huddle and cower on the deck.

But I won't do that. Not with Sail strung up like that. I suppose a person has limits, and this is mine.

It's easy, so easy to make it across the ship. To pass by without anyone bothering to even look my way. It's the arrogance of men, to think so little of women. And it'll be their downfall too.

Past hooks of weapons, past coils of rope, past pirates hauling loot, I veer around it all. Until I make it all the way to the bow. Right behind the captain.

All twenty-four of my ribbons move like tentacles. All down my spinal cord, growing in perfect symmetry out of my skin, the inch-wide satin strips rise up on either side of my spine, from the bottom of my neck, to the dimples above my butt.

Their long lengths are like snakes ready to strike. Not at the captain, but to Sail, to the ropes that bind him to the pole.

Some of the saddles in the middle of the ship see me and cast nervous looks around, some of them inch forward to get a better look through the wind-driven rain.

I stand at the base of the wooden post, looking up, directing, moving each ribbon with determined intent.

Even as they get sodden and heavy with rain, they deftly tug out knots. When that's not enough, their edges harden, no longer soft like satin, but sharp—as sharp as the edge of a blade. Golden silk battles against corded twine, ripping and yanking, slicing into the strands like they're nothing.

"Oy!"

I ignore the shout that snags the attention of the pirates, ignore them as they finally see me, see what I'm doing. My ribbons keep shredding, keep tugging.

When the first pirate gets to me and snags my arm, a ribbon is already there to intercept him. It lashes out, slices into his arm, cutting through his thick furs like they're as thin as a petal.

A muffled yelp of surprise escapes him as he stumbles back and lets go of me to put a hand over his wound, but I pay him no mind. My eyes are still up, my attention ensnared on Sail's body.

Down. I want to get him *down*.

My ribbons work viciously, directed with barely a thought, fueled by anger as red as a fire claw's flames, despite the fact that they're soaked-through and heavy.

One after another, the bindings fall away from Sail's body, until someone grabs me from behind and spins me around.

I come face-to-face with Captain Fane, his brown eyes searing, his face uncovered. "What the fuck do you think you're doing?" he snarls.

His hands grip my arms so tightly that he pinches my skin despite the layers of my sleeves covering me. I shove at him, but the slaps of my hands do nothing against him. He barely even notices it, because he's too busy looking behind me, looking up.

To where my ribbons are cutting through the last of the ropes.

The captain's eyes widen. "Shi—"

Before he can finish his curse, Sail's body is falling.

It crashes over us, cold flesh and stiff muscles knocking us down, tearing me out from the captain's hold.

I land in a jolted heap, Sail's legs sprawled over my torso. The sound of footsteps pound toward us, voices yelling through the whipped wind.

I roll out from under Sail and outstretch my ribbons again, making them wrap around his body. Around and around they go, until he's bound from neck to hip, and then I start to *pull*.

He's heavy and both of us are soaking wet, but my ribbons pull as hard as they can, refusing to let go. Inch by inch, they drag him across the puddling deck.

The strain is instant along my spine, the muscles at my back burning with every tug, already exhausted. But I have no time to slow, no time to rest between heaves, because the Red Raids are coming for me, the captain is snarling, vile anger in his expression as I pull Sail's body toward the edge of the ship.

"Stop!" Captain Fane shouts—not at me, but at his men. "I'll fucking deal with her."

Dread swarms around me, but I don't let it show on my face, I don't let it stumble my steps.

Because I don't care.

I don't care that the captain has a promise of punishment on his face as he stalks toward me. I don't care what he'll do to me for this. Because he killed my friend. He killed him, and I couldn't stop it.

But I can stop *this*. I can stop the Red Raids from dishonoring Sail's body. So I will.

With gritted teeth, with sweat and sleet dripping down my temples, I heave. I keep two ribbons loose, poised at my sides, ready to lash out at any who approach or try to stop me.

But the pirates backed off at Captain Fane's order, so it's just me. Just me, dragging Sail's body slowly—too slowly—as the captain stomps toward me, fists clenched and eyes raving.

My back hits the railing of the ship, and I waste no time to lean down, placing my hands under Sail's arms. I pull as hard as I can, ribbons straining with me as we try to get him up.

Heavy. So damn heavy.

My back sags against the railing, panted breath butchering through my chest, the wind and rain making it hard to breathe, to see. My body is frozen through, my fingers slippery and numb.

Being this spent and labored is a consequence of my own idleness. I was too useless, too passive, all those years in my cage. My ribbons slip around Sail.

Weak, I'm so damn *weak*.

My golden eyes find the saddles where they're standing off to the side, huddling in their circle, as if they can keep out the weather, the world. "Help me," I beg them.

My eyes go to Polly, who managed to get my golden coat again, the gold fur wrapped around her to help ward off the rain. But she stays still, unmoving, unwilling.

"Please," I plead, finding Rissa next. But she doesn't move either. Maybe Rosh… But he looks away as soon as my gaze finds him.

Outsider. Even when I'm trying to help one of our guards, a guard who was kind to each and every one of them, I'm the outsider. I'm on my own.

Captain Fane laughs. "Not even your fellow whores are willing to help you." His voice is so thoroughly pleased.

I sniff, forcing myself to keep it together, to not give up. Sail didn't give up, not for a second. I can do no less for him.

I *will* do this.

I heave again, ribbons straining, pulling at the skin of my back, like sewing needles threaded through the muscles.

Captain Fane takes a taunting step closer to me. Close, but not close enough for my ribbons to lash at him.

He studies them, taking in the way they curl, the way they tug. Vile eyes flick up, a crooked smile showing off those few wooden teeth. "Look, Reds. A true fuck puppet. She even comes with her own strings."

Mocking mirth surrounds me. Their laughter horrible, their words worse.

I block it all out, my teeth clenched so tightly together that my jaw jumps. Amidst the ongoing snickering, I manage another hefty tug, and I get Sail's body propped up at last.

My back screams with fire, while rain and sweat drip along my spine, but it's nearly enough...it's nearly there...

The captain's mouth curves up in cruel amusement as he watches me continue to struggle. I must look pitiful, pulling a guard who's nearly a hundred pounds heavier than me, soaking wet in a puddle.

"Are you trying to jump overboard and ride your dead guard like a sled?" the captain asks, making some of the pirates behind him chuckle.

He holds up his arms and turns full circle, displaying the desolate land all around. "Hate to break it to you, but we're in the middle of the Barrens, you stupid cunt. You're not going anywhere."

My body shakes, my ribbons strain. But I don't give up. I don't give in.

The captain steps closer, testing my boundaries, pecking at me, looking for an opening.

In a snap decision, I wrap the remaining two ribbons

290

around Sail, leaving me defenseless to the captain's advances. All of this will be pointless if I don't.

The last two ribbons give me the extra strength I need.

Captain Fane lunges for me, but he's too late, because I've hauled Sail's body up and over the side. The second I do, my ribbons unwind from his body, passing him over to gravity's clutches, and he falls.

Falls, falls, falls, landing right in a pile of pillowed snow far below.

I lean over, watching, chest heaving, dropping icicle tears into the rain as our ship slides past.

A blink, and Captain Fane is there, snatching my ribbons in a viselike grip. He crushes them together in his fist, yanking them tight against my spine, my back arching painfully.

"You foolish bitch. All that fuss, and you failed. Couldn't even manage to make the jump."

He yanks me away from the railing and starts to drag me away, but he's wrong. I wasn't trying to escape. I never intended to jump. I couldn't survive the fall anyway, and they'd only catch me if I managed to somehow make it.

No, I accomplished exactly what I meant to. I got Sail away from here. Away from these pirates, off this ship.

His place of rest might be a mound of snow in the middle of the Barrens, but it's better than the alternative. I couldn't let him stay strung up for a second longer.

I get pulled harshly, quickly across the deck, toward the captain's quarters, toward that punishment his eyes promised.

"You can't disrespect his body anymore," I say boldly. Bright side. It's the only bright side I have right now to cling to, as bleak and grim as it is.

Captain Fane's grip tightens on my ribbons in anger at my words. They're tired, wet, and wilted, crushed in his hold and sapped of strength, same as me.

"Fine," he says against my neck as he leads me on. "Then I suppose I'll just disrespect *yours*."

CHAPTER 30

*I*f *my poor ribbons weren't* crumpled and stuffed in Captain Fane's fists like wet parchment, if they weren't so exhausted and waterlogged, I might be able to rip them from his grasp and defend myself. I might be able to fight back.

Unfortunately, his hold is firm, pulling so harshly that my muscles and skin burn with every movement. If he pulls any harder, it feels as if he'll rip them clean from my back, like yanking off a finger or plucking out an eye.

I try and fail to get them to rip out of his hands, but they're too smashed, too wet, too tired. I've expended all my pitiful strength on getting Sail's body off this cursed ship.

But at least I managed it.

I make myself a promise right here and now though. If I somehow make it through this, if the Red Raids don't ruin me completely, I won't allow myself to be stagnant anymore. I won't allow myself to be so weak and inept.

I should've known better, after my childhood, after all the things I've been through. I should've known better than to become so complacent or languid.

If I could go back, I'd shake myself. I became like Coin, that solid gold bird forever resting on his roost. I clipped my own wings, I stayed listless on my perch.

So if I make it through this, if I live, I vow to myself that I won't let it happen again. I won't sit idly by and keep letting men crush me in their fists.

With the scar at my throat as a stark reminder, I firm up, crystallizing into a hardened rock of resolve. The healed line tingles, and my mind shifts to Digby. Did the Red Raids kill the scout who saw their movement? Did Digby and the others unwittingly follow the scout right into death?

I don't know, and I don't dare ask. Partly because if Digby and the others are still out there safe, I don't want to tip the captain off. But another reason, a darker reason, is that I can't bear to be told that the pirates killed them. Not yet. I can't face that just yet.

For now, my mind needs for Digby to be out there, living and breathing. Maybe he'll find Sail, in that grave of flurried snow, and lay some sort of tribute at his burial, one to stay with him in this desolate place while his spirit moves on to the great After.

It's a nice thought, anyway.

His hold still rough, Captain Fane finishes dragging me to the back of the ship. I get hauled up a short five steps from the main deck, to the higher captain's quarters. The wall is plain, save for a red slash marked down the door, a short eave jutting off the gable above.

My face is shoved against the closed door, my cheek pressed into the white weathered wood, splinters threatening to splice through my skin.

He holds me there with his forearm crushing my back, one fist still holding my satiny strands like a leash on a dog. With his other hand, he fishes into his pocket and pulls out a key, shoving it into the lock of the door.

I start struggling, though my efforts are weary. But I know for a fact that I don't want to go inside. The moment I cross that threshold, things will happen—bad things.

"Hold still, or you'll only make this worse for yourself," he snaps.

Of course, that just makes me try to get away even more, but he shoves his hips against me, using his legs to pin me in place so I have nowhere to go, no way to move. I want to cry at the helplessness of it all, but I swallow that down. There's no time for that, no time to break down.

He turns the lock with a click, shoving the key back into his pocket. But before he can turn the handle, Quarter calls for his attention. "Cap! We got a hawk!"

Captain Fane turns to look, keeping me stuck shoved against the door. I can't see him, but I hear Quarter stomping up the stairs.

"Just came, Cap," Quarter says as he stops beside us.

From the corner of my eye, I can see a large tawny hawk with a black beak sitting on Quarter's forearm, talons digging into the fur.

The captain grabs a small metal vial off the bird's leg and unrolls it, careful to keep it held beneath the eave, blocking it from the haggard rain. It's a short piece of parchment, though its length grows as he unrolls it. All I can see is a messy scrawl of black, but the captain's brows draw down, water dripping off his beaded beard as he reads.

Captain Fane mutters something I don't catch and then shoves the parchment and vial into Quarter's chest. "We need to send a reply?" Quarter questions.

"No. They'll be here before the hawk could deliver it, anyway."

Quarter frowns at the captain before replacing the empty vial on the hawk's leg. As soon as it's secure, the bird takes flight, shooting up into the sheet of rain and disappearing from view without a sound.

"Who's going to be here?" Quarter asks.

Instead of answering, Captain Fane holds out a hand. "Give me your sash." Quarter blinks for a moment before he reaches beneath his furs and begins to loosen the white sash tucked around his torso.

Captain Fane turns his attention to me. Without a word, he starts to wrap my ribbons around my torso, pulling them so taut that it makes me grit my teeth in pain. He wraps them around and around, until their long lengths are completely bound around my middle, and then he ties the ends all in a knot, so tightly that I can't move them at all.

"Get all the saddles in the kitchens and put them to work. Cook needs to get a dinner ready to be served within the hour. We have guests coming."

He holds out his hand again, and Quarter quickly passes over the sash. The captain wraps it around me, just as tightly as he wrapped my ribbons, and ties that off too. Another deterrent in place to keep my ribbons immobile.

The captain spins me around and lowers himself so we're eye-to-eye. His expression is angry, severe. "If *any* of the saddles try anything or disobey in any way...I want them stripped, whipped, and tossed overboard."

Quarter nods at him, though his eyes are on me. Even with his red band over his face, I can tell he's grinning. "Aye, Cap."

With one last lingering glare my way, Captain Fane shoves me toward Quarter before storming off to the front of the ship, shouting orders about changing course.

"Alright, come on, you. And don't even think about fucking up with those puppet strings of yours, or I'll slice them clean off your back."

The skin along my spine flinches, like the ribbons heard the threat.

With a grip on my arm, Quarter leads me down to the main deck again, straight over to the huddled saddles. "Right, you cunts! Follow me!"

Quarter doesn't wait to see if they listen as he turns us, heading for a set of stairs in the middle of the ship that leads below deck. I can hear footsteps trail after us as Quarter and I make our way down the creaking stairs.

We pass through a narrow corridor, and then we go deeper into the back of the ship where we enter a long galley kitchen that reeks of potatoes and smoke.

At least we're out of the storm and the kitchen is warm, thanks to the cast iron oven with roaring flames inside its belly. The walls and floors are made from the same white wood as everything else, except it's been stained, black with soot in some places, splatters of old food stuck on others.

Standing over the iron oven is the cook, the only pirate I've seen so far who isn't dressed in the same white fur as everyone else. He's in a simple white leather vest and trousers instead, his meaty arms bare and littered with sloppy tattoos. He's stout and short, with a crooked jaw that juts to the side, and a low brow that makes me wonder how well he can see above the pot he's stirring.

A scowl crosses his ruddy face when he notices us enter. "What the damned hell I got women in my galley for?"

"Cap's orders, Cook," Quarter replies. "We got guests coming, apparently. We need a meal served up deck." He jerks his head in our direction, where all of us are grouped together near the doorway. "They're your help."

Cook lets out a garbled string of curses, but Quarter pays it no mind. "Cap wants it ready by the hour." Cook sends him a crude gesture but starts to yank out tinned supplies from the cupboards.

Another pirate comes in and leans against the wall, a dagger held in one hand as he stares at us. A guard dog to watch us and attack, if necessary.

Quarter looks back at us. "I'll warn you now. Cook's the meanest bastard of all of us. Getting whipped and tossed overboard will be the least of your worries if you fuck up in here."

With those lovely parting words, Quarter pushes past us and walks out, leaving us alone.

Cook takes one look at us and narrows his eyes, using a rag to swipe over his sweat-lined face. "Well? What the fuck are you waiting for? I'll boil your fucking hands if you don't get to work. This meal ain't gonna cook itself."

I tense and so do the others, but then Rissa strides ahead, leading the way once again, getting the others to follow suit.

I stay at the back of the group, trying not to flinch every time Cook screams at us or tosses food our way. We hustle to do everything he says, even with our teeth chattering, our clothes and hair sopping wet. When one of the saddles accidentally makes a puddle on the floor, he kicks her down and makes her sop it up with a tiny, useless rag.

And all the while, as I chop and stir and wipe, with Cook snarling and the pirate guard watching, I try to work my ribbons loose, try to get the knots undone bit by bit without anyone seeing.

I have no idea who sent that messenger hawk to the captain, or who's coming here, but I know the options are bleak. No one good would come to dine with the Red Raids.

Yet no matter who's coming, I'm grateful for the interruption. If it weren't for that letter, I would be in the captain's clutches right now. The thought makes me shudder.

Even so, I know that this reprieve is temporary. Fleeting. I know that before this long, horrible night is through, I'll be stuck in the captain's clutches again. So all I can do is try to work my ribbons, and hope I don't get caught.

CHAPTER 31

Quarter wasn't exaggerating when he said that Cook was a mean bastard. The only sort of direction we get are pans thrown across the room when we don't move fast enough or a snarl if we dare to ask him a question.

We all rush around the narrow galley like chickens with our heads cut off, throwing things together with shouted directions barely more detailed than, "Go make the fucking biscuits," despite the fact that none of us have ever worked in a kitchen and have no idea how to make anything.

The room grows hot and humid from the steam and smoke, sweat gathering to mix with the rainwater on our already wet bodies. It's uncomfortable to say the least, but Cook doesn't give us an inch to slow down, and none of us dare to look idle.

The entire hour is anxiety-ridden and feverish, and it

seems like we make enough food to feed the entire ship twice over. When the ship rocks to a sudden stop, our only warning is the booming growls of the fire claws that preclude it.

Everyone lurches on their feet as our momentum comes to a skidding halt, but we barely have time to get our bearings before Cook is yelling at us to start bringing up the serving ware above deck.

With tin plates and tankards in hand, we file out, following our watchdog who leads the way. When we get upstairs, I find that the storm has ebbed, leaving only a stubborn wind behind.

We follow the pirate through puddled spots on the deck, to the door located to the right of the ship, all the way to the back, past the captain's quarters. Inside is a small dining area, though it's packed tight with rows of wooden tables and built-in benches. There's barely room enough to walk between them, but we all slip down the aisles sideways, quickly unloading everything.

I somehow end up beside Mist, and the woman gives me an ugly glare sharp enough to prick my skin. She slams down her plates in front of me, apparently unwilling to stand next to me any longer than necessary.

She elbows her way past me to leave, the other saddles shooting me looks as Mist storms out. With a sigh, I pick up the pile of dishes she left and start to distribute them on the table. I'm the last one to finish, the rest of them already filing out to return to the kitchen and get the food. I follow several steps behind them, and the pirate watching us smirks as I walk past.

I still haven't been able to take out a single knot in my ribbon. Aside from them being wrapped so tight, they're still damp, and it's making the task that much more difficult.

Frustration makes my lips press into a thin line, yet that frustration sizzles out when I get onto the main deck and notice that the saddles have stopped dead in front of me. And there's also something...different.

It takes a moment for me to realize that it's the silence.

The constant noise of shouting and growling, as well as the sound of the ships skating across the Barrens with the pelting rain and whipping wind is gone. All is quiet. I skirt around the saddles, squeezing between their group and the railing to get a better look, to see what's brought on this muted stillness.

When I push my way to the side, my eyes sweep over the scene. All the Red Raids are gathered together at the middle of the ship, each and every one facing the lowered gangplank.

Captain Fane stands at the center, his band still hanging around his neck but his hat proudly sitting on his head. Quarter stands slightly behind him to the right, his hand resting on the hilt of his sword.

Tension—the kind specific to anticipation—is pushing its presence around to everyone. It's pushing even more incessantly than the bitter wind, keeping us still and silent. My heart starts to beat quickly, nervously, though I have no idea what awaits.

But something...something is coming.

I glance around, confirming that no one is looking my way, everyone too caught up in whatever the captain is waiting for, on whoever sent him that messenger hawk. Even the guard dog pirate is standing on the other side of the saddles, watching the ramp. I can't waste this distraction.

Wedged on the outskirts between the side railing of the ship and the saddles' turned backs, I turn my body slightly. I'm still cold and damp, but at least my time in the kitchen dried me slightly, and the wind now, although cold, is whipping around my limp hair and dress, drying even more of me.

Using the diversion, I concentrate on my ribbons again, attempting to untwist the gnarled loops. The ends struggle to move, pulling weakly, tiredly. Captain Fane knotted them so tightly that every tug hurts, like pressing on a bruise.

Taking a risk, I carefully bring one hand behind my back and shove it under Quarter's sash. The fabric is taut, but somewhat stretchy, so I'm able to delve beneath, my searching fingers finding the cluster of tangles.

With a quick glance, I angle my back even more to the railing, trying to look as inconspicuous as possible as I bring my second arm behind me. Fingers meeting, I feel for the largest, most tender knot. With my face left carefully blank, head pointed in the same direction as everyone else, I start to work the tangles, praying to the Divine that no one looks my way.

But amidst that heavy tension of wait, something changes. Something interrupts the hush.

The sound of booted steps starts to clamor up the wooden ramp. One set, then two, then more, all of them walking in near perfect symmetry up the gangplank, their footsteps growing louder and louder as they get closer.

Stomp, stomp, stomp.

The Red Raids go rigid, and the pirate captain stands up a little bit taller. I start to tug more frantically, the feeling of impending danger spurring me into a frenzy to get myself undone.

Accompanying the footsteps, I can hear metal armor, rattling like the tails of desert snakes. And where chain mail and chest plates are, swords and daggers won't be far behind.

I keep trying to get unbound, but I'm struggling to make even a single loop loose enough that I can pull it properly. My heart pounds in time with their steps.

I need to get free, I need to get these knots *out*, I need—

A dozen soldiers appear on the ramp, marching straight onto the ship, two by two. They stop in front of Captain Fane in a formidable formation that flares out like a pyramid.

It's an imposing sight. Black armor as dark and flat as burnt coals, brown leather pants and straps that criss-cross over their chests. Onyx sheaths are belted around their waists, their sword hilts made of gnarled deadwood tree bark contorted wickedly. Heads covered in helmets, postures threatening, my mouth goes dry at the sight of them.

Because there, carved at the center of their midnight chest plates, between the leather straps, is their kingdom's sigil. That twisted, misshapen tree with thorned roots, stripped of all leaves, four crooked branches reaching out like the devil's claws.

These are Fourth Kingdom's soldiers. *King Rot's* soldiers.

And they're an awful long way from their borders.

My hands go still on my ribbons, my eyes go wide. King Ravinger's army is the most feared in all six kingdoms. I've heard plenty of stories telling of their viciousness on the battlefield. I find myself wanting to inch backward, as if I can try to fade into the shadows, though my feet are frozen where I stand.

No one speaks. No one moves. Even with the twelve soldiers standing there, Captain Fane waits, though I don't know why.

My brows pull together in a questioning frown, until I hear it—a single pair of footsteps.

A thirteenth man stomps up the ramp, passing his soldiers who stand at attention on either side of him like brick walls. He's tall, his very presence demanding of attention. Yet despite the fact that he's wearing the same black armor and brown leather as the others, he has a very distinct difference.

"Are those...*spikes*?"

I hear the hissed whisper from a saddle to my right. I hear the murmurings of *cursed* and *evil*. I hear them explain how King Ravinger created him from the rotted wastes, turning his body into something unnatural for one purpose: to command his army.

But they're wrong.

The commander with spikes jutting from his spine and arms isn't cursed. The male who stops at the front of the group, so tall that Captain Fane has to tip his head up to look, isn't some result of King Ravinger's powers perverting his body.

No, the man standing there, whose body basks in menace, is one thing and one thing only.

Fae.

CHAPTER 32

There weren't always six kingdoms in Orea. At one time, there were seven.

A thousand years ago, Seventh Kingdom ruled at the edge of the world. Past the Pitching Pines, past the frozen mountain of Highbell, far past the Barrens and even the arctic sea.

Way out at the end, so far that even the sun and moon only skimmed its horizon. So distant that the flat earth ended in a precipice with nothing below. Seventh Kingdom lived in perpetual gray, no light, no dark, no beyond. But it was here where the bridge was found.

Lemuria. The bridge that led to nowhere.

The bridge was just a track of gray, empty dirt that stretched over the edge of the world, past what the eye could see. That strip of land kept going, with nothing below or around it, nothing existing at all except for the dark, sightless void.

It was said that if you were to step off the bridge, you would fall forever, and not even the Divine gods and goddesses could find you to give you the reprieve of death.

But Seventh Kingdom's monarchs were scholars. They didn't believe in myths or unknowns. So they sent soldiers and explorers onto the bridge of Lemuria to find out what was beyond, to discover where the bridge led.

For years, hundreds of Oreans journeyed on the bridge, only to never be seen again. Most believed it was a fruitless endeavor, one the monarchs should give up. A suicide mission. A task soon given to thieves and debtors instead. A venture that never led to anything.

Until one day, a woman walked back across.

She wasn't a soldier or an explorer or a scholar or a thief. She wasn't sent by the monarchs. She was a stowaway. An orphan girl whose father had gone over the bridge and never returned.

At age ten, she slipped past the guards who stood at the start of the bridge and ran silently, determinedly, into that void to search for her father.

No one ever knew. No one ever saw.

She walked through time and space, battling madness and starvation and thirst. Where all others finally caved and tossed themselves off the bridge, giving in, she pressed on. Where every other Orean man had failed, she succeeded.

GILD

*Saira Turley did the one thing that no others had—
she walked the bridge of Lemuria, and came back to tell
the tale.*

But she didn't return alone.

*Because the bridge, that narrow road in the nothing,
led to a new world. A world of magic.*

*She might not have found her father, but Saira did
find Annwyn—the territory in the realm beyond.*

The realm of fae.

*Saira fell through their ground and landed on their
sky. Bird, they called her. Broken-winged bird.*

*A group of fae took her in, cared for her, and she was
amazed at these people with their remarkable power. She
found a new family in the magical paradise, made a life
there.*

*But her heart was always in Orea, the place where
her mother was buried, where she had fond memories of
her father.*

*When she turned nineteen, Saira fell in love with a
fae male—the prince of Lydia. It was said that their love
was deeper than all the seas of Annwyn, that music was
made from the song of their hearts.*

*And before they married, the prince gave her a wed-
ding gift.*

*He couldn't bring back her father for her, but he
could bring back her home. So the prince took her to the
bridge of Lemuria once more, at the edge of their glittering sky, and he bound it.*

Through space and time, he found the thread that connected their realms through this voided bridge. With his great powers, he yanked it closer to Annwyn, to the fae kingdom, so that Saira could return home to Orea whenever she wished.

Orea and Annwyn became sister realms. It was a celebration for all seven kingdoms when fae and Oreans united.

After that great joining, Lemuria was no longer that voided, endless path of death, but a true bridge between the realms, one that only took minutes to cross.

And for hundreds of years, we coexisted. Mingled. It's where Orean magic still comes from, mixing with the fae. But year by year, that magic dies out a little bit more because no more fae come here. And no more Oreans cross into Annwyn. They haven't for three hundred years.

Because the fae betrayed Orea.

A new monarch rose, long after Saira Turley and her prince drew their last breaths. A king who spoke against cohabiting with Oreans, against mixing with lesser beings. He snapped the thread that Saira's husband had tied with love, severing the bridge, and cleaving the realms in one mighty swipe.

Seventh Kingdom, vulnerable there at the edge of the world, was swallowed whole from the force of the magical cut. The land and people were never seen again. And the bridge of Lemuria fell into that void, crumbled to nothing.

So Orea has the fae to thank for the magic that still exists here. But it's a bitter gift that's laced with betrayal.

Because there is no Seventh Kingdom anymore. There is no peaceful alliance. There is no bridge to Annwyn. There are no more fae.

...Or so people think.

CHAPTER 33

*D*rums.

My heartbeat feels like drums beating through my veins, too loud, too fast, too harsh.

I'd always thought that the stories of the commander, even the written accounts in Highbell's library, were exaggerations. Dramatics to overemphasize the terror of his presence and justify people's cowardice when they buckled in fear of him.

The commander—who people call Rip for his predisposition to literally *rip* soldiers' heads from their bodies—became a modern legend, someone to be feared, just like King Rot himself. But I didn't expect Commander Rip to actually be this frightening.

Of course, there were rumors that he was fae—more fae than any other Orean. But again, I thought they were just that. Rumors. Gossip. Embellishments. More exaggerations spread, probably by King Ravinger himself, to make his commander seem that much more frightening.

But now that I see him for myself, I can tell that he's not just another Orean with a watered-down magical bloodline from long-ago fae ancestors.

He's *more*.

The spikes prove it. Most written accounts made it sound like it was just a part of his armor, another dramatic elaboration. But I can tell that it's not. The spikes, the height, the menacing presence, it's all real.

I don't know what to think of it.

My eyes can't seem to leave him, and I find myself counting the black spikes that trail down his spine. Starting from between his shoulder blades to his lower back, he has six of them, each one shorter than the one above. They're curved in a slight downward arc, popping right through his armor, a vicious gleam to them that reflects the red-burning lanterns.

The ones on his outer forearms are much shorter, but look no less sharp and deadly, four leading from above his wrist to below the curve of his elbow.

I'm too terrified to wonder what he looks like without his helmet. Some accounts have said he has horns on his head or vile scars ripped down his face. Some have alleged that he has fangs, while other written records swear that he can kill a person just by looking at them with his burning red eyes.

I don't want to find out if any of those are true.

But what I *do* want to find out is why he's here, in the Barrens, meeting with the Red Raids.

"Captain Fane," a low, deep voice rumbles out. The saddles beside me stiffen at the sound.

"Commander Rip," the captain replies in greeting with a slight tilt of his head. "I'm surprised to see you so far from Fourth. Your message was unexpected."

"Hmm."

Captain Fane's attempt to fish for information is fruitless, but he doesn't seem deterred. "We heard there was trouble at your borders."

The commander cocks his head. "No more than a nuisance. But the king doesn't tolerate attacks on his land."

"Of course not. No true leader does."

I nearly swallow my own tongue at Captain Fane's obvious suck-up.

"How are the Barrens and Breakwater Port? I assume pirateering is still paying well."

The captain smirks. "Can't complain."

"You're not usually this far north in the fall."

It's not a question, but even I can hear the demand for information.

Captain Fane shares a brief look with Quarter before replying. "We had a tip. It pulled us back this way, and fortunately, it paid off. We'll return to the docks soon enough."

My hands, still frozen on my ribbons, drop down to my sides.

We had a tip.

A tip? A tip to bring him here? Frowning, I look at the captain, as if staring at him hard enough will give me answers.

"Interesting," Commander Rip replies. He shifts his arms, the scarlet light catching on those spikes of his, drawing the captain's eye. "And would this *tip* have anything to do with the dozen messenger hawks you sent out a couple of hours ago?"

Captain Fane stiffens. "How do you know about that?"

Instead of answering, the commander holds up his fist. He opens it, letting a piece of rolled parchment fall to the deck...followed by his soldiers behind him *also* opening their hands and tossing down eleven more.

The captain's expression turns outraged. His mouth opens and shuts, a gaping fish without water. "What... How did you—"

The commander tosses up a pouch in the air, and Quarter barely catches it in time. "Compensation. For the hawks."

Quarter and Captain Fane stare at the commander, completely caught off guard.

"You intercepted *all* of my messages?" the captain demands, fury coating his throat.

The commander tilts his head. "I did."

Captain Fane's jaw tightens, wooden teeth grinding. "And do you want to tell me *why*? That's an act of enmity, Commander. My Reds have killed for far less."

The threat does nothing to affect the commander or the soldiers behind him. If anything, it's the Red Raids who appear nervous, exchanging glances with one another, as if dreading a fight between them and Fourth's soldiers.

"There's no need for bloodshed between us," the commander replies evenly, unruffled. "In fact, I'll be helping you."

"And how's that?" the captain snaps.

Commander Rip takes a single step forward. One step, such a negligible thing, and yet, the menace of that stolen space between them has the captain's hand going to the hilt of his knife—the same one he used to plunge into Sail's heart.

"You were all too eager to write to potential buyers, bragging of the spoils you pilfered. But I'm going to do you one better, Fane, and make it easier for you." His voice is no louder than before, but for some reason, the tone makes me wince, makes my teeth capture my bottom lip in worry. "You have Midas's traveling party. I'll buy them."

Captain Fane gapes. "*You*? Why?"

Even though he still has his helmet on, I somehow get the feeling that the commander grins. "That's between Midas and Ravinger."

My stomach twists in a corkscrew, like it wants to wring itself out and dig itself down. I hear one of the saddles gasp, the sound full of dread.

It's one thing to be stolen by vile pirates. But it's

another thing entirely to be bought by King Rot's commander. The male is notorious for his heartlessness on the battlefield, the entire army itself a brutal force that has never been defeated.

And now he wants us.

That's between Midas and Ravinger.

With that vague explanation, there's not a single doubt in my mind of why Commander Rip is way out here in the Barrens, why he's striking this deal. King Ravinger sent his army to confront Midas. And we just fell into the palm of his hand.

Captain Fane shares a look with Quarter, the glance loaded and considering. When he turns back, he drops the hand away from his hilt.

"As I'm sure you read in all of my letters," the captain begins testily, "I have Midas's royal whores, plus a few of his soldiers who lived. I was planning on bringing them to the coast to be split up and sold."

The commander finally looks away from the captain. His head turns, and I swear, I *feel* his eyes land right on me. My breath gets stuck against that gaze, like a fly to sap. I'm trapped, unable to move, unable to escape. My pulse skips ahead.

But then he just continues his visual sweep, head turning, those hidden eyes passing over the group of saddles with bored consideration. I'm finally capable of letting a shaky breath slip through my lips, a fly ripping free from the clinging trap.

"Like I said, I'd be saving you the trouble," Commander Rip says, facing the captain once more. "I'll buy all of them. The horses too, though you can keep their gaudy gold armor. They'll have no need of it."

Captain Fane narrows his eyes, as if suspicious of just how much information the commander seems to have.

"It'll be a hefty sum. I was anticipating multiple offers."

"I'm sure we can come to an agreement," the commander says with bold certainty.

Captain Fane shifts on his feet. "My men were expecting at least a couple of weeks to enjoy our prizes before I sold them off."

That wringing in my stomach tightens and twists. Captain Fane has no shame, complaining that he and his men won't get to play with us if he sells us straightaway. The thought, the debasement of it, makes bile burn in my throat, hot enough that I want to breathe fire and scorch him where he stands.

"As I said, I think we can come to an agreement, Fane."

Silence ticks by. The wind is the only thing that moves or makes noise. Everyone else watches, saddles, pirates, soldiers. Every eye trained on the commander and captain, waiting to see what will happen.

Above us, the night carries on, as bleak and dark as ever. It makes me wonder if it will ever ebb or if I'm doomed to be stuck in these bleak shadows forever, to go from one bad circumstance to a worse one.

RAVEN KENNEDY

Finally, Captain Fane nods. "Alright, then. A meal is in order, I think. I always say an agreement is best made over wine and food."

The commander tips his head and lifts an arm. "Then lead the way, Captain, and you can tell me all about what transpired this night. I'm sure we'll have a lot to talk about."

Captain Fane grins. "Aye. When Midas finds out that you and your king have his men *and* his whores, he's going to lose his head."

A dark, gravelly chuckle comes from behind the dark helmet, sending chills down my arms. "I'm counting on it, Captain."

CHAPTER 34

I 've seen foxes in a henhouse before. Bursting in on the poor birds, stalking them when they were just trying to do their job and lay their eggs. The foxes taunted them, tried to make them fly. I've seen an entire coop get destroyed in an explosion of feathers and noise and fear.

This dinner is a lot like that.

The Red Raids are the foxes, taunting and groping, trying to see if they can make one of the saddles attempt to fly away in a panic.

But this dinner doesn't just have foxes. We have wolves too.

Commander Rip's twelve soldiers take up an entire bench in the dining room. They sit, squeezed together, shoulder-to-shoulder, dark and looming and entirely too big for the space. They've taken off their helmets to eat, but they're quiet. Watchful. Stalking wolves amidst the rabble.

"Not you."

I get stopped by the guard dog before I can go into the dining room, my hands full with two pitchers of wine.

"What?"

He looks to Rissa behind me and tips his head. "You. Take the pitchers in for her."

Rissa arches a blonde brow. "I'm already carrying this tray," she points out.

"Do I look like I give a shit? I said take them."

Rissa's lips press together, but she flicks her eyes to me and gestures to the tray full of hard biscuits. "Stack them on."

I pile the biscuits on one side as best I can, and then set the pitchers on top. As soon as she has it all, her load considerably heavier, Rissa sweeps past us, heading into the dining room where the rest of the saddles are already serving, some of them pulled onto laps, enduring hands slipping up skirts.

I stand awkwardly outside the doorway, shooting a glance at the pirate. "What am I supposed to do?"

My guard dog leans against the outside wall and pulls out his knife, edging the blade beneath his nails to clean them. "Don't know. Cap'n just said you weren't allowed in there while Fourth's men are here."

Realization dawns like a cold morning. "The captain doesn't want the commander to see me."

The pirate just smirks, continuing to clean his disgusting nails.

I look into the brightly lit room, the ship oddly quiet at its continuous standstill. From my vantage point, I can see Fourth's soldiers at the bench closest to the door. Captain Fane and Commander Rip are at the front of the room, sitting at a small, two-person table where they can look out at the long benches before them, their backs facing me.

The commander has his helmet off, but at this angle, I'm unable to see his face. I can rule out the horns, though. Instead, all I see is thick, short black hair on top of his head.

"I'll just go grab more stuff from the kitchens," I mumble, turning to walk away.

Unfortunately, my guard dog follows, so I don't get a chance to slip away, not that I was expecting anything to be that easy.

When I make it back to the galley, I'm barely through the door when something comes flying at my face. I duck, hearing the splat of a rag landing on the wall where my face just was.

"Get to cleaning," Cook barks from the other end of the room.

I suppress a sigh before pulling off my one remaining glove and slipping it into my dress pocket. I pick up the wet rag and start scrubbing the long countertop, surreptitiously working on my ribbons all the while.

Finally, with my back hunched over and sweat gathering at my neck, I get a knot undone. My heart races at the small but worthy victory. I chance a look over my shoulder, but the two pirates aren't looking at my back. Cook is too busy eating his meal alone in the corner, and my guard dog is now picking at his teeth with the same knife he cleaned his nails with.

Head facing forward again, I continue to scrub, continue to unknot. Persistence. It just takes persistence.

I'm almost through scouring the place when Polly comes in, her cheeks flushed and her eyes shiny. "They want more ale," she says dully, her tone beaten flat like overworked dough.

"What do I look like, a serving wench?" Cook barks at her. "Go fucking get it, then."

Polly looks at a loss, so I quickly straighten up and toss the rag down. "It's over here," I tell her, leading the way.

She follows me to the pantry where I show her the tankard and the last remaining pitchers. I feel her gaze on me, the questions brimming as she glances at me from the corner of her eyes. "Can you use those things? To hurt them? To escape?" Her question is no more than a hum, secrets spoken with barely a breath, but I know what she means.

I don't dare look over my shoulder at the pirates to see if they're watching us. "No. The captain knotted them. I can't get them out yet."

She breathes out through her nose, a small sound of disappointment, a deflation of hope rushing out.

"I need to bring more ale than this," she says, voice

at normal level now as she hefts the full pitchers in her arms. "Can you carry the other two?"

I hesitate for a moment, but then nod and fill two more. Together, we carry the pitchers out, Cook glaring at us as we go, the guard dog on our heels.

When we're just outside the dining room, I stop. "I'm not allowed inside."

Polly looks over at me with a frustrated sigh. "Fine. I'll send someone else out to grab those."

She takes a breath before going inside, trying to hold her head up high, trying to keep an easy smile on her face. She barely even flinches when one of them smacks her ass as she leans over to pour for him. A performance. It's all a performance.

The room is rowdy and loud, the pirates obviously deep into their cups, the food already eaten. I see Polly head over to Rissa, saying something in her ear in passing. Rissa glances over at me before she rushes over to grab the last two pitchers.

"They sure do drink a lot," I say quietly as I pass them over to her.

"Good for us," she murmurs with a wink. "If we can get them drunk enough, some of them might pass out. One less bastard to deal with tonight."

She turns away with a sultry smile plastered on her face, her act ready to appease them, ready to work the room to the best of her ability so she can come out unscathed.

Like she told the others earlier, they're professionals, and it shows in every smirk, every tease, every sway of their hips. Fawns forced to gratify the predators. To entice them to watch, to appreciate. Persuading them to not harm, not bite.

I just hope it works.

My vision of the room gets cut off when a furious face steps in front of me. Mist's black hair hangs in limp knots around her, the bodice of her dress sagging, either from the earlier rain, or some attention she received in here. "Typical," she says with a snort. "The favored doesn't even have to serve like the rest of us."

"I'm not al—"

"Save it," she snaps. "Can you at least take these dirty dishes back to the galley, or are you too good to even do that much?"

My teeth grind. "I understand your anger, I do," I begin. "But instead of being so nasty toward me, save your energy for *them*," I say, nodding toward the quiet soldiers.

"As if you care."

I do, of course, but she won't believe me no matter what I say.

She shoves the dirty dishes into my arms before spinning around again. I take my armful to the kitchen, where I stay for the next hour in front of a bucket of cold, barely sudsy water and scrub every dish clean.

The saddles file in one after another, bringing me

more to wash until my back is aching, my hands chapped and numb. But I use my time well. I scrub out my frustration on the dishes while my ribbons keep plucking at the knots, inch by sluggish inch. I use the sash to my advantage, hiding their every move.

Keep going. All I can do is keep going.

When I'm finally done washing, the guard dog hoists me up by the arm. "Come on, I want to get up there to see what's happening."

I wipe my wet, freezing hands on the front of my dress, feet tripping to keep up with his impatience. He's obviously bored of being my babysitter.

"Stay at my side and keep your mouth shut, got it?"

With a nod, I follow beside him as we go upstairs to the main deck, where I find all of the saddles lined up in front of me.

Soon, they'll all be gone. They'll leave with Fourth's men, and I'll be left here. I'll be trapped, kept without any bars, but no less captive.

I don't know which is worse. Wolves or foxes. Merciless pirates or enemy soldiers.

I wish Midas were here.

The thought surges into me so violently that tears fill my eyes. I would give *anything* to see him right now. For him to swoop in, to rescue us, to protect me once more. Just like he saved me from those raiders all those years ago. My vagabond savior. My champion king.

But Midas isn't here.

He's not coming, because he has no idea I'm even in any trouble. And by the time he finds out, it'll be too late. Far, far too late.

CHAPTER 35

My hands twist in front of me, as tangled as the knots at my back.

This is a crossroads, forged on the deck of a pirate ship. I don't know which fate is worse or which captors are more brutal.

Better the devil you know, but what happens when the devils are always new? Always strangers creeping up unexpectedly to snatch you away?

Short of Midas coming in to rescue me, I have no hope of escaping the pirates or the soldiers. And where would I go if I did? We're in the middle of the frozen Barrens, miles of arctic waste all around. I could wander for days on my own, easily get lost in the white blanketed wind, or caught up in a blizzard and never find my way.

But maybe that would be better. Maybe it would be a blessing to fall into the snowbanks and never wake up. A gentler embrace than what these men have in mind, that's for sure.

Despite not knowing which captor is worse, I do know that the thought of being split up from everyone I know fills me with panic. Even though the saddles don't like me—some might even hate me—at least they're a part of home. A reminder of safety.

A particularly large knot at my back makes my ribbon stab with pain, but I suppress my wince and keep at it as I stand on the deck. Alone. I'm going to be here, used by the captain, completely alone. If I can just get my ribbons undone, I might have a chance. Maybe just enough to buy me some time.

Near the middle of the ship, Captain Fane and the commander are deep in discussion, the commander once again wearing his black helmet.

They go back and forth for a while—negotiating it seems—until at last, the captain nods. A deal is struck. Just as a previous pact was made—one made between two kings.

Men making deals on the behalf of women never seems to go very well for the women.

I see the commander nod over his shoulder, and one of his soldiers walks forward holding a trunk. Captain Fane opens it, eyes glinting and mouth dropping wide at the overflowing coins inside.

He grins, his mouth curling in wicked gratification. "Well, you have yourself a deal."

He starts to take the trunk, except the soldier doesn't let go. Captain Fane shoots a look at the commander. "Problem?"

"I'll take my purchases now."

The captain nods. "Of course. Quarter will accompany you to the other two ships. You'll find Midas's men and horses there."

The commander nods, and his soldier releases the trunk at last. The captain takes hold of it with a grunt, before quickly passing it off to two of his pirates to haul off.

"Enjoy the rest of your night, Commander. Give your king my best," the captain says with a tip of his hat.

"One moment, Fane."

The captain stops, turns. The pirates carrying the loot pause. My wringing hands waver.

"The amount agreed upon is for *all* of Midas's people," the commander announces.

The captain blinks, brows pulling together in a frown. He's confused for a split second, but I know. I know it a moment before the commander's helmet-clad head turns in my direction, cutting through the people standing in front of me, as if he were aware I was standing here all along.

A gauntlet raises, a finger pointing at me. My heart freezes in the center of my chest. "That includes *her*."

Captain Fane gapes as understanding crashes over him like an unforgiving wave. "No," he begins with a sharp shake of his head, his black feather wavering on the top of his hat. "She isn't for sale. Never was, because I'm keeping her. You bought all the others."

Commander Rip's hand lowers as he looks at the captain. Even from this distance, I can sense his displeasure. "I said *all*, Fane, and I meant it." That rocky, jagged voice is as harsh as the Barrens' cold. "Did you actually think I was giving you a trunk's worth of gold just for some saddles, snow stallions, and half-dead soldiers?" A shake of his head. "No. Midas's favored will be coming with us as well."

My chest goes tight, stuck, like the weight of that coin-filled trunk just slammed down on top of me. My drum-beat heart rhythm is back in full force, reverberating in my ears.

Captain Fane's fists clench at his sides, eyes blazing. "And if I refuse?"

A callous, cruel chuckle comes from the commander. It's the kind of sound you hear before being tortured by a madman. The kind of laugh from a cold-blooded villain. "You won't like what happens if you refuse. But by all means, the choice is yours."

A tic appears in the captain's jaw as he takes in the soldiers standing at attention, their stoic postures unwavering. Even though the pirates outnumber them, I have a feeling it doesn't matter. "How did you know about her? I didn't mention her in any of the messages I sent."

"You had your tip, and I had mine."

I have no idea what that dubious answer means, but my palms begin to sweat.

Quarter says something in the captain's ear, but he just shrugs the man off, expression seething. He shifts on his feet, and the two leaders become locked in a stare-off.

If I thought there was tension before, it's nothing compared to this. Even Rip's soldiers seem more rigid, like they're ready for a fight to break out. My eyes bounce between the two of them, worry gnawing at my bottom lip.

I don't know who I'd rather stay with, if I had the choice. Would I rather be left with the depraved Red Raids, or be sold to the terrifying commander of Ravinger's army? I'm stuck between a rock and a hard, spiked place.

Finally, Captain Fane answers. "Fine." The word comes out bitter, like a snap of reproach. Just like that, I get tossed down the lane of the crossroads. My fate sealed.

"Quarter, let them inspect the soldiers and horses first, make sure they're to the commander's liking," Captain Fane bites out. "Then come back for the saddles so they aren't standing around in the snow." He gives the commander a look. "Wouldn't want your goods to freeze before you've even gotten off the Barrens."

The commander says nothing.

Quarter clears his throat and comes forward. "Right. I'll take you to the other ships if you're ready."

The commander pauses, casting a glance at the saddles, at me.

"Fine," he says, nodding tersely. "Captain, my soldiers and I will be moving out on the hour." With that, he turns and walks down the ramp, six of his soldiers following behind him. The other six stay where they are, hands clasped in front of them, heads straight ahead to stand watch.

Captain Fane's mouth tightens, but he turns to his men. "Put the trunk in my quarters."

The two carrying the trunk immediately rush off to follow his order.

The captain casts a look at the saddles, eyes lingering on the ones with their eyes cast downward, their dresses still torn, shivering in still-damp clothes.

He glances down the line at a couple of his men. "Put the whores in the dining room until the commander returns for them. We don't need one of them trying to get any ideas about jumping overboard so they don't have to go with him. He's already paid, and I'm not giving any of that gold back."

I'm not certain, but I think I hear one of the soldiers snort.

"Aye, Cap."

The saddles turn and dutifully begin to head toward the kitchen, three Red Raids leading the way. I go with the herd, my head lowered, my mind spinning. I almost make it to the dining room when my arm is grabbed, as is Rissa's beside me.

"Quiet." Captain Fane snaps the word to us like a whip, his grip unyielding.

The saddles near us glance over, but with the look of the captain's face, they quickly look away. Without a sound, Rissa and I are pulled from the group and led toward the captain's quarters instead. We're lost in the mix, so the soldiers don't see—or maybe they just don't care.

My heart stutters in place, my feet stumbling their steps. A cold sweat breaks over my skin, chilling me instantly.

"Rip might think he's so fucking clever, but I'll be damned if I don't enjoy you before he takes you with him," Captain Fane mutters.

Terror splits me in half, threatens to topple me. Beside me, Rissa's back stiffens.

"I went through a lot of fucking trouble to get here in time. I've earned a taste," he grumbles, as if talking to himself.

My fear mixes with resentment. Anger.

This was supposed to be my *one* measly reprieve— mine and the saddles'. It's only fair. If we get sold to the devil, the demons shouldn't get to torment us.

But as I'm dragged closer and closer to the captain's quarters, it becomes abundantly clear that there will be no such reprieve. I'm not escaping Captain Fane's abuse.

All because he wants a *taste*.

Like we're something to digest, to consume, to devour.

Why am I so cursed to endure the greed of men? Is

it simply the gild of my skin? Or is it something more, something deeper, something inside of me that brought me this life?

The answer, I suppose, doesn't matter. But the question still burns. It burns just as much as the scar on my throat.

I share a look with Rissa. Her blue eyes troubled, her brows lowered down, both of us trying to keep up with the constant spin of our fate.

The captain stops us at his door and fishes out his key, while the two pirates carrying the trunk of coins wait off to the side. As the captain shoves his key into the lock and lets the men in to deposit the trunk, my face lifts to the sky, my eyes searching, seeking.

But just like every time when anything bad has ever happened to me, there are no stars out. No light. No soft, glimmering shine. Just murky clouds over an endless night.

I keep waiting for rescue to come, for a dawn to bloom, for a star to hatch, for a hope to surface.

But it doesn't.

It doesn't, and I'm pulled into the room, away from the sky, like a candle's flame snuffed at its wick.

CHAPTER 36

The captain's quarters aren't much to look at.

Although, I've probably inherited some unreasonable expectations. Living in a solid gold castle will do that to a girl.

But I take in the room, every inch of it, focusing my eyes with unwavering intent, because I need the distraction—the focus. Any diversion other than the captain locking the door behind us. It sounds louder than my cage ever did.

I keep my gaze forward, fixated on the best part of the room. It's a large set of windows that spans the back of the ship from ceiling to floor, revealing a sea of shadowed snow beyond. Outside, the sky is lightening ever so slightly. This incessant night finally beginning to ebb away.

To the left is a desk, littered with papers and maps. Barrels and stacked trunks are shoved against walls, each of them closed tight, keeping whatever is inside hidden from view. Some are being used as tables, and stuck on top, the weeping of the candle's tears has overflowed, hardened wax molded against its pillar in frozen trickles.

To the right, at the space where I don't want to look, is the bed. It lies in wait, shaded partially by the heavy red drapery covering the corners of the posts. The blankets are rumpled, several of the pillows forgotten on the floor, and I *really* hope the stain on the sheets is ale.

Rissa and I stand by warily as the captain walks to his desk and removes his hat. He rips the red band from around his neck and tosses that too, before picking up a silver flask and tipping it back into his mouth.

His eyes watch us as he takes sloppy gulps. My body begins to shake, like the needles of a Pitching Pine before they're ripped from their branches and plunge into the ground like stakes.

"Performance," Rissa murmurs beside me, so low that I almost don't hear her. A reminder to play a part. To slip into an act, to keep my real self separate from the horrors and closed off inside me, where he can't reach. Perform. Just perform so we can get through this.

Her low murmur of encouragement is enough to make me stop shaking. To take a full breath. I'm grateful for it, for the way it grounds me and reminds me that I'm not alone, even though I wish she'd been spared of this.

"Captain, your cabin has quite an...amass of belongings," Rissa says, bringing out her easy, sultry voice. It's her attempt to lessen the tension, to set the tone of this encounter. Everything she does, from her voice to her movements, is calculated. Purposeful.

Captain Fane ignores her comment as he tosses off his furs over the desk and sets down his flask. "Unfortunately, I don't have time to play long," he says, eyeing her body. "Strip and get on the bed."

I see Rissa's throat bob, but she doesn't balk. "Of course, Captain," she purrs.

Calm, collected, sensual. She's performing as the embodiment of desire.

Walking over to the bed, she slowly strips with gracefulness and provocative ease. As the captain watches her, I watch him. I see his carnal hunger spike, see him lick his lips.

Rissa doesn't belong here, on this stained bed, in a room that reeks of alcohol, with maps stuck to the walls with old wax. She's all soft skin and beauty and poise, and this place is dingy and harsh, with no admiration for her level of worth.

As soon as her nimble fingers release the last button and her dress falls, she climbs onto the bed and waits expectantly for his next order, her blonde hair lying prettily against her skin as she rests on her ankles.

I've seen her naked hundreds of times with Midas of course, so I'm used to it, but for a moment, Captain Fane is entranced.

Then he pounces, making it across the room in five long strides.

He's on her in an instant, crowding over her on the bed. But just when I think he's going to kiss her, he grabs her by the hair instead and spins her around.

She yelps in surprise as she's placed on her knees, but the noise is smothered out when he presses her face into the mattress.

My heart starts to race, but Rissa tries to recover, tries to meet him on the battlefield and redirect the act. She turns her head, cheek to pillow, back arched, while groping hands squeeze her bared bottom, pinching her pink. "Oh, Captain, I do like a man who knows how to take charge," she says in an admiring husky tone.

"Quiet," he snaps.

Not bothering to remove his tunic, he undoes his belt and loosens his leather pants until they drop to his knees where he's kneeling behind her. Without warning, he roughly thrusts himself into her.

Hand still fisted in her hair, he moves in and out quickly, like the harsh rap of a hammer. Somehow, Rissa doesn't flinch or shirk. Instead, she manages to arch back, to pretend, to move with him. She lifts her head up from the pillow and braces her hands on the mattress, continuing to play the part.

But when she lets out a moan to appease him, Captain Fane's mouth twists down, his eyes flash. He jerks her hair and then releases it to wrap his hand around her mouth instead, cutting the noise off. And it becomes apparent then—he's not interested in her having pleasure, not even pretending to.

He reaches up the length of her body, his fingers curling around her jaw. When a strangled breath escapes her, his hold on her mouth tightens. "I said stay fucking quiet," he snaps, the thrusts never slowing.

I'm frozen at the door, my back pressed against it like I'm stuck to the wood, ribbons writhing against endless knots.

While darkness retreats outside, it seems to grow in here. The captain uses her, making everything feel dirty, cruel. At least with Midas, even with my constant simmer of jealousy, the act never made me cringe, never made me hurt for them.

But I hurt for Rissa now.

Captain Fane has lost his entranced look, lost his appreciative gaze. With his teeth gritted and hairy body jerking, all Rissa can do is hold on and stay quiet. But he tries to make her slip up, tries to bring the sounds out so that he can hurt her even more.

Every time a noise slips out of her, even when it's just a shaken breath, he gets rougher, faster, meaner. Until her blue eyes find me, tears brimming over with the brutality of it all.

She might be a saddle, but she's a *royal* saddle. And say what you will about Midas, but he's not a brute. He doesn't abuse his saddles. Uses them for his pleasure, sure, but he doesn't get off on violence.

Her pained, teary face kills me, makes my own eyes burn. I can't stand to keep watching, standing idly by.

"Captain…" I say, taking a step forward. "You're hurting her."

He casts a dark look over his shoulder at me, blond hair in greasy tendrils that hang down to his ears. "Yeah, and you're next, fuck puppet."

Fear lodges in my stomach like a stone. It scratches all the way around as it rolls, making me go raw. But when he slams into Rissa so hard that her head smacks against the headboard, I find myself taking two more steps, find myself speaking again. "Stop it."

Surprise crosses both of their faces at my daring. But the captain's expression is replaced with his promise of punishment—the same one he gave me before.

He pulls out of Rissa suddenly, making her body fall onto the mattress with a heavy slump. And then he's coming for me, expression dark, brows drawn.

The backdrop of windows behind him shows that the sky is lighter. The black cloak of night is finally peeling away, revealing the approach of a graying dawn. Captain Fane is a dark figure before it, his silhouette shrouded by the impending morning.

As he rounds the bed and stalks closer, my feet want to retreat, but I hold my ground. I tip up my chin.

He disrespected Sail's body, and now he's disrespecting Rissa's. Rissa, who's willing to do anything to make it through. Rissa, who would've performed and taken everything he threw at her like a professional, because that's how strong she is.

But as I've come to find, I have my limits.

"I told you I wanted *quiet*."

Captain Fane backhands me before I can even tense.

The blow sends me flying. I can't catch myself before I slam down onto the wooden floor.

Pain bursts behind my eyes like shattering lanterns, but I don't have time to recover before a boot is kicked into my ribs. *Hard*.

I cry out, a strangled cry ripping out of me like an embedded string. It pulls loose, stripped from my throat, leaving the taste of copper in my mouth.

With me on the floor in a pained daze, I barely feel it when he reaches down and tears the front of my dress. I fight him off, curling over into a ball, my body instinctively trying to protect itself, my arms coming up to hold the bodice of my gown together.

He straightens up with a cruel scoff. "Midas obviously didn't know how to train his whores," he says as his hands drop down to the pants still wrapped around his ankles. "Good thing I do. Now stay there and watch silently, pet."

With a cruel smirk shot in my direction, he picks up his leather belt and stalks over to Rissa. For no reason other than to be a complete and utter bastard, he swings it, cracking the leather against her back in a brutal hit.

A shout pours out of her mouth, and the depraved asshole snarls at her to be quiet again, as if this is *her* fault. His mouth curls, his dick bobs, and then he's shoving into her again, like he actually idolizes her agonized cries.

Still sprawled on the floor, my entire side radiates pain from where he kicked me. I tenderly feel the spot where his boot landed, and I hiss out a breath. It hurts, but I have to get up. I *have* to, because Rissa is sobbing, because the windows are finally glowing with light, the sun finally dawning, bringing forth an ashen day.

I force myself to breathe as I struggle to my feet. My cheek throbs, my side screams in protest, but I manage to get up—even if I am slightly hunched over. I pull up my torn bodice, trying to keep it from falling off my chest, forcing my hands to stop shaking.

I look to the bed again and see that the captain has wrapped his belt around Rissa's throat as he fucks her, her tears soaking the hair at her temples.

Anger appears in me, like my own rising dawn.

My hands fist and my jaw locks. I know it the second that the sun officially crests the horizon, because with it, so does my resolve.

My skin prickles.

I move forward, the murky morning filling the room with a dimmed haze. But even with such weak daylight, I feel better. Like I always said, I'm a bright side kind of girl.

The moment I step into the stream of muted dawn, the prickling on my skin intensifies, warming me up. My shoes scrape against the wooden floor as I limp toward the bed.

Rissa's shiny eyes find me, her face wrinkled in pain, red from the pressure he's cinching around her windpipe. My fingers straighten and flex.

When Captain Fane groans in pleasure, the sound digs into the soil of my fury and makes it sprout into a bud of hate.

He notices Rissa's attention on me, because he turns his head, following her gaze. When he sees me walking toward him, he smirks. "Can't wait your turn, hmm? Fine. I'll have you now. See what all the fuss is about with Midas's Golden Cunt."

He drops his hold on the belt, making Rissa fall back coughing and choking. He starts to approach me with an excited gleam in his eye. "I'm going to enjoy making you hurt."

His fist comes up, ready to hit, or grab my hair, or make me kneel, or toss me down. I don't know for sure what he means to do as that hand comes for me so fast, but it doesn't matter.

Because I'm faster.

Without hesitating, without thinking, I rush, not away from him, but closer. I cut the gap between us like a knife plunging forward, and then I slap my bare palm against the skin at his neck.

That's all it takes.

Even though he doesn't realize it yet.

The captain blinks at me, like he's confused, like he's wondering why his raised hand has stopped, why it isn't coming down to punish, why he isn't already subduing me.

Our faces are inches away, and I can feel his putrid, alcohol-laced breath puff out. I can feel the shudder that travels the length of his body.

His lips part, like he wants to ask what the hell is happening, but all that comes out is a mangled choke. It stutters from his throat for a split second before cutting off unnaturally.

He goes still as my hand squeezes tighter around his neck. Behind me, I hear Rissa gasp. Because there, at the spot beneath my palm, a change starts to spread across his skin.

Like a ripple, it extends from his neck where I'm touching. It billows out, like smooth water, cresting over his shoulders, pouring down his arms, spreading over his torso, dripping down his legs. I feel it seep beneath, sinking past his skin, puddling into his organs, flooding through his veins.

His face is the last to go.

Because I want him to watch. I want him to *see*. I want him to look at me and know that my eyes are *his* punishing promise.

The last thing Captain Fane is able to do is widen his gaze in shock. But he doesn't have time to blink or breathe. Not again. Not ever.

One second, his skin is ruddy, his tunic stained, his cock purple, his eyes brown. And the next, he's frozen in time, every inch of him, from the beads on his beard to the toes in his boots, all of it gleaming, resplendent, vindictive.

Because I just turned the motherfucker solid gold.

CHAPTER 37

The gold beneath my hand is cold and solid, no give, no warmth. It feels the way only lifeless, insentient things can feel to the touch. Like a rock left at the bottom of a sea.

I stare at the face with the slightly curled lip, the barely visible grains in the teeth, the panicked stare. My heart pounds in my chest, but not with regret. It thrums with the truth of what I've done. With what I've revealed.

I peel away my fingers from his throat one by one, until I've released the metal husk of a man, letting my arm drop to my side.

"You...you—what did you *do*?"

My eyes pass over to Rissa who's sitting frozen on the bed, gaping at me in horror. Her eyes keep flitting from me back to the gold statue of Captain Fane's body, like she isn't sure which one is more of a threat.

Her breath is coming in quick pants, but I don't

know if it's from what I just did, what she endured from the captain, or if she's just in shock from it all.

"Are you okay?" I ask.

She only blinks at me, mouth open, hair disheveled, tears drying on her cheeks.

My head is beginning to swim, an ache blooming out through my temples, while a heaviness is threatening to settle over me. I rub my forehead for a moment, as if I can ease the oncoming headache. It feels like all of my strength is dripping out of me, like a tree oozing sap.

I gesture to the late captain. "He's much better like this, don't you think? No more talking or moving..." I glance down at his cock that's still standing at attention, my lips pursed in thought. "I bet we could even hack that thing off with a hammer if you wanted to."

She makes a choking noise, though I'm not sure if she wants to scream, sob, or laugh. Maybe a combination of all three.

Ripping the belt from her throat, she rubs at the red marks marring her skin before shakily getting to her feet and pointing. "How did you do that, Auren?"

"Umm..."

She walks over, unbothered by her nudity as she circles around the captain, her trembling hand reaching toward his chest. She makes a fist and knocks on it before snatching it back. "Great Divine, he really is solid gold," she breathes. Her uneasy eyes lift to me. "And he's... dead?"

"Oh, yes," I assure her. "Very, *very* dead."

A weighted exhale tremors through her body. "But King Midas…"

Her words trail off and fall at our feet, but I don't pick them up for her. I've already revealed far too much. I can't explain how it all works, with Midas and me. I can't let her know anything more than she already does.

She shifts on her feet, and the wooden boards beneath us give an ominous creak. We both freeze and look down, where the floor is sagging beneath the weight of the captain.

I wince. "That…that's probably not good," I admit.

She gives me a vexed look. "You think?"

If the captain breaks the floor, it will be incredibly loud. And if it's loud, then the pirates will come running. I can't let that happen, because I can't let anyone see what I've done. Doing this in front of Rissa was bad enough. But if the pirates find out…a shiver travels through me at the thought.

"Rissa," I say, forcing her eyes to lift and focus on me. "You can't tell anyone. Ever," I stress, my expression hard, my tone absolute. "You have to keep it a secret. Please."

I can see her mind working, her cogs turning, and I wish I knew what she was thinking.

"You told him to stop hurting me."

I nod carefully. "I did."

She considers me for a moment. "The last time you tried to help me, you chucked a book at my head."

353

I grimace a little. "I'm a bit impulsive."

She looks at the captain. "I'll say."

Worry gnaws on my bones like a starved mutt as silence stretches between us. Sure, I tried to stand up to the captain, but she'd already been hurt. Despite everything that's happened tonight, I can't assume I've earned any kind of loyalty from her.

But she finally nods. "Okay."

For now, that okay will have to do.

I blow out a breath, shaking out the tremble in my hands, trying to push back the aching tiredness and anxiety pouring over me. "Alright. Now, we don't have much time before the commander comes for us. We can't let anyone see this."

Rissa shoots me an exasperated look. "And how in the world are we supposed to hide him?"

I bite my lip, praying to the Divine gods that the floorboards don't buckle as I look around the room. But it's not as if I can simply toss a blanket over him or shove him under the bed. The Red Raids are going to notice when their captain doesn't emerge from his room.

My eyes catch on the trunk of gold coins next to his desk, and my mind sparks. "I have an idea," I tell her. "Get dressed."

Rissa spurs into action and goes to gather her gown from the bed, while I go to the captain's open closet and snag a pair of thick gloves left on the floor. As soon as I slip them over my hands, the white changes color, like the leather was soaked in a vat of gold.

Since the captain tore the front of my dress, I snag a short brown overcoat on a peg near my head. Unlike the white leathers and furs that dominate the rest of his clothing, this one has large brown feathers down the back and the sleeves.

Despite how light it is, it's surprisingly warm with the feathery down adding another layer of protection. It's also short enough in the back that it's not a detriment to my ribbons, and when I button up the front, it holds my ripped bodice in place.

As soon as Rissa is dressed, she looks over. "Alright. What do we do now?"

My eyes go from the captain to the windows behind him. Rissa follows my gaze and shakes her head. "It's not possible."

"It's the only thing we can do," I argue. "He can't be found like this. Under *any* circumstance."

She lets out a puff of breath like she wants to argue some more, but settles for muttering under her breath. She then ties her hair up out of her face while I go to the bed and snatch up the sheets.

In all honesty, she's probably right about this being impossible, but it's the only chance I've got. I'm damn lucky he's close enough to the window to even attempt it, or there would be no hope of this. Even so, there's a good chance I won't be able to shove the bastard out the window.

But I have to try.

With Rissa's help, the two of us move as fast as we can, knowing that our time is running out. We tie two sheets around the captain's neck like a noose, leaving ourselves plenty of length to use as a rope.

I secure my sheet and then rush to the window and unclasp it, thanking all the Divines above that both of them open easily. With them now open, it lets in a blast of cold wind, soft snow flurries peppering across the floor.

I feel Rissa's attention on me, casting clandestine looks. I know she's brimming with questions, but I can't afford to have her voice them, and we don't have the time anyway.

I check to make sure the sheets are secure once more, and we circle around the captain until the window is at our backs. "So...the plan is to just pull like hell and hope we tip the bastard over?" she asks, doubtful.

"Pretty much."

She shakes her head before rubbing her hands together. The two of us both grip our sheets, wrapping them around our hands.

"On three," I tell her. "One, two, three!"

Together, we pull with all our might. Hands fisted, arms bunched, back straining, legs planted, we pull. Rissa grunts as she yanks, but it doesn't move. Not even a bit.

We both let go of our sheets at the same time, panting and cursing.

GILD

"Shit," I mutter as panic begins to bubble up in me. I can't leave him here like this. I *can't*. It's not an option.

"Shit, shit, shit…" Full of frustration, I kick the captain hard in the shin. Not the best thing to do, considering he's solid gold. I curse again at the pain that shoots through my toes.

Rissa cocks a blonde brow at me. "Maybe *don't* kick the solid gold man statue, okay?"

"It was kind of worth it," I grumble.

She cocks her head, considering. Then she turns and brings the meat of her fist down onto the captain's dick with an impressive hit. It would've definitely hurt if he were still made of flesh. And alive.

"Ow," she says, frowning at the unmoving gold phallus. She rubs her sore hand and looks at me. "Hmm. You're right. That was worth it."

"Yeah," I sigh.

Both Rissa and I look around, puzzling over what to do. The window looks so close and yet so damn far. My eyes catch on a pair of hooks bolted to the wall beside the windows, where one of the captain's swords is being displayed. My mind spins and clicks.

I rush forward, snatching the sword off the wall and tossing it onto the bed. Then I'm taking the length of sheets and wrapping it around the hooks, tugging to test how secure it is.

"What are you doing?" Rissa asks.

I lift my whole body off the floor by hanging from

357

the sheet, and the hooks don't budge. That's a good sign. I just hope this works.

"Grab the captain's chair and put it behind him. This hook will act like a pulley," I say, showing her the sheet in my hands that goes from his neck, to the hook to me. "I'll pull as hard as I can to tip him from the front, while you stand and push at his head from the back. Hopefully it'll be enough to topple him, and then gravity can do the rest."

She nods and hurries around the desk to grab his chair. Once she has it next to the captain, she stands on top of the seat, giving herself the extra height.

I take my place at the wall and grip the sheet. Four of my ribbons—the only ones I've managed to unknot—come up, wrapping around the sheet as well, but they're tired and aching. I don't know how much strength they can lend me.

Rissa's gaze flicks over them with both wariness and fascination.

"Ready?" I say, cutting off anything she might want to ask.

In reply, she braces her hands against the captain's head and plants her feet, while my grip tightens on the sheet.

I count down. "One...two...three..."

She pushes. I pull. The floor creaks. The wind blows. The statue doesn't move an inch.

My entire body strains as I use every bit of strength

358

and determination I've got. My sore side twinges in pain, but I ignore it. My poor ribbons feel as fragile as butterfly wings, and my spine is screaming, the muscles pulling.

"*Come...on...*"

I'm going to either black out or tip this bastard over. There's no in-between. I hold my breath and just keep pulling, pulling, refusing to stop, refusing to fail.

This has to work. It *has* to.

I hear Rissa make a frustrated noise as she heaves, and sweat breaks out over my body. Dizziness swoops over me, like a bird circling my head.

We're giving this every bit of strength we have. And if we stop, we won't be able to start again. This is it. I know it, she knows it, even the frigid wind knows it.

But the captain doesn't tip.

Tears flood my eyes, and my stomach drops. We can't do it. *I* can't do it.

The impulsive decision I made to kill the bastard probably forfeited my own life as well.

The realization cripples me. That this is all for nothing, that there's no way I can do this. The utter failure of it all makes dread slump my shoulders. It pushes me down, hunches me over, bowing me with the weight of what's to come.

With a growl of resistance, my teeth clench so hard together I'm worried I might actually break them. My entire body shakes, my head swims with black dots, but

I keep pulling. All I get in return is the sound of the sheet ripping, the floorboards creaking in threat.

A sob escapes my throat. Rissa makes a strangled, painful grunt. The last of my hope starts to slip out of my grasp as the sheet continues to tear.

But then, like some sort of divine miracle, my ribbons start to glow.

It's dim, like the softest beam of light below a pond of water, but it's there. It's the same glow of silken warmth that woke me up in the carriage after the attack.

A gasp escapes me as the four silky strands seem to come alive with a second wave of strength I didn't know they were capable of. The lengths whip out, releasing the sheet and grabbing straight onto the captain's torso, wrapping around with a metallic clink.

They pull with such force that I cry out in pain, my spine feeling like it's about to snap.

But with their massive strength, Captain Fane begins to tip. And that slight movement is all we need to make him topple.

Rissa lets out a surprised yelp and falls forward as the statue goes tipping toward the open window. With a crash, his shins hit the lip of the window frame, but gravity has him in her clutches now and she's not letting go.

My ribbons unravel in a flash, and the captain falls, like a massive tree cut at its trunk. He spins in his descent, and I lean over, watching as he plummets to the ground, the sheets around his neck flapping as he goes.

He hits the ground hard, sending up a spray of snow, like a body diving into water.

Rissa and I both blink down, staring silently, as we realize that we actually succeeded.

I cast a quick glance around, but luckily, the other pirate ships aren't behind us, and the dawn is still meek enough that the landscape is barely lit.

Our breaths are jagged as we continue to look out the window, staring at where he's landed cock-up in the snow.

Rissa's lips curl up in satisfaction. "A fitting end, I think."

I give a tired snort.

Even though all my body wants to do is collapse on the floor, I force myself to go over to the desk and grab the handle of the coin trunk. It's heavier than I can lift, and my aching body barks in protest, but Rissa hurries over to help me, and we both chuck that out the window too.

We watch as it lands a few feet away from the captain, snowfall already spreading over them like confetti.

"Explain to me why we just tossed out all that gold?"

"Motive," I say distractedly, my voice weary.

Snow is piling up on the floor, so I do my best to sweep most of it out before I yank the windows closed again. My only hope is that they'll believe my story, that the ships will move before anyone sees.

I give one last look at the gleaming captain below. He's cursed to forever have shock in his eyes and pants around his ankles. He's also richer than he ever dreamed, but too dead to appreciate it. For a man solely motivated by coin and pleasure, that thought makes me immensely satisfied.

I turn away from the window with an exhausted sigh, barely able to hold my back straight. My ribbons hang limp and feeble behind me, no glow left in their golden lengths.

But we did it. It actually worked.

"Alright?" Rissa asks me.

I shrug in return. That was only half the battle, and we barely managed it.

All I can do now is hope that the snow keeps falling, that my lie is believed, that the ships move on, and that the gleaming truth stays hidden beneath a mound of smothering snow.

But even if we manage all of that, our lives are still in danger.

I might have ended the captain of the Red Raids, but we're going from being the captives of greedy pirates to being the captives of bloodthirsty soldiers.

I don't know which is worse.

But I'm about to find out.

CHAPTER 38

A knock sounds on the captain's door, making me nearly jump out of my shoes.

"Cap'n, they're coming back!" one of the pirate's voice hollers through the door.

Rissa's eyes go wide in worry as she mouths, *What do we do?*

Spurred into action, I point to the bed, and Rissa and I waste no time rushing over to it. "Lie down," I whisper to her.

She quickly complies, and I toss the captain's discarded belt to her. "Secure your wrist to the bedpost."

She gives me a look. "Really?"

"Just trust me. And mess up your dress."

She gives a huff, but with her free hand, she does as I say, making her bodice sag, her skirt hiked up and disheveled.

I put myself on the floor next to the bed and as gently

as I can, coax one of my ribbons to wrap around my wrist before attaching it to the post. Every curl they make aches like a strained muscle or bruised bone, but I know this needs to look somewhat believable.

With my free hand, I undo the buttons of the captain's feathered overcoat, not exposing myself fully, but leaving a gap so they can see the torn bodice beneath. I hike up my thick skirts to rest against my upper thigh too, hoping that enough skin will distract them from questioning anything too much.

Another knock sounds at the door. "Cap'n, you coming out? They're heading up the ramp."

I look up toward the bed. "If you can cry on command, now would be the time," I murmur.

Rissa scoffs. "Of course I can cry on command."

"Cap'n? You alright in there?"

Murmured voices sound behind the door, then heavy footfalls come closer. I hear the sound of Quarter's voice calling for Captain Fane just as Rissa snaps her fingers at me. "What?" I ask her.

Instead of answering, she shakes a pointed finger toward the captain's desk.

With a frown, my eyes skate over to it, only to see that the captain's hat and coat are still lying there.

"*Shit*," I hiss.

I debate getting up and trying to throw them out the window, but it's too late. Quarter is already pounding on the door.

"Cap? Cap! I'm coming in!"

I hear Rissa sniffle as the pirates outside begin to kick at the door. I flinch with each hit, until the doorframe splinters and the door comes crashing open.

Three pirates stalk in, Quarter at the lead. Their eyes immediately find Rissa and me, but their heads swivel around, looking for Captain Fane.

"Cap?" Quarter calls.

When it's obvious the captain isn't in here, his expression darkens, and he stalks over to the bed.

"Where is he?" he demands.

Rissa starts crying. Really loud, wailing, hiccupping cries. Either she's a terrific actress, or she was holding it all in.

I make sure to keep a scared look on my face, which isn't difficult, considering I'm terrified.

Quarter stops in front of me and looks between the two of us. "I said where the fuck is he?"

"Captain Fane...he...he..." Rissa's voice breaks off into wracking sobs.

Quarter growls in frustration and looks down at me, kicking me in the shin with his boot and making me hiss out in pain. "Somebody better fucking speak!"

I pretend to struggle against the ribbon tying me to the post. "After he...took us, he tied us up. Then he told us to stay quiet, and he grabbed the trunk full of coins," I say quickly, my voice shaky and high-pitched. "He took it and snuck out. Locked us in here."

Behind him, the other two pirates go tense and share a look between them.

"Snuck out." Quarter repeats evenly.

I nod my head, anxiety nipping at my heels.

Just believe me. Please believe it.

Quarter pulls away and starts looking around the room. My heart rate soars as he circles around the desk where the captain's hat and coat are lying. It pounds even faster and harder when he passes by the window.

Don't look out there. I beg all the Divines. *Please don't let him look out.*

"Where was the trunk?" he barks.

One of the other pirates points. "We set it just there, Quarter."

Quarter curses and kicks at a nearby barrel, sending it flying across the room and cracking against the wall. "He fucking took the coin for himself and jilted us!"

"Where would he go without a ship?" the pirate asks.

"He obviously planned this," Quarter snaps. "Took a fire claw or conspired with those Fourth soldier fucks." Another string of curses batters out of his mouth, smacking into the room with vicious force. "That sneaky bastard. I'll run him through if I ever see—"

"Quarter." A different pirate appears in the doorway. "The commander is waiting. He's getting impatient."

"Fuck!" Quarter tugs at his hair in frustration before spinning on his heel and looking at us.

My body goes tense, worry pounding against my skull, magnifying my headache tenfold.

"What do you want to do, Quarter?"

He lets out a thin, gritted exhale. "If we tell the Reds the captain took off with our pay *and* the commander left with our whores, we're going to have a fucking mutiny on our hands." He sends a hated, dark look in our direction. "Get them to the commander."

The pirate opens his mouth to argue. "But—"

"Now," Quarter snaps. "You think we can survive an attack from Fourth's soldiers if we try to renege on the deal? He paid, whether we have the coins or not. He won't leave without them. Especially not the gilded bitch."

The pirates glance at one another, clearly displeased, but they stalk over to us. "Come on, you cunts," one of them mutters.

I quickly lift my hand to the ribbon that's wrapped around the post and pretend to undo it so that he doesn't attempt anything like tearing or cutting into it.

He grabs me by my arm just as I get the ribbon undone, his fingers pressing hard through the material of my sleeve as he hauls me out the door while the other pirate takes Rissa.

Just as we're led out of the room, I hear, "Wait a minute, isn't that the cap's coat? Why would he leave without his coat?"

Rissa stumbles behind me, and alarm bells go off in my head.

"Oy! Stop!"

The pirates escorting us jolt us to a halt and step aside just outside the room. Quarter's footsteps stalk over, and I turn to face him as he approaches, my knees shaking beneath my skirt.

He stops in front of us, holding up the captain's coat and hat. "You two wanna tell me about this?" he says, looking back and forth between us. I don't dare look at Rissa.

My eyes flicker down to the coat as he shakes the fur in front of me. "Wh-what about it?" I ask, trying to sound as confused and pitiful as possible.

"You're telling me that the captain snuck out with the trunk, during a snowstorm, but didn't even bother to wear his fucking coat?" he snarls.

I flinch from the anger in his voice, but I manage to get out a shaky answer. "I—I don't know. Maybe he was in a hurry?"

Quarter narrows his eyes and then takes a threatening step toward me. I cower back instinctively, my back nearly hitting the wall. I turn my face away from him.

Don't touch me, don't touch me...

His eyes flash with viciousness. "You're fucking lying, aren't you? What are you lying about?"

My knees nearly buckle right then and there. My chest goes tight, and it has nothing to do with my knotted ribbons and everything to do with the grip that fear has around my ribs.

"I…" Whatever excuses and lies I was going to try to spin collapse against my tongue.

My mouth is dry, my head is pounding, and I'm so tired…so incredibly *weak*. I expended a lot of energy—too much—and my body is ready to collapse. I probably would have already if adrenaline weren't coursing through me.

Quarter leans down close to my cheek, and I freeze. "If you don't start talking, I'll stuff something in that useless mouth of yours, and then I'll fill you with so much cum, it'll corrode your plated pussy, do you fucking understand? What happened to Captain Fane?" His tone is dark and murderous.

Black dots burst at the edges of vision. My mind scrambles to fix this, to solidify my original story, but after the night I've had, it's like my mind is sputtering out.

Why did I think I could get away with this? The threads of my lies are snapping one by one, and all I can do is try to hold onto the weak strings with a desperate grip.

Quarter growls next to my face, making my eyes squeeze shut. "Fine. I'll *make* you talk, and then—"

Before Quarter can finish his sentence or go through with his threat, a cold, smooth voice cuts through the air like a boom, a volcano erupting in the middle of a silent twilight.

"What do you think you're doing?"

CHAPTER 39

At the sound of the commander's voice, Quarter's head whips over, and my eyes snap open in surprise.

Commander Rip is standing there, flanked by two of his soldiers. The three of them are menacing and dark, like obscure shadows spreading their darkness. Even with the helmet obscuring his face, I can tell that the commander is seething.

"Move away from the favored. Now."

No room for argument, no politeness in the commander's tone. He doesn't even have to raise his voice to sound frightening.

Quarter straightens up at the command. "She's lying about something, and I'll be finishing this discussion before you take her."

To be honest, I'm too shocked at Quarter's courage to be nervous for myself. But beside me, I hear Rissa whimper, like she's afraid we're about to be caught up in a deadly fight, and maybe we are, because the three pirates behind Quarter grasp the hilts of their swords nervously.

But the soldiers behind Commander Rip don't move an inch. The commander himself also doesn't grip his gnarled hilt. He doesn't take a step forward. He doesn't even argue.

No, the commander *laughs*.

The sound pours out of his helmet and pools in the air between us, making the pirates go tense. It's the sound of a warning. It's the laugh of a madman, one set on the promise of blood.

A threatening aura as thick as tar pulses off him, making my skin bead with an unnatural chill. The spikes on the commander's arms gleam black like a chasm's throat ready to swallow Quarter whole, and I nearly feel sick with fear.

This is the monster that King Ravinger unleashes on Orea. This is the male terror that the legends and gossip and tales are derived from. No wonder no one wants to meet him on a battlefield.

Beside me, Quarter blanches behind his mask, his eyes widening like prey who vastly underestimated the predator.

"Fine, take her," Quarter blurts, his voice gruff, caught between fear and a feeble attempt to sound confident. "I can't trust the words from a whore's mouth, anyway."

"Good choice." The commander's voice is like a sinister purr.

Quarter grinds his teeth, irked with the patronizing tone, but he turns and stalks off, retreating into the captain's rooms like a dog with his tail between his legs. Smart man. The other three pirates shoot glares at the soldiers before they also turn and follow behind him.

I stare at the commander, barely able to breathe. Too affected by his palpable menace to be relieved that I'm escaping Quarter's questions.

"Let's go." The commander speaks the order quietly but firmly.

He turns and walks off, while the two soldiers with him wait for Rissa and me. We peel ourselves away from our frozen spots near the captain's quarters and begin to walk, my steps lagging slightly.

As we walk across the deck, the gazes of the Red Raids follow us, their masks like sneers. But Fourth's soldiers don't pay them any mind, don't even seem to care as they escort Rissa and me toward the ramp, a light dusting of snow covering the gangplank.

I let my eyes scan the faceless red masks of the pirates one last time, my gaze catching on the pole where they'd strung up Sail. I have the biggest urge to spit at their feet, but I hold it in.

I face forward as the commander begins to walk down the ramp, his boots making prints over the wood as he descends. Rissa and I follow quietly behind him, the other two soldiers at our backs.

But exhaustion is rebelling through my body,

threatening to take over. My weary, stumbled steps don't go well together with the steep incline of the gangplank, especially when it's slippery.

I try to focus each step, going slow and careful, but even so, my legs are shaking, my energy sapped. So I'm not even surprised when my boot hits a patch of ice and I go tripping forward, unable to catch myself.

I nearly knock into Rissa, but I manage to jerk my body to the left before I run into her. Of course, that only makes me toss myself right over the side of the ramp, and I go flying off.

Luckily, I'm near the bottom, at least. Bright side.

On my short fall toward the ground, my arms and loose ribbons thrust in front of me in an attempt to catch myself, and I brace myself for the impact.

I land hard, my hands and knees bursting with pain as I hit the thick snow. Wet cold immediately soaks into my skirt and gloves. My ribbons nearly collapse beneath my weight, the hardened contours pulsing with a sharp ache, but at least I didn't land flat on my face.

For a moment, my dizziness and exhaustion is so great that I worry I'm not going to be able to pick myself back up, that I'm just going to collapse in the snow. But I can't let that happen. I'm entirely too exposed and vulnerable here, beneath the veil of a clouded morning.

I startle when the crack of a whip shatters the air, followed by the thunderous sound of countless fire claws growling.

Behind me, the ships of the snow pirates begin to slowly drag away, wooden hulls scraping against waves of ice, my prostrate body so close to them that the ground trembles beneath me.

But beyond the ships that are inching away, gaining momentum by their fiery beasts, I see a sea of white landscape that's clogged with hundreds, maybe even thousands, of Fourth Kingdom's soldiers.

Like craggy rocks littered throughout the once pristine landscape, they're *everywhere*. With these numbers, it becomes blatantly obvious why the pirates didn't dare fight the commander. With this might at his back, they would be slaughtered.

My stomach churns inside me as my eyes scan the sight of them, but I'm unable to even comprehend their numbers. This isn't just a reconnaissance mission. This isn't the commander traveling to Midas with a small group of soldiers to deliver a royal message.

No, this is the might of King Ravinger's army, come to wage war.

I escaped the Red Raids only to be caught by the enemy marching toward my king. I fell into the commander's hand like a shiny bargaining chip.

My dread churns so thick in my stomach that I worry I'm going to be sick. When a pair of black boots appears in my line of vision where I'm still braced awkwardly on the ground, all I can do is blink, my body frozen there in the snow.

This is bad. Very, very bad.

The commander's voice grates down my back as sharp as his spikes. "Well, this is very...interesting."

My throat bobs with a dry swallow, and then my eyes lift up where the commander stands looming over me. Behind him, the army begins to move, though I don't watch them. I'm too focused on *him*. Because his helmet is off, tucked under his arm, and I can see his face for the very first time.

He has no horns. No glowing, murderous eyes. Not even a terrifying scar is ripped down his cheek.

No, all of those things were just nightmarish gossip, the imagining of something demonic. Orea is probably in too much denial to face the truth, too separated from our land's long-ago history, too afraid to think that we have full-blooded fae in our midst. They use King Rot's power as the excuse, they believe falsehoods, spread misinformation, or discard it all as rumors.

But Commander Rip isn't a demon, and he hasn't been twisted by Ravinger's magic. He's a presence all his own, and I can't help but stare at him, taking in every detail.

His irises are black. As black as midnight shrouding the world, starless, moonless, no differentiating between iris and pupil. Thick, arched black eyebrows are set above those desolate eyes, making his expression fierce and grim.

Above the hairline of each eyebrow is a line of

tiny, very short spikes. The same black as the spikes on his back and arms, though these ones don't curve, look slightly more blunted at the tips, and are only about a centimeter tall.

His nose is strong and straight, his teeth are bright white, showing a hint of slightly sharp and elongated canines. Along his temples and curving down his cheekbones, he has a subtle dusting of gray, nearly iridescent scales, like the scales of the lizards that live in the Ash Dunes.

He has thick black hair, a rough black beard over pale skin, and a strong square jaw—a jaw that leads up to subtly pointed ears. And all of this on a body standing six and a half feet tall, thick with muscles and an aura ripe with menace.

He's terrifying. He's ethereal. He's so very, very fae.

The rest of Orea might have forgotten what true fae look and feel like, might like to pretend that all we have left of the fae is what little magic that still passes down in bloodlines, but the commander's presence disproves that.

Orea feels betrayed by the fae, but fear is the predominant emotion. It's why only those with magic are allowed to rule. It's why Queen Malina had to give up control of her throne and marry Midas for his magical power. Because if the fae ever do come back to finish what they started, we need rulers who can protect their kingdoms.

I wonder if King Ravinger knows exactly what kind

of beast he has on his leash. I wonder if he can feel the commander's power brimming beneath the surface, sense his suffocating atmosphere.

I'm vulnerable here at his feet, with the commander's eyes locked on my weak ribbons that are still trying to help hold me up. His unwanted attention makes my heart gallop.

With a mental push, I'm somehow able to collect the shattered pieces of my strength and force myself to my feet. As soon as I stand, my loose ribbons hang limp and dull behind me in the snow, no strength left to even wrap themselves around me.

The commander's head cocks in an animalistic way as he regards me with a slow drag of his eyes from bottom to top, making the sheen of the barely-there scales over his cheekbones ripple in the gray dawn.

When his gaze finally lifts to my face, my wary gold eyes get caught by his intense black ones.

The pirate ships pull further away, the army continues to move, but the commander and I continue to stand there, watching each other.

From this close, I can see flakes of snow getting caught on his thick black lashes. I can see the polished gleam of the spikes over his brow. I wouldn't call him handsome, he's far too wicked looking for that, but the savage grace of him is as magnificent as it is utterly alarming.

Even though I'm freezing, my palms begin to sweat

inside my gloves, my pulse pounding so hard I expect it to knock pinprick holes through my veins. The wind picks up, ruffling the brown feathers along my stolen coat, making it look as if my whole body is trembling.

Strong. His presence is so damn *strong* and full of death, like even his aura knows how destructive he is.

Finally, he speaks again. "So, *this* is King Midas's pet." He glances down at the feathers on my sleeves, the gold ribbons bereft in the snow, and his black eyes flash with interest as they lift again to my face. "I have to admit, I didn't expect to find a goldfinch."

I'm not sure why hearing him call me a pet bothers me, but I find my hands fisting the fabric of my skirts.

"I know what you are," I say with a sharp tone, my accusation escaping with a puff of hazy air between us.

A slow smirk spreads over his mouth, a menacing curl of his lips that makes my heart stumble. He takes a single step forward, a simple move that somehow sucks all the air out of the world.

He leans in, his aura pushing at me, testing, feeling, overwhelming. And despite the frigid air of the Barrens, despite the deafening noises of the scraping ships and the marching army, his voice presses hot and resonant against my ear as he speaks. "Funny, I was about to say the same thing to *you*."

CHAPTER 40

KING MIDAS

I've been to every single kingdom in Orea.

First Kingdom is a tepid jungle, flooded with pretentious fools who fancy themselves masters of the arts. Second is an arid expanse of sand and not much more, the monarchs a dull, puritanical lot.

Third Kingdom holds more interest, their coasts speckled with private islands only to be visited upon invitation of the monarchs. Their only blight is that they share a murky border of swampland with Fourth, but King Rot's kingdom holds no interest to me at all.

Fifth Kingdom, however, I've grown increasingly fond of.

I look out below me, my hands braced on the balcony

railing. The ground glitters silver and white, but my focus is on the ice sculptures in the courtyard, maintained as religiously as any royal garden, every curve chiseled, every inch shaped to perfection.

What a wonder it will look like once all the ice has been touched with gold.

I don't have ice sculptures in Highbell. The blizzards and storms are far too vicious for that. But here in Fifth Kingdom, the everlasting cold is much more mild, only light dustings of snow gracing its sparkling ground.

I watch the sculptors continue to carve for a moment longer before I turn and head back inside, letting the balcony doors snick shut behind me. I've been given the south suites of Ranhold Castle to stay in, the interior all decorated in whites and purples, with gray rock and black iron fortifying its structure. It's lavish and entirely respectable enough for a visiting monarch.

Except, I don't intend to simply visit.

I sit down at the desk set into the corner of the room, fresh blue winter blossoms set cheerfully on top, its stem resting in frosted water.

I'm deep in a stack of papers when the knock sounds on my door, and my advisor, Odo, shuffles in.

"Your Majesty, a letter has arrived for you."

I hold out my hand, my attention split on the roster in front of me as he places the rolled parchment in my palm.

Breaking the wax seal, I unroll the message, my eyes distractedly skimming over the words. But then I stop. Go back. Start over.

I read it once, and my body goes rigid. I read it a second time, and my jaw clenches tight. By the third time, I'm seeing red.

"Sire?"

My eyes snap to Odo where he waits in front of the desk, no doubt wondering if I need to send a reply.

There will be no reply.

My hand crumples the paper. "They have her."

My voice is dark and low, words formed between barely separated teeth. The realization pounding in tandem with my enraged pulse.

Odo hesitates. "Who has who, Your Majesty?"

In a blink, I'm on my feet. My arms sweep everything off the desk in a terrific crash. Books slam against the floor, papers go flying, the frosted vase of the flowers shatters against the wall.

My advisor flinches back, wide eyes on me as I pace back and forth across the room. My fists are clenched so tightly at my sides that it's a wonder I don't snap the bones in my fingers.

"King Midas?" Odo questions hesitantly.

But I barely hear him, nor my guards who come into the room because of the noise, their swords drawn against a threat that isn't here.

A cloud of fury gathers in my head, a heavy storm

of thoughts pummeling behind my temples and dripping down my limbs.

No one dares move or question me further as I continue to pace, probably in fear that I'll solidify their heads and leave their golden skulls on a frozen spike outside the gates.

I don't feel it when I stop and slam my fist into the wall. I don't care when my knuckles split and blood stains the white carpet in furious blots of red.

I don't feel it, and I don't care, because the thing that matters the most to me in this world has been taken from me.

My favored. My gilded. My precious. She's been stolen from me and is being held in an enemy's clutches.

I turn to my guards, my anger rising like boiling water, sending a thick haze of fury over my vision. The precision of my planned annihilation against King Fulke will be *nothing* compared to those who dared take Auren from me.

She's mine.

And I'll destroy everyone in my path to get her back.

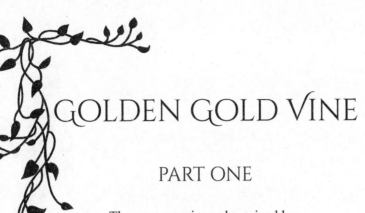

GOLDEN GOLD VINE

PART ONE

There was a miser who prized her,
this golden gold vine.
This sapling so gilded,
her leaflings did shine.
The moment he saw her,
he let out a whisper of *"mine."*

He'd found her in rubble,
along a plain road.
Unburied, he took her,
in pocket he stowed.

Back to his house,
where he stared at her gleam.
Hands curled to covet,
want stitched to seam.

What a chance this was,
the chance for much more.
So he planted her there,
right outside his front door.

Kept under secrets and hidden she lay.
This old miser did find her,
did steal her away.

Brought to the yard,
he planted her there.
Fenced her all in
to shelter her glare.

Soon she grew tiny buds,
glinting with gold.
He plucked them by one,
went to town to be sold.

He paid off his debts,
bought whatever he sought.
But it wasn't enough,
whatever he got.

For greed had been planted
beside her thin roots.
Want had leafed out,
along with her shoots.

Yet although he watered,
soon she did wilt.
Her golden did dull
and worry he spilt.

For his most prized possession
looked right to be culled.
She wasted away,
while he fretted and mulled.

It wasn't til so angry,
he pulled out his hair.
Brown clumps all fallen
on the vine bare,
that her color suddenly glistened,
her vine did then surge.
She grew ever much
from his body he'd purged.

Ecstatic, he knew, what he must do.
So this miser clip-clipped,
and gold flowers then bloomed.
His hair he snip-snipped,
gladly shedding his plume.

For she would not grow
without sacrifice.
Only pieces of him
would ever suffice.
For her to keep growing,
that was her price.
This golden gold vine
was the miser's own vice.

TO BE CONTINUED...

ACKNOWLEDGMENTS

I thought it would get easier over time to release new books, but I can say it never does. I want to thank my family and friends for your love and unending support.

To my husband, for being such a rock star every single day. I couldn't do this without you, and I love you so much.

To my daughter, I'm sorry for all the times I have to work instead of play, but I want you to know that I adore you more than all the waves in the sea.

To my dad, you watch every single book release, and even though you're not allowed to read them, you have cheered me on and celebrated every word. Thank you.

To my mom, you read my first ever book drafts and told me they were good even though they were probably garbage. Your encouragement helped me not give up and to keep going.

To my sister, I would never have gone on this writing journey if it weren't for you. I gained my first steps of confidence by writing at your side and I learned so much and had so much fun.

To Ives aka Ivy Asher, you help me make every single book better, you let me whine to you when writing is hard, and you have my back in every facet of the book world. I am so damn lucky to have you.

To Ann Denton and CR Jane for being beta reader extraordinaires, thank you so much for helping me with *Gild* and giving me the confidence boost I needed. Still not gonna give you spoilers though.

Thank you to Helayna for polishing *Gild* (see what I did there?)

And most importantly, to YOU, the reader. I know *Gild* is somewhat different from some of the other things I've written, and I'm just so thankful that you took a chance on it. All of the support, posts, reviews, and comments I receive mean the world to me, and your enthusiasm encourages me to keep going. Thank you from the bottom of my heart.

—Raven

Raven Kennedy

ABOUT THE AUTHOR

Raven Kennedy is a California girl born and raised, whose love for books pushed her into creating her own worlds.

Her debut series was a rom-com fantasy about a cupid looking for love. She has since gone on to write in a range of genres, including the adult dark fantasy romance The Plated Prisoner Series, which has become a #1 international bestseller with over two million books sold worldwide.

Whether she makes you laugh or cry, or whether the series is about a cupid or a gold-touched woman in a castle, she hopes to create characters that readers can root for.

When Raven isn't writing, she's reading or spending time with her husband and daughters.

You can connect with Raven on her social media, and visit her website: ravenkennedybooks.com